Hellgate

Hellgate
Awakening a Runner's Soul

By
Roger A. Sutton

E-BookTime, LLC
Montgomery, Alabama

Hellgate
Awakening a Runner's Soul

Library of Congress Control Number: 2006939670

ISBN: 1-59824-404-3

First Edition
Published December 2006
E-BookTime, LLC
6598 Pumpkin Road
Montgomery, AL 36108
www.e-booktime.com

Contents

Author's Note

"Hellgate" is a fictional story but it is based upon a real race held each December in Virginia.

Although most of the characters are also fictional, those of you who have been my teammates and friends over the past 30 years will recognize many of the places, events and even the stories as quite real. There are also many references to real people, such as Hellgate race director David Horton. When possible, these individuals were contacted and shown content for approval.

Blending real events into a fictional story was made easier by the advice of my friends and family who provided me with their views on how it all happened. In particular, I want to thank my parents, Jim and Norma Sutton for their unwavering support, as I pursued my goals through high school and college. My wife Jill, who has, in recent years put up with the endless inconveniences that my running schedule creates. In addition, for the last year I have added the horror of writing a book about it which, I'm sure, has tested her patience. As for my friends, I know it appears as if I have just vanished for the past year. I appreciate your patience as well, so please keep a beer cold for me, because I'll be back.

A special thanks, in no particular order, to my High School coach, Wayne Feder, my college coach, John Randolph, my college teammates who pushed me to improve, Mike Blaney, Bill Cason, Eric Joffre, Ray Wunderlich, Keith Brantley and John Rogerson, the Gainesville runners that I shared thousands of miles with, Norm Hommen, Barry Brown, Greg King and Ernie McKee, the Raleigh/Durham ultra runners and friends who introduced me to trail running, Scott Scheodler, Steve Leopard, Jim Claubusch, Chris Shields, Steven Fraser, Rachel Toor and Steve Wright, the Croom trail regulars who have shown me the local trails since my

7

move to Florida, Chase Squires for providing several suggestions, my sister and newbie runner Jennie, my brother Ron whose skills at multiple sports helped inspire me to become some type of athlete, and my good non-running friends who I hope to fish, golf and drink beer with until we're all a bunch of hundred year old droolers, Brad, Jennifer, Lance, Stephanie, Jeff, Brad, Lori, Dave, Dawn and all the rest of you losers, you know who you are!

And finally, if I can blame someone for the year I spent writing "Hellgate" it's a Georgia redneck by the name of Chuck Hutchins. Send all complaints to him since it was his crazy notion that we should each write a book that got this started. Thanks again to all of you.

Roger Sutton

ELEVATION PROFILE
(with Boston Marathon comparison)

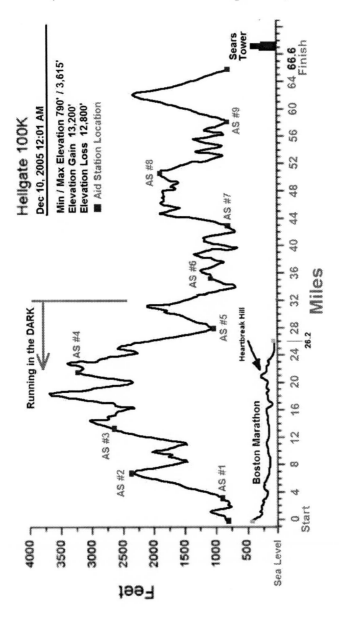

Hellgate 100K

Dec 10, 2005 12:01 AM

Min / Max Elevation 790' / 3,615'
Elevation Gain 13,200'
Elevation Loss 12,800'
■ Aid Station Location

Running in the DARK

AS #2   AS #3   AS #4   AS #5   AS #6   AS #7   AS #8   AS #9

AS #1

Boston Marathon

Heartbreak Hill

Sears Tower

Finish

Feet

4000   3500   3000   2500   2000   1500   1000   500   Sea Level

Miles

0   4   8   12   16   20   24   28   32   36   40   44   48   52   56   60   64   66.6
Start   26.2

9

Desperation Road

"I don't know about psychology; I'm a runner."

— Steve Jones
Marathon World Record holder in 1984

Dec 10th, 2005, 3:05am   Jefferson National Forest, VA

The cold wind is howling as Josh watches his flashlight disappear over the side of the road and fall into the darkness. The pain radiating from his knee keeps him alert, and in the moment, as he scrambles across the ice covered road to the edge of the drop-off. He moans when he sees that his light has tumbled far down the steep, snow covered embankment. He quickly considers his options but knows any attempt to retrieve it would be foolish.

"Shit," Josh mutters as he tries to push himself into a sitting position with his back to the wind. *I can't believe I lost my light with five hours until sunrise.* The black and yellow, hi-tech clothing he wears is only meant to keep him warm while exercising and within seconds he feels the frigid air work through the multiple layers to his skin. The thin gloves are also of little help and he can feel the cold attacking his fingers. Frustrated by his misfortune, he sits on the ice, takes a few deep breaths, and begins to make a swift inventory check. Only the handheld flashlight is missing. He still has his water, food and batteries.

He feels the enormity of his task begin to overwhelm him and tries to convince himself that, although it seems like it at first, the lost light isn't a total catastrophe. In fact, it's the only item he has a backup for. He touches his forehead for reassurance, thankful that the small headlamp, which looks like something that a miner

11

would wear, hasn't been damaged. He's not hurt and is still able to continue but the missing flashlight had a powerful halogen beam and, up to this point, had been irreplaceable on the rugged portions of this technical trail. During his months of practice, he had discovered that he's just not as comfortable running with only the weak glow of a few LED's to light his path. Now, that's all he'll have for the next five hours.

He had hoped it would be different. Three hours ago, as he ran to the top of the first ridge, he only used the headlamp and thought his eyes would eventually adjust. They didn't. With no nearby cities to light the sky, it was quite a shock to find out how much darker it was on this remote mountainside than on the trails close to his home in Florida. He tried several times but no matter how he adjusted the small headlamp, it only put out a narrow ribbon of light, which gave him a claustrophobic feeling, especially when he was going through the woods. Anxious and paranoid, he had fallen back on the halogen light to get him through the night. So now, as he lies on the ground looking down at the bright light shining uselessly under the snow, out of reach, he knows he's in trouble. He feels the familiar pounding in his chest increase in intensity and an uneasy tightness in his stomach. *Calm down.* Josh takes a deep breath to fight against the rising feeling of anxiety and tries to force his heart rate back to normal. *Forget about it and just get up and keep moving,* he thinks.

The angle of the road makes it difficult, but he struggles to his feet and stands unsteadily on the ice. Like a deer caught in a car's headlights, Josh waits motionless. He wants to run but, still stunned by the latest in a series of falls, he elects to exercise extreme caution and tests the traction on the road surface by balancing on his left foot and pushing with the tip of his right shoe. His foot doesn't catch on anything and slides freely across the glazed path. "Come on, there's no grip at all," he mumbles. He's high in the mountains, surrounded by huge open spaces and long distance views, but his entire world has been reduced to the tiny cone of illumination. Everything else has faded into the background.

He's still breathing hard from the long climb up to this elevation and, in the sub-freezing temperature, his breathe creates a fog that obscures his limited view whenever the tiny headlamp shines through it. Everything around him looks surreal and dreamlike, and his feet slip slightly whenever he shifts his weight. Unsure of what to do, he bends over and carefully begins brushing the snow from his legs. When he realizes he's just wasting time, he quits the useless activity and tries to regain his resolve to continue. The cold wind bites into his face as he looks up at the clear sky and wonders if he'll make it to sunrise. He needs to get moving.

Having temporarily regained his balance, he just stares straight ahead still afraid to take a step on the treacherous road. Motion to his right catches his attention and he turns toward the sound of footsteps crunching on the crusty surface of the snow near the drop-off. There's another light moving methodically uphill toward him. Desperate for any kind of contact, he decides to wait and, as the dark figure approaches, the bobbing light flashes across Josh's face. Instinctively, he spins away and, much too late, puts his hands up to shade his eyes. There's a brief explosion of pain and he's temporarily blinded. While struggling to adapt to the gloom, his pupils had been fully dilated, trying to soak up every bit of available light, and now he could only see a very large orange spot floating in the darkness in front of him. Shutting his eyes does little good, but he hears the footsteps continue to come closer. When the movement stops, for a moment, Josh hears nothing but the wind blowing through the trees.

"Turn your light off!" Josh yells.

The wind makes the stranger sound distant even though they are now very close.

"Yeah. Sorry. Hey man, are you all right? That looked like a nasty header."

Josh still can't see anything but can sense the shadow moving closer. "Yeah, no problem. I'll be fine."

"Are you sure you're not hurt?"

Josh instinctively flexes his leg wondering if there's any damage. "Hell, who knows."

"I saw you go down a couple of times so I thought I should check."

"Well, I've knocked the crap out of my knee but I think I'll get through to the next aid station."

"Can I help with anything?" the new arrival asked.

"No, I just need to get off of this ice before I break something important."

The stranger's light came back on at a lower setting and stopped a couple of feet away from Josh. "Yeah, this road sucks, but I think the trail gets better after we get off of this side of the mountain. Just walk for a while. If you're lucky, after a few minutes your knee will just go numb and you'll be able to run again."

The idea of walking on this exposed road for any amount of time makes Josh cringe. "Yeah, thanks. I guess I'll just try to stay close to the edge where there's a little snow for traction."

"Oh man! Are those your regular training shoes?" the voice asked.

Josh was confused by the question and looked down at his feet before answering. "Yeah. Why?"

"You didn't put sheet metal screws into the soles for traction?"

Josh pivoted away from the cold, gusting wind and pulled his hat tighter onto his head before answering. "Screws? No, I've never heard of that."

"Well, it doesn't make much of a difference in the snow but it really helps on the ice." The voice still sounded troubled. "I can certainly see why you're falling so often."

Another mistake, Josh thought. *I've made too many of them already without adding another to the list.*

He was only a few hours into one of the east coast's most hazardous trail ultra-marathons and knew that there was no margin for error. This was no local 5k road race or even a marathon with a possible Oprah sighting. Josh was racing 66 miles, more than two and a half consecutive marathons, on harsh mountain trails. He was running at his limit and needed to be perfect. So far, he'd made a mess of it.

Ultra-marathons.

Where do you go for new challenges once you've had your fill of road racing and marathons? It may be off-road for any of the hundreds of trail races that blanket the backcountry each year. If you have the need to be more extreme, you can leap beyond the marathon distance of 26 miles and test yourself with an ultra-marathon. The beginner distance is 50 kilometers, about 31 miles, but most runners consider *real* ultras to be in the 40 miles or higher realm. Surprisingly, being a talented and accomplished road racer at distances up to the marathon does not necessarily translate to success in ultras. Some say that a good runner is a good runner, no matter what the distance. Maybe that's true, but the training differences force you to make a choice. Do you want to be fast in a 5 mile road race or in a 100 mile mountain race? You can't have both.

Josh was making mistakes and when you're competing in races over 50 miles in length the mistakes don't go away. They accumulate and haunt you all the way to the finish. It's like making a navigation error of a few degrees on a sailboat. If you're going across the lake, the error won't make much of a difference, but if you plan to cross an ocean, the blunder could land you on the wrong continent. Each mistake would significantly reduce his chances of making it to the finish line and they were piling up. Patience, caution and preparation were pre-requisites for this type of race. Regrettably, Josh had very little of the first two traits and not as much as he needed of the third.

"I live in Florida," Josh hastily explained, "and we don't really get conditions like this. I guess the snow and ice just caught me unprepared."

"This must be your first time at Hellgate."

"It's that obvious, huh?"

"Yeah, I wish I could help but I guess you just need to take your time and try to get past this section without hurting yourself."

As Josh's eyes adjusted, the person behind the voice was starting to come into view. "What's your name?" Josh asked.

"Jeff, and you?"

"Josh," he responded.

"It's nice to meet you Josh," he said while extending a gloved hand.

"Same here," Josh said. "You know, I appreciate you stopping but I don't want to slow you down. Go on ahead and I'll try to catch up later."

"All right Josh," he said. "Have fun."

Fun? Josh thought. *Is he being serious?*

As Jeff turned away to continue his trek up the hill he noticed that Josh was shaking from the cold. "Look, you've gotta keep moving until things get better. Standing in one spot isn't helping you at all." The wind made it hard to hear the last words. "Relentless Forward Motion. Remember that. Relentless Forward Motion."

"Right. Thanks. Have a good one."

With an almost inaudible, "You too", the stranger and his blinding light headed up the incline and into the darkness.

Despite what he had said to Jeff about being able to make it to the next aid station, Josh was becoming concerned. *I'm not moving fast enough to stay warm anymore and at least six falls on this ice has really trashed my knee.* He was unprepared. The snow and ice storm had come out of nowhere about 18 hours before the race and he had not made any adjustments to his race preparation. It was a stupid mistake. Josh had run in competition hundreds of times and knew better. Whenever you're racing you have to be flexible and willing to change plans at a moments notice when the weather doesn't cooperate. If he was running at home on an unseasonably hot and humid day he absolutely would have compensated for it and changed plans. *Why did I let this happen?* he wondered.

He had fallen repeatedly as he power hiked up the incline and the sore knee that had plagued Josh during his training was being battered. Everything leaned away from the drop-off and the constant camber of the road caused him to fall to the left every time. As a result, each time he went down he landed on the same spot of his left knee. It was like taking a pounding blow from a hammer over and over in the same spot. Needless to say, it hurt every time, but the last fall had been particularly painful. *If I land on that knee one more time, I'm done.* All of his planning for Hellgate, almost four months worth, was falling apart. He looked up at the outline of the mountain that loomed up in front of him, barely visible in the faint moonlight. Jeff was right. Standing around and freezing was his immediate problem. For now, the clock didn't matter. He was cold and starting to tighten up badly. If he was going to make it, he had to get his heart rate back up. *Relentless forward motion.* He said to himself. *Relentless forward motion.*

Josh took a few cautious steps and tried to regain some of his lost confidence. Soon, he was moving again but he was also seriously behind schedule and he knew that Jill, who was waiting several miles ahead, would be assuming the worst. She always thought that any overdue arrival at a checkpoint meant he was either injured or lost. Of course, she had every reason to think that, ever since his incident on the Appalachian Trail a couple of years earlier. Some things are never forgotten. Although she was supportive of his unusual addiction, his wife rarely came to races and right now it seemed certain that this was not the best choice for a weekend trip together. She would expect him to meet her on time, but he knew already, that to try and stick to a schedule at Hellgate was utterly ridiculous. *If I make it under the time limit to the first checkpoint, I'll tell her to go back to the hotel* he thought. *In fact, maybe I should just go with her. Damn, that sounds nice.*

Josh was still a relative newbie when it came to long races but he had already had numerous opportunities to take an early ride back to the hotel. He'd never done it. It wasn't that he was immune to the temptation, in fact, when you're cold, tired and your legs ache it can sound like the only sane thing to do. The darkness makes it even harder to pass up a warm bed, leave a checkpoint, and head back into the mountains. Josh never thought about why he kept going. He just did. Like nearly every other competitor in this race, once he starts, he's fully committed. Mile after mile, they all push themselves beyond what seems conceivable or sensible. Each checkpoint is merely a brief stop on the way to fulfilling their goal. In most cases, only medical professionals forcing the issue or a missed cutoff time will take an entrant out of the race. To simply quit would injure pride more than anything but that tiny bruising of ego is usually enough to keep everyone moving. The thought was in and out of his head with little consideration. It certainly never occurred to Josh that someday, maybe even tonight, he might actually take that ride into town.

Scott was also here, somewhere behind Josh on the trail. His friend and training buddy was more than partially responsible for Josh coming to the mountains of Virginia. Of course, it hadn't been that hard to convince him, especially after smoothing him over with a few beers first. It was easy because Josh, like every long distance trail runner on the east coast, had already heard numerous stories about this race long before Scott suggested they run the damn thing. Jill argued, quite effectively, that it was a long trip up from central Florida just for a race, but the allure of Hellgate was something that couldn't be denied.

At 43 years of age, Josh Stanton had been running competitively for over 30 years. Ranging from the short races they allow children to run in elementary school to the elite level of NCAA Division 1 track. At one time, he was one of the fastest 10,000 meter runners in the Southeastern United States but his results had disintegrated over the years as injuries and age began to take their toll on speed and stamina. Even so, for many years past his prime, he was still pretty fast and new challenges were always presenting themselves. Still, he doesn't like to lose and, as the wins became more infrequent, the desire to compete faded away. Of course, he had always remained active but only a few years earlier, he would have told you that his competitive days were behind him and that he would never race again. It was only a chance meeting with a group of ultra marathon runners that changed his mind, and now, ultra distance trail racing had become a new addition to his racing resume. His new friends had been teaching him the nuances of this extreme sport and, today, as he had done many times before, he was putting into practice what he had learned.

Only this time, cold and lonely on a Virginia mountainside, and visibly limping with over 50 miles between him and the finish line, Hellgate was kicking his ass.

River Run

"It was a big ego trip. All the kids I hung around with were impressed. But then I took about a five year layoff."

— **Don Kardong**
*Fourth place finisher in the 1976 Olympic Marathon,
Speaking about a 4-mile run to his grandmother's
house when he was 10 years old*

Summer, 1971, Central Nebraska

Neither Josh nor his family could remember a time when he was not a runner. From the moment he stopped crawling and made his first awkward steps, he seemed to run. His parents always told him that as a child he had constantly been in motion. It started as a toddler when he drove his mother crazy by running all around the house. When he got older, the pattern continued as he ran to the playground and then, while other kids rode bikes, he would run to and from school. If he needed anything from anywhere in the small Nebraska town that they lived in, he never needed to find a ride. Instead, he would just head out the door and go on foot. After school and in the summer, he ran to baseball practice, the city park and even to the public golf course to play with his dad. He ran everywhere. It wasn't as if his parents couldn't afford a bike or that he couldn't get a ride, in fact, he turned down lots of rides and he had a nice bike. He just preferred to leave it at home and cut through backyards and across fields on foot instead of riding on the street. This fascination with running wasn't the calculated choice of an adult training to win an age group award at a local road race. In fact, they barely existed in the 1960's. Josh was just a kid and, at the time, he was totally unaware of all the things that would someday be required in order for him to become a competitive distance runner. None of that mattered. He didn't care because he had absolutely no interest in such things. It was just natural to him. Birds fly, fish swim and Josh, well, he just liked to run.

Josh had an exciting and active childhood. He loved to be outside with his friends and often would be gone for the entire day. They roamed all over the small town doing an assortment of activities. Most of the time it was just routine kid stuff but when you're young, seemingly meaningless events can unexpectedly influence behavior and even affect the choices that are made as you grow older. The mundane things that make up every day are forgotten. No one can recall the peanut butter sandwich they ate when they were 6 years old but childhood triumphs and defeats, traumatic events, can certainly become the basis of a person's earliest memorable experiences. Almost anyone could tell you the day they learned to ride a bike or about the day they went off of the high board for the first time at the local pool. Josh was not an exception to this rule. Like everyone else, he knew all about his first bike ride but he could also tell you about his first real trail run which happened to take place on a day that featured a surprising triumph combined with heartbreaking failure.

Just after Josh's ninth birthday, he was allowed to go to a Boy Scout camp in central Nebraska. He truly loved the trips that his troop went on and this was no exception. The scenic location in the woods was so different from the farmlands that surrounded his parent's home. The troop had set up a nice campground and there were activities around every corner. They spent countless hours riding horses, cooking meals over the fire and shooting on the archery range. It would have been perfect except for one thing, the swim test. Every year, one of the most popular outings at the camp was an inner-tubing trip down a nearby river. Everyone was eager to go and the only requirement was that you first pass a seemingly simple swimming test.

It sounded so easy but Josh felt panicky as he went to the pool with his friends because he knew he was not a good swimmer. This was Nebraska, not a costal state where everyone learns to swim at an early age. He hoped it would be a short distance so that he wouldn't look too foolish but when he learned the details of the test, his heart sank. Each scout would have to swim the full length of an Olympic size pool and back without assistance. Touching the side of the pool, even for a moment, was not allowed. Josh had never swum that far in his life.

The glassy smooth water appeared to stretch to the horizon in front of him and just standing on the edge made him feel anxious. When directed by the adults that were walking up and down the length of the pool, he reluctantly entered the water and waited for his group's turn. As soon as they blew the whistle, he and his friends began swimming toward the opposite end of the pool. Josh flailed his arms and thrashed through the water. He could swim, but it wasn't pretty and it took a lot of effort for him to cover a mere 20 or 30 yards. As hard as it was for him, he wasn't a quitter and he did his best to swim two lengths unaided, but he didn't have the technique or strength and could not make it without grabbing the side to rest. The lifeguards were sympathetic and, after allowing him to take some time to regain his composure, they decided to let him try again, but it was no use. He was just not strong enough to swim that distance. He was told that it wasn't a big deal, he wasn't alone, and that there were others that had been unable to finish the second lap.

"Look Josh," his troop leader said. "I heard that it was a long swim and that not very many are going to make it through this test. So, don't worry about it. I know you wanted to go on the tubing trip but I'm sure you'll make it next year."

"You're all going without me?"

The troop leader looked uncomfortable. "Yes, I'm taking everyone that passed."

"What do I do?" Josh asked.

"Whatever you want. It'll only be a couple of hours. Why don't you just hang out at the campsite or, maybe, go back to the archery range for a while," he suggested.

"They'll be others still here?"

"Definitely."

Josh nodded his head and walked away but his suspicion that they were lying seemed to be confirmed later when he found out that everyone else in his troop had passed the test and that they were all cleared to go tubing. He was left, alone and ashamed, in camp, as the bus, full of his friends, left for the river.

It was humiliating to fail the swim test and Josh stormed around the camp for a while disgusted with himself. He was angry and he could feel the tension building in his chest. He was a ball of energy and, as his face became flushed and his breathing more rapid, he had to do something. Most kids would have screamed or thrown objects around the camp, but not Josh. He released the energy the way he always had, by running. Without thinking about where he was going, he bolted out of camp and headed down the nearest trail. The path through the woods was perfect single track that wound through a hardwood forest with rolling hills and steep ravines cut by small fast moving streams, but Josh didn't notice those details. He simply ran, with no thought at all of saving energy for a return trip to camp.

It was a beautiful afternoon and, within a few minutes of leaving camp, he was alone on the trail. Surrounded by the sounds of nature, he heard the birds, insects and the rustling of the wind through the trees. Running through the forest felt easy at first, as the frustration of the botched test fueled him, but soon, his breathing became more labored and he felt fatigue creeping into his legs. He pushed on and the rolling hills and frequent turns kept him focused as he ran further and further from camp. At first the route seemed random but he soon realized that, unconsciously, he had taken a trail towards the river. He wasn't exactly sure how to get there so he just continued to run in what he felt was the general direction. Several turns took him to dead ends but having to backtrack did not discourage him at all. He just kept running away from the camp.

Inevitably, he was unable to keep up the pace and he started to walk the uphill sections but, as soon as he crested the tops, he would lower his head and resume running. As the trees and branches flew past, sometimes cutting into his arms and legs, Josh kept at his task. He didn't even think about allowing the dry throat and dull throbbing from his legs to slow his forward progress. He just ran. The sun continued its trek across the sky but with no watch or time reference, Josh had no idea how long he had been on the trail. He never considered retreating and when he finally heard the roaring water he knew that it was not the sound of one of the many streams he had crossed earlier. It was the sound of a large river. He felt excitement taking the place of his anger and ran even harder toward the increasingly loud drone of water falling over rock. As he burst out of the forest onto the bank he staggered to a stop, spent from the effort, and immediately bent at the waist and grabbed his knees, gasping for air. Even as he let his lungs drink in the cool air, his eyes scanned up and down the river looking for tubes. It looked like it might be the spot but he had no idea if this was actually where they would float past. He wasn't even sure if this was the right river but, now that he was there, he watched expectantly.

The run had begun out of frustration and, at first, he had just wanted to get to the water but, now that he was there, he knew running to the river was not the real goal, it was to cross. For some reason, he felt that he had to make up for the swim test by proving he could swim across the river. Even with no one to witness the accomplishment, he had to make it to the opposite bank, only then could he go back to camp satisfied. For ten minutes, he walked up and down the muddy bank looking for the best spot to cross and then, after finding a good location and catching his breath, he took off his shoes and plunged into the cold water. He was a little scared so he tried to walk out as far as he could before pushing off into the faster moving current. As could be expected, a long run to the river had not magically transformed him into a good swimmer but there was no way he was going to fail again. The swift water grabbed at him and for a moment he thought he'd made a terrible mistake. Maybe this was too much, too soon. He tried to push the negative thoughts out of his head and focused on a large tree in the distance. He pummeled the water with his arms and kicked frantically, trying to make some forward progress. It wasn't nearly as far across the river as the length of the pool but the water was swirling around him and he had to fight to keep his head up so that he could keep the opposite bank in sight. Josh awkwardly fought against the current until he felt the surging water release him and he knew he was going to make it across. A few seconds later, he was relieved to feel the ground under his feet again.

He pulled himself out of the water and, as the mud squeezed between his toes, looked back at the river and smiled. With his inner demons temporarily satisfied, he searched for a good place to rest. An hour later, he was sitting on a tree hanging over the water, wondering how he was going to get back across, when his friends came floating around the bend on their tubes. Within minutes, they saw him.

"Hey, it's Josh!" One of his friends yelled. "Jump on a tube!"

Josh was excited to see them but knew he wasn't allowed to tube. "I can't. I didn't pass the swim test and they won't let me go with you," Josh hollered back.

"Oh, come on!"

About that time, his troop leader came into view and he wasn't very pleased to see the scout he had left in camp all the way down at the river. "Josh! I told you to wait back in the camp. How'd you get here?"

Josh carefully climbed down from the tree. "I ran the trails," he answered.

"You couldn't have," the troop leader said while shaking his head, "the camp is at least seven or eight miles from here."

Josh just shrugged. "I don't know how far it is. I didn't have anything to do and I just felt like running here, so I did." Josh was annoyed by the apparent disbelief that his troop leader was exhibiting.

"And I suppose that means that you also swam across to this side?" he said as he grabbed the tree and pulled himself ashore.

Josh looked at him and answered quietly, "Yes." The guy seemed angry. Josh hadn't even considered that he might get in trouble for this.

The troop leader looked back at the river and the cluster of tubes that had collected near the tree and appeared to reconsider the possibility that Josh had run there. "Well, there are no roads so I guess that's the only way here. Obviously, you can swim well enough to ride on a tube. I don't understand why they told me that you couldn't swim. Anyway, jump on with someone. You might as well float the rest of the way with us."

"Thanks!" Josh yelled.

As Josh walked back into the water, he realized that the failed swim test was forgotten. He had wiped it from their memories by simply running to the river which was, in their minds, an unthinkable task. He was no longer the weak kid that they had pitied earlier. He was years away from being a competitive runner but he already knew that he was capable of something that others thought of as difficult. Still, despite the attention that he received for his effort, for the 9-year-old kid it was just a run. He really didn't care about anything but the feeling he had when he first pulled himself out of the water and knew he had done it. How far he had gone or how fast he ran the trail made no difference and, in fact, no one asked. All that mattered to Josh was making it there. It was personal. He had just wanted to finish.

Committed

"Racing teaches us to challenge ourselves. It teaches us to push beyond where we thought we could go. It helps us to find out what we are made of. This is what we do. This is what it's all about."

— Patti Sue Plummer
U.S. Olympian and former 5k American Record Holder

September 2005, Ocala, Florida,
Countdown to Hellgate – 12 weeks

The Tin Cup Tavern is a small pub on the downtown square. On weekends, local rock bands play, and the place is packed with a mix of tourists and students. The rest of the week, it's a place for locals. On those week days the music isn't as loud and the beer, which turns over at a slower rate, seems colder. It's a great spot to hang out with friends and talk about the past and plan the future. Of course, as with most watering holes, the conversation is always more energetic as the bar tab starts to pile up and that was the case tonight. The small table towards the back is a favorite spot for Josh, Scott and their friends who come in to drink beer and tell lies about what they did when they were younger. On Wednesday nights, they're regulars.

Not everyone at the table is a runner, but among the ones that are, Josh's position in the group as top dog is understood. Although he's now in his 40's, during his long career, he has run faster than them at every distance and has won more races than they have even entered. The unspoken position is, for the most part, unchangeable. It's respect due someone who has invested a lifetime of effort into the pursuit of speed without motorized

26

assistance. Josh doesn't talk about it, and he certainly doesn't ask for it, but he still loves the fact that they know the order. He likes being the top dog.

Scott Leopard is a different story altogether. Josh's friend is a classic ultra distance trail runner. Although he claims that he isn't interested in racing at all, Scott has managed to put together some remarkable performances. Over the past 15 years, he has run just about every 100 mile trail race in the country. Like many ultra runners, his passion is taking on the most difficult courses in the most inhospitable locations. He always tells Josh that he doesn't care about his times or his place. He's more interested in the pursuit of his personal goals. He'll go on and on about *discovering what he's capable of* and *traversing trails and enjoying vistas that mainstream runners will never see as they pound away across asphalt America* but that doesn't change that fact that he kicks the crap out of just about everyone. In short, despite his efforts to be just another guy out enjoying the trail, when it comes to racing, Scott is nearly an unstoppable force.

Given Scott's love for trails, it was no surprise that four years earlier, it had been his enthusiasm for trail running that pulled Josh, a retired road racer, into this offshoot of the sport that he had abandoned for so long. And now Josh was hooked on distance running again.

Anyone who trains with them will tell you that it's an unusual pairing. The mindset Josh takes into training and racing is the result of years of competitive track and road racing. It drives Scott crazy that Josh has never been able to let go of his old habit of trying to finish every race and even workout in front. It seems like he doesn't just want to beat the competition, he wants to dominate it, in training, as well as in racing. Scott is just the opposite. He is non-confrontational, despises the roads, and hasn't been on the track for speed work in years. That doesn't mean his training is any easier, it's just that he sees the path to success differently. It's a constant battle between them as Josh pushes for more speed in their workouts while Scott argues for more consistency and longer weekend runs. It's an athletic version of the odd couple, but the funny thing is that they both excel at the sport and expect to eventually convince the other of the errors of his ways.

The first time Scott mentioned Hellgate it was over beers at the Tin Cup. He just threw it out there like it was no big deal.

"Hey, Josh, I'm thinking about running Hellgate this year." All the runners at the table stopped talking and looked at Scott, while the non-runners gave no noticeable reaction. "I've spoken to a few people that ran it last year and it appears to be on its way to becoming a classic."

"Hellgate's a 100 kilometer race. That's a little short for you," Josh said.

"Yeah, I know. It's only 62 miles long but everyone that I've talked to says it feels more like a 100 mile race and there aren't too many 100 kilometer races that can make that claim."

Their non-running friends, who favored golf and fishing for their outdoor activities, had heard enough about ultra-marathoning over the years to, at least, appreciate the athletic challenge. That doesn't mean they understood why Josh and Scott wanted to run them but at least they no longer said things like "I don't even want to drive my car that far" and "What do you think about when you run?". Now when they hear distances like "100 miles" bandied about by these guys, like it was as normal as slipping on your shoes and going to the store for milk, they keep those annoying comments to themselves.

Hellgate. Josh repeated it in his head a few times.

Only a few years old and already Hellgate has an almost mystical quality. The few veterans who have completed the race talk about it with the respect that is due a feared adversary. Meanwhile, the newbies cringe as tales of pain and disappointment pour in at an alarming rate. For a race that's less than 100 miles to gain a reputation as such a complete test of endurance after such a short life is remarkable. Especially in a sport where extreme is the name of the game.

Ultra runners are always looking for the most challenging physical and mental tests. Badwater, Leadville, Hardrock and the Barkley are names that every ultra-marathoner recognizes. Each is at least 100 miles long and they present challenges of extreme temperature, altitude and terrain. What could possibly convince

Scott to put Hellgate into their class? Typically, a race of 62 miles would not normally be viewed with such trepidation by the ultra running community. But this was not a normal race.

"That's a Horton race, right?" asked a slightly drunk Josh.

"Right, it's David Horton's race. That means two things," Scott explained. "First, you know it will be well organized and, second, you know it will be tough. After all, this is the guy that's been directing the Mountain Masochist 50 miler for over 20 years."

"Oh, one more thing," Scott continued. "It also means it's probably longer than the advertised 62 miles. I've heard it's more like 66 miles. He says he doesn't do that on purpose but it's typical Horton."

David Horton doesn't just direct races, he runs, like few people in the world ever have. In 1991 he set the speed record on the Appalachian Trail, covering the rock strewn 2,144 miles in just over 52 days. A few years later, he ran across America in the third fastest time in history. To top it off, in 2005 at the age of 53, he broke the speed record for the Pacific Crest Trail, a remote route over soaring rugged mountains, across frigid snowfalls and through countless fast moving rivers. He ran the 2,666 mile length of this trail from Mexico to Canada in a paltry 66 days. Horton won't ask you to do anything in his races he wouldn't do himself. Unfortunately, that doesn't leave much out.

"Sounds like a hoot, I'm in," Josh said.

Scott smiled; he knew Josh would enter the race. He also knew that Josh had no idea what he was signing up for. "Great! We'll start putting a training plan together tomorrow."

"Done. Anyone else wanna go?" Josh asked the other runners at the table. There was no response. "No? Fine, Scott and I will take full responsibility for the representation of Florida."

"Maybe you should write yourself a note so you remember in the morning," Scott suggested.

"Don't you worry, I'll remember," Josh said as he raised his glass. "To Hellgate!"

The next day, a sober Josh did remember and realized he needed to tell Jill that his friend had talked him into running a race out of state. *If we make a vacation out of it she might like the idea a bit more.* No, they had tried that in the past. This was no vacation and she would see through the weak attempt at misdirection right away. She'd let him go and run the race, she always did. It's just easier if she views it as a nice getaway for herself as well. It's always been a common theme amongst runners to try and schedule vacations and races together. They always try to act casual about it, like it's just a coincidence. You know, "since we're going there anyway, I might as well run the race". Their spouses see through it immediately and, after a few attempts, the runners give up on the ploy.

"Why do we have to go to Virginia for a race? Why can't you just run something closer to home?" Jill asked when Josh eventually told her about Hellgate.

"Because there are no races like this in Florida."

"So, what makes this so special?" She was clearly unhappy at the prospect of using vacation time to go to a race. Scott, who was supposed to be helping him, sat quietly, nursing his beer and trying to keep from laughing. He knew that Josh was going to have a hard time with this one.

"Well, a lot of things. Look, we're down here in Florida running in the heat and humidity on flat, sandy trails month after month. Even the longest, toughest hill in the area takes less than a minute to run. We need a change. Scott says that these mountain trails are spectacular, nothing like our trails. They're rocky and steep. In fact, some of the climbs and descents could take well over an hour to complete. Obviously, there will be some fantastic scenery. The type of views you rarely get to see without browsing through postcards."

Jill could tell they really wanted to go and was running out of objections. "But it's in December. I'm a southern girl, but even I know its cold in the mountains that time of year. You're not good in the cold and you know it."

"You're right, the weather will be tough, but I don't care about that. I'm sure it will be cold and wet but that's what we're looking for. It's kind of an anti-Florida race where everything will be different than what we're used to. If it meets our expectations, it will be more of a physical and mental test than anything we can get at home," Josh explained.

"Scott, why are you trying to talk him into this?"

Scott looked uncomfortable at being pulled into the argument. "Sorry Jill, I just said I was going. As soon as he heard about the race, and the midnight start, he jumped at it."

"A midnight start? You've got to be kidding. That's nuts."

Scott jumped back in without thinking. "Not really, you see most races start in the morning and finish before dark. If they are long enough to run past sunset, it usually favors the faster runners who can finish early in the evening while others are required to run long into the night. Hellgate starts at one minute past Midnight so that everyone has to run the same amount in the dark. The late sunrise during the winter means that everyone will cover seven and a half hours in the dark. It's really a fair way to do it." As he finished his explanation, Scott glanced at Josh and wondered if he was helping or hurting the pitch.

Jill looked dejected. "Great, so were talking about staying up all night, in the cold, for an early December, 60 plus mile race deep in the Virginia Mountains with a midnight start. That's very nice. I think you're both crazy."

Hearing his wife lay it out like that caused Josh to pause briefly but then he jumped right back into the pitch.

"Maybe you're right, maybe it is crazy, but you just can't find this anywhere. This race has over 27,000 feet of elevation change. That's unheard of for a race on the east coast. Normally, you'd have to go all the way to the Rockies for that kind of vertical," Josh said excitedly.

"27,000 feet of elevation change?" Jill stood up and began pacing. "Josh, what's the highest hill around here?" she asked.

"Well, there's a big one at Croom and another on the Santos trails. I'd say they're about the same size. Maybe, 40 feet. Why?"

These boys aren't thinking right. "Ok, Scott, get out your pencil and tell me how many times you'd have to run that hill to get 27,000 feet," Jill said.

Scott reluctantly grabbed a napkin and began to do the calculation. Jill waited.

"You'd have to run our *big* hill about 675 times." Scott announced.

Jill chuckled. She had hoped, even expected, that it would convince them to give up the idea but it didn't have the affect Jill intended.

"Really?" Josh asked.

"Really!" Scott was smiling from ear to ear. "It'll be brutal!"

Josh was returning the grin and, seeing that, Jill gave up trying to reach the rational part of their brains. It was clear to Jill that she didn't understand these two at all but at least she knew by their voices that they were committed. For some incomprehensible reason it was important to them.

"All right, I'll take some vacation time so that we can go out a day early. I know you'll be worthless afterward so I won't plan any tourist stuff. As usual, you owe me for this one."

With Jill's blessing, it was official, they were going to Hellgate. Somewhat lost in the shuffle was the fact that it would be the longest run of Josh's life. Two years earlier he had completed a 50-mile race and this would be considerably longer. It had been a gradual process to work up to 50 and, over the years, each time he bumped the number up a little higher it had been for a different reason. Indeed, Josh had learned from experience that there are a lot of things that influence a runner to do any long run, especially when it's further than they've ever gone before. Sometimes they are meticulously planned, like Hellgate would be, other times they are the whimsical result of circumstance, necessity or even anger and frustration. At one time or another, Josh had experienced each of them.

Whatever the reason for starting, at the end of each one you may or may not view the world differently, but you will have a better appreciation for your capabilities and what it means to push boundaries.

Although he didn't really recognize why, one thing was certainly true about Josh, he loved to push boundaries.

The Mile

"Almost every part of the mile is tactically important – you can never let down, never stop thinking, and you can be beaten at almost any point. I suppose you could say it is like life."

— **John Landy**
Former World Record holder in the Mile run and, in 1954, the 2ⁿᵈ person to break the 4 minute mile barrier (only five weeks after Roger Bannister)

Spring 1977, Woodbury, MN

Josh's family moved from central Nebraska to Minnesota during the summer of 1976. As soon as they arrived, he was thrown into a new school far from his childhood friends. Being the new kid in school is always difficult but it was exceptionally hard for Josh who was not very outgoing and had always had trouble making new friends. In the past, sports, and running in particular, had helped him get through similar transitions and meet others his age.

Whether it's football, hockey, or even horseshoes, most athletes learn the fundamentals of sports early and Josh was no exception. He found out at a young age that he had good hand eye coordination skills but he was little and, when it came to team sports, his lack of strength caused problems for him. Just a few pickup games proved that he was too small for football and several summers of little league had convinced him that baseball was not going to be his sport either. His older brother was bigger, more talented, and seemed to be able to play every sport. It was intimidating and Josh, in an attempt to measure up, was willing to

33

try as many sports as necessary to figure out which one he was going to pursue. The criteria was simple, he wanted to find a sport where he could make an immediate impact. He wanted to be good at something like his brother. Once he finally gave up on team sports the list of remaining options was short but, as he had seen many times growing up, running had always come very naturally to him. So, when he entered the ninth grade, he signed up to run on the high school freshman track team. It was an unforced fit given his size and after only a few weeks he realized that he had some talent. Maybe track would be his sport.

Josh's only problem was that quality coaching didn't really exist at this level. Since he had no idea what type of training to do to improve, he just ran around the neighborhood and did whatever he thought was best. For the most part it was just a guessing game but, even though he had no idea why, the training and his natural ability combined to make him faster. Soon it became apparent that he could be competitive. After the first month, when he started to outrun the other guys on the team, more and more people talked to him. He had been noticed. As a new kid in school he had been an unknown and now, all of the sudden, he had something that made him special. He didn't realize it at the time but the attention and acceptance that came his way, because of his running ability, would fuel his efforts and provide a competitive drive for the next several years.

This was all new to Josh but the first thing he had to do was choose an event. Former world record holder Sebastian Coe once said that "theatrically, the mile is just the right length – beginning, middle, end, a story unfolding." It's always been one of the most glamorous events in track but Josh didn't know that. His logic was very simple. In Minnesota, high school freshmen are not allowed to race distances over a mile and, since he wanted to run as far as possible, that's what Josh chose.

He had already been training for almost two months on his own and, leading up to the first meet, he had been running in a pair of Converse basketball shoes which were falling apart from the pounding. Unfortunately, he had no money for new shoes.

Josh went to his mother. "Mom, I need new shoes for track."

"For track? What's wrong with the shoes you have?"

"Nothings wrong with them for going to school but I can't run in them anymore. They're just not right for it. There's not enough cushion and they don't have any grip at all," Josh explained.

Josh's mother had been through this before with her two sons. They wanted something new but after a few weeks went by they would be on to the next adventure. The item that they *had to have* would be casually thrown into a closet or a corner of the garage. It had been like that with almost every activity that they took up over the past ten years.

"I'll tell you what Josh. If you stay on this track team all the way to the end of the season, we'll get you a new pair of running shoes for the summer."

That wasn't what Josh wanted at all. "That's too late! I need them for our first meet. It's this Saturday."

"Ok, Ok, how about we see how you do in the first meet and then we decide. Maybe you won't even like running on the track team."

"Yes I will!" Josh argued.

"Well, if you do, then I won't have any problem buying you a special pair of shoes but I'm not doing that until we know more about it."

Josh knew he wouldn't get a better deal. "Fine. I'll run in these for a while."

The first race of the season, which was on a cinder track, was run in his high top basketball shoes. No one talked to Josh before the race and he didn't really have a plan at all. When the starter's pistol fired, he just ran. The track had a deep groove in lane one so Josh ran behind a couple of kids on the line between lanes one and two. After the second lap, Josh had passed the leaders and started to pull away. He started to hurt on the last lap but no one caught him and he was shocked when he not only won the race but he also ran a time of 5:31 which was only a few seconds slower than his school's freshman record.

A week later it was more of the same as Josh won the race going away in a new school record of 5:24. Another week went by and Josh got his first taste of defeat. He ran faster than ever, but lowering his freshman record to 5:14 wasn't enough to win.

Still, he was learning how to race and each week he was a little bit faster and his confidence improved. The high school varsity coach was in the stands the following Saturday to see Josh run a dominate time of 5:03 and win again. He had only missed the freshman district record by a few steps and the coach had watched intently. He was amused and impressed that Josh had been able to run that fast in basketball shoes. As the weeks passed by, the season was going great. Josh had made some friends on the team and, having won most of his races, began to look forward to the end of the spring when the District Championships would determine the best freshmen runners in the St. Paul area.

As the meet drew nearer, for the first time, Josh was nervous. He was just 14 and yet people were talking about him and a level of expectation was building. He started to feel like he was letting them down if he didn't win even though winning every race was incredibly unrealistic. The truth was that there were a couple of kids in the district that had run very fast in cross country and both were undefeated in the mile this season. Since Josh had raced each of them earlier in the year and lost, he was certain that they were not thinking about him at all. Everyone knew that the ninth grade district mile record of 5:01 was definitely in jeopardy. This would be a showdown between the two undefeated runners and Josh hoped that no one actually considered him a legitimate contender for the victory. He wasn't ready for that kind of pressure.

Josh's mother was proud of him and, after seeing him win several races, she finally relented and he had gotten his first new pair of actual running shoes. He warmed up sporting a brand new pair of Pumas and decided that he would try and stay with the favorites as long as he could. As soon as the race started Mike Moran, who would go on to win back to back State Championships in the 800 meters during his junior and senior seasons, took the lead immediately. He was followed down the backstretch by his rival Bill Field while Josh and everyone else jostled for position back in the pack. Bill had been the faster runner during cross country the past fall but earlier in the track season Mike appeared to have more speed in the mile. Josh tried to stay close and ran hard, all the way out in lane three, trying to pass the clump of runners between him and the leaders.

Josh didn't want to get boxed in and focused on passing cleanly. He went around the group and by the end of the first lap he had moved into third place and was closing on Bill. As expected, the second quarter mile was slower than the first since the inexperienced runners still hadn't learned how to pace themselves for long races yet. Seeing the young runners struggle with race tactics didn't make it any less exciting as Josh and Bill both cut into Mike's lead.

After slowly closing the gap down the front straight, the three runners were all together going into the third lap but the rest of the field was out of it. Without the other runners, it seemed eerily quiet as they went down the backstretch for the third time. He followed Mike and Bill through the turn and down the back straight but by the time they entered the second turn Josh was tying up. Although he started to lose ground, he fought hard to maintain contact as they approached the line for the bell lap.

The final lap was a blur to Josh. He had gone out hard and was paying for it now. Mike and Bill were running away from him and he couldn't do anything about it. He kept pushing himself around the track and, as Mike powered down the home stretch, Josh was trying to hang on to third place. When he crossed the line, Mike and Bill were already bent over grabbing theirs knees and seriously gasping for air. They both looked up and slapped Josh on the back as he staggered past and gave him an appraising look that he hadn't warranted earlier in the year. For the first time, he had made an impression on them and, in the coming years, they would all become friends as well as rivals.

The freshman district record for the mile, which had stood for 12 years, was shattered. Mike had won in 4:41 with Bill only a few seconds back. Josh's mile time of 4 minutes and 51 seconds had broken his own school record by 12 seconds and, even though he placed third, he was also 10 seconds under the previous district record.

Unfortunately, although all three had showed the speed for it, in Minnesota freshmen weren't allowed to run in any of the high school championships so, with little fanfare, the season was over almost as quickly as it started. But for Josh, who had found a way to make friends and get noticed, it was only beginning.

The summer between his freshman and sophomore years he did planned training for the first time in his life. He tried to run every day. He knew he had to because in only a few months the races would be much tougher. The cross country races would lengthen from two miles to three miles and the competition would be better. He'd be racing kids that were bigger, stronger, and in some cases, four years older than he was.

The high school coaches had watched his 4:51 mile and immediately started making preparations to fit him into the varsity team with their star runner Sean Nicols. He was going to be a sophomore but he could tell that they wanted him to run like he was a senior right away. Josh immediately felt the pressure and months before the first official practice he was already out on his own, running too hard and too far. He needed advice on how to prepare, physically and mentally, but there was no one to give it to him. Once again, he had no direction and just did whatever he thought was best.

High expectations followed him as he moved up to the high school varsity team the next fall for Cross Country season.

Morning Run

"A lot of people don't realize that about 98 percent of the running that I put in is anything but glamorous: 2 percent joyful participation, 98 percent dedication! It's a tough formula. Getting out in the forest in the biting cold and the flattening heat, and putting in kilometer after kilometer."

— **Rob de Castella**
3-time Olympian and 1983 Marathon World Champion

September 2005, Croom Tract, Central Florida
Countdown to Hellgate – 10 weeks

Josh was late getting to the trailhead and although it was still dark he could see Scott's truck parked in the usual spot. The older runner was already adjusting his headlamp and filling water bottles. He looked like he was preparing for a long camping trip. The back of the truck was loaded with all types of gear. There were bottles, food, sunscreen, bug repellant and an assortment of colored packages. As if that isn't enough, water drops, shoe changes and blister control, are also all part of the logistics of a 35-mile trail run.

"'Mornin' slacker, how ya feelin'?"

"How'm I supposed to feel at 4 a.m.?" Josh responded sluggishly.

Scott has had the same discussion with every new ultra runner he's ever trained with. "I know it sucks but so does running when its 97 degrees."

"Ever heard of a treadmill? 72 degrees all day long and you get to watch *Gilligan's Island* reruns until you puke."

39

"Come on, you know you need time on the trail for Hellgate and today we'll have the added bonus of getting to practice running in the dark with our headlamps. You know you need that."

Josh rolled his eyes and started filling his bottles with multi-colored electrolyte drinks. "Knowing it's the right thing to do doesn't make it any easier to get out of bed. And, by the way, it's not surprising that everyone thinks we're lunatics. This isn't normal behavior."

"Of course it's not normal, who wants to be normal?"

"Not me. Hey, speaking of not normal, do you have any duct tape? I need to do some work on my feet if I'm going to survive this little jaunt through the woods."

Scott started searching the side pockets of his bag. "Hey, you play golf, right? I saw Tiger Woods on SportsCenter last night and he had duct tape on his fingers. It almost made me feel like taping our feet with it isn't that strange." He found a roll and tossed it to Josh.

"Thanks. Yeah, you're right. If NASCAR can use Duct tape to hold a car together at 200 miles per hour, I guess it ought to hold our feet together. On second thought, it's all the lubricants that you have in that bag that would really freak people out," Josh responded.

"That may be true, but once you've seen all of the crazy spots that you can chafe and blister on a five-hour run, like I have, you'll agree that a little lubrication can be your best friend."

Josh grabbed a tube of *Body Glide* from his own bag and applied the ointment to several of his favorite locations. "You won't get an argument from me," Josh agreed.

It looked like overkill to go for a run but they knew they would pay dearly if they missed any step in the ritual. They organized drinks and figured out how many calories they would need to consume. Laying it all out so later they could quickly get what they needed. It was a hot and humid day so extra shoes and socks would be waiting as well. The battle against blisters would be waged on many fronts. Obviously, the feet are a prime concern and even a small blister can derail training for several days. When training runs push past the marathon distance you can't be too careful. Everything rubs and the salt in your sweat attacks any unprotected skin. Bandaids are placed over the nipples to reduce friction. Without them you'll finish with blood soaked shirts and be in pain for a week. Toenails have to be trimmed as short as possible, but even then most trail runners are missing at least one at any given time. After a 100-mile trail race your toes can look like they were attacked by an insane carpenter trying to pound your feet to the floor. In other words, if purple is your favorite color you won't need any fancy nail polish. The chafing can be endless and only experience will identify where you'll need protection which means you have to suffer at least once while learning. Josh and Scott have both made plenty of mistakes in the past so today they carefully work through the mental checklist hoping that nothing new or unexpected slips in to ruin the plan.

The conversation continues as they prepare for the workout but most of it seems to be in a code that only others in their sport would recognize. If they were overheard the listener would find, like anyone who has spent way too much time together, the two runners could talk for hours about absolutely nothing. This morning's run, a nice steady 35 miles through the Withalachochee Wildlife Management Area, would be filled with non-stop inane chatter.

Like all distance runners, they start each run concerned about two things, weather and terrain. It doesn't matter if it's high mountains, scorching deserts, sweltering heat or blinding snow, they all present problems that must be overcome.

Unlike some of the fair weather locations around the United States, the oppressive heat and humidity make Florida a tough place for a distance runner to train, but it can be done. You almost have to equate it to training at high altitude. Just as in the mountains, you have to make adjustments to your workouts to allow for the increased effort required to run in the oxygen depleted air. For most of the year, it meant early morning or late evening runs. Although Scott couldn't stomach it, Josh was content to train indoors on a treadmill during the week so that he could avoid the heat and also to accurately control the pace he was running. It was hard for him to take an "easy" day without the treadmills accurate speed settings as a means to force him to maintain a slower pace. To break up the boredom, he'd head for the trails every weekend and, when possible, for a mid week long run.

Josh was keenly aware that the biggest danger of running outside in the heat and humidity was dehydration and he had been on the wrong side of the equation enough times to learn his lesson. In fact, proper hydration, enough but not too much, combined with the right amount of electrolytes is a battle that every runner in Florida is intimately familiar with. If you get it wrong, you're in for a tough day, and worse, an extended recovery period before you can resume hard training.

In fact, ultra distance running may be the only sport in existence where the athletes monitor the color of their urine. Light yellow and it's all systems go. Dark yellow and you're entering the danger zone. If you are unable to get the fluids back under control, be prepared for a downward spiral that includes energy loss, cramping, dry heaves, disorientation and even kidney failure. If it makes it all the way to brown, you can expect a trip to the hospital or worse.

So what do you do? The first instinct is to follow the old rule of *drink early and often.* It's a great idea but, if all you drink is water, additional danger lurks. Too much water combined with massive sweat loss can cause an imbalance in the electrolyte, or salt level in your system. The results can be deadly. Your brain can swell and without medical attention you can actually die from over-hydrating.

It's scary to be 8 miles from your car on a 95 degree day and realize that you've screwed it up. You have to stay calm and get back by any means possible. The last time it happened to Josh he flagged down a car and asked if they could drive him to a store for water. It doesn't take a genius to figure out that if you're on a remote trail that option disappears. To avoid this problem you have to do one very important thing. Plan. On more than one occasion Josh had missed that step.

Quite simply, if you move anywhere in the Deep South, severe dehydration and heat stroke are part of the landscape. It's like being dropped in the ocean, you have to learn how to swim fast or you're going to drown. Even after you've learned, you still know there's danger but you're more confident that you can handle it.

In Florida, the terrain is a much easier problem to deal with than the weather.

There's no doubt that the southern peninsula is identified more by it's beaches than it's trails, but Josh was lucky enough to live in Ocala, which is located in the midst of the rolling hills that dominate the central part of the state. It's only a few miles from his house to the Cross Florida Greenway. Once there, the Santos Trailhead gives him direct access to over a hundred miles of single track trail through a variety of eco-systems. Similar parks and trails are available within a short drive in every direction. All of them are unique, and nice in their own way, but his favorite was the location of today's morning run. They were going to run the Croom Tract of the Withalachochee Wildlife Management Area.

The Croom Tract has close to 22 miles of surprisingly hilly hiking trails along with another 55 miles of mountain bike trails. The footing varies from firm packed dirt with tree roots and rocks sprinkled in to deep sugar sand on the hills that are remnants of ancient sand dunes.

The sand is a persistent nuisance. Although it sounds relaxing, running at the beach is only fun the first time. No one in their right mind would do it twice. At Croom, the fine grained sand saps your energy with incredible efficiency. Nothing's solid. Your feet slide in all directions and you have to fight for balance. Even worse, it sticks all over your already damp skin and quickly finds its way into shoes and clothing causing friction and exacerbating blister problems. When it rains, it turns to mud, when it's dry, it's like running in baby powder, when it's hot, it mirrors the heat back into the air like a blast furnace. Sandy beaches may be romantic, but sandy trails suck.

Hills in Florida are not significant by any stretch of the imagination. If you want a really long hill, that is, one that takes more than 30 seconds to run up, you go to the inter-costal waterway and run the bridges. That doesn't mean the hills at Croom don't hurt. It just means that they only hurt for 30 seconds each. So there are no hour long climbs to sap your strength, instead it's the unrelenting series of hills that eventually wears you down. None are steep enough to require a walk break, so you're running continuously, and after a few hours you really feel them tearing into your reserves. It won't prepare you for the mountainous terrain found in many trail ultras but it's still tough and ultra runners from all over central Florida flock there every weekend to prepare themselves, as best they can, for those mountain 100-milers. Every now and then, if someone is really serious about getting some mountainous trail running in, they make the seven-hour drive to North Georgia and test their strength against the Appalachian Trail.

"You ready yet?" Scott asked as he started walking towards the trailhead.

"Yeah, Yeah, I'm ready."

"Let's go. I'll lead for a while, until I get sick of knocking down spider webs for you." Scott was already shuffling into a slow jog. "Try to keep up."

"It won't be hard. Just make sure to yell loud when you fall so I don't step on you."

The spiders are everywhere this time of year. Each morning they build their thick sticky webs across the trail and wait for prey. These aren't tiny spiders that you barely see. They're huge and the webs adhere to your face like glue. The spider's long legs are two to five inches across and connect to a body that can be the size of a silver dollar. Without warning, they come out of the darkness and cling to you as you frantically swipe at the messy remains of their liar. If your luck is bad, you get one right in the face. Big enough that it could be mistaken for a pirate's eye patch. It's not unusual to think you've gotten through a large web cleanly only to have a gigantic spider work its way off your shirt to the sensitive skin of your neck. It's an unmistakable feeling that really gets the adrenaline flowing.

Early on, Scott seemed to be immune and had earned the nickname of "Spiderman". Josh had eventually developed a tolerance for them and could now plow through the webs without so much as a single curse.

They started downhill from the parking lot on a stretch of single track that was covered with leaves and tree roots. It was tricky footing and you had to stay focused to avoid falling. They had run it many times and you would think that they would know every step of it, but at night it was another world. Only two minutes out, Scott went off the hiking trail and ran a hundred yards down a bike trail that crossed it. Cutting across, through the thick underbrush, to the correct trail would never work. They would have to backtrack to the point of the error. Josh could have made the same mistake but he laughed at Scott for the next 10 minutes anyway. It was going to be a long morning.

Running at 4 a.m. is unnatural and Josh feels lousy as they work their way through the first 10 to 15 minutes. The small amount of stretching had done very little to alleviate the tightness in his achilles and hamstring. Pains that were leftovers from his mid-week speed session. Even his lungs feel bad. The early pace is easy but he breathes heavily as if he's hammering out intervals on the track. It's always that way. After a few miles, the body recognizes what's going on and starts to bring dormant systems to life. Blood will start to surge into cold, tight muscles and tendons. The oxygen delivery systems will begin to do their jobs with ruthless efficiency. By the time Josh's eyes are wide open and he feels fully awake, the aches and pains of the first few miles will have faded away. Neither runner talks about how they feel. Instead, they run into the dark woods in the midst of a fervent debate concerning college football.

Scott loved running at night while Josh barely tolerated it as a necessary part of living in Florida. For Josh, it was eerie and more than a little scary to run through a remote part of the woods alone at night. Visions of the Blair Witch and every slasher movie ever made lodge themselves in your memory. Josh didn't always think about those things, but one evening, as Josh was heading to the trails for a night run, Jill made an unsolicited and unnecessary remark.

"Wasn't Danny Rollings, you know, the Gainesville serial killer, living in the woods when he mutilated all those college students?" she asked innocently.

"Why in the hell would you ask that? You know that's only 30 miles from here. Why would you want to even bring that up?" Josh asked.

His run that night was horrendous.

Once those thoughts get in your head, you jump at every noise expecting something horrible behind each tree and around every corner. The experience of night time trail running will quickly convince you that when you're alone in the dark, with no way to get help, your imagination is something that you'd like to be able to turn off, but you can't.

Even if you don't have random thoughts of terror, the noises will still drive you crazy. The first time you do a night run it's unnerving because you expect tranquility and silence but you quickly find that the darkness is bursting with the sounds of nature. No matter how many times you've run a loop, at night, your favorite trail won't look even remotely familiar and it will probably scare the shit out of you.

They ran single file, in the dark, over the rolling hills and through the bottom of several primeval sinkholes that are scattered through the area. After a while the never changing beam of light gives them tunnel vision and everything outside of the small faint beam fades into impenetrable blackness. The terrain changes slightly as they head into a marshland section near a couple of ponds. The sounds change as well. Soon they hear frogs, birds, and other animals splashing in and out of the water. Occasionally, when they come close to the ponds during the wet season, they'll hear the unmistakable sound of larger animals in the water. Alligators inhabit just about every body of water in Florida and they are known to lie near the trails at night. They're also very fast. The ponds tend to overflow when the rains come during hurricane season and, at times, the trails and new pond boundaries intersect. Stepping on the back of a 10 foot gator at night is not a pleasant thought so Josh and Scott are always a little more alert when they are in close proximity to any water.

Having someone else with you definitely makes night running a lot easier on your mind. A little bit of conversation keeps the ever present light from hypnotizing you into a zombie like state and running off course. Not being out there solo also eliminates some of the fear factor. You still worry about falling, which happens almost every time, but at least someone knows where you're at if you get injured or, in Josh's case, have an unexpected panic attack.

Just over an hour into the run they cross a paved road that they had driven down on their way to the trailhead. It was a convenient place to leave some supplies. As usual, they had hidden water, extra batteries and some energy drinks in a small cooler just off of the road and out of sight. This isn't a race and they take their time crossing the road and making their way to the stash. They want time on their feet to prepare for Hellgate but they don't really want to run hard enough to get out of breath. The general rule is that if it gets hard to talk they're running too fast. The idea is to teach the body to conserve carbohydrates while burning fat for fuel.

Josh is feeling good now. After just over eight miles, the rust has been knocked off and they've settled into a pace that feels easy. It's the part of the run where he feels like he could go forever. There's no pain at all.

This early in the morning it's still relatively cool, not even 75 degrees yet, and steam is rising off of the tops of their heads as they briefly stop to refill their bottles.

"Any damage?" Josh inquires.

"None. Just the normal minor cuts from the bushes and vines. I tell ya, it's nice to get through that section without a fall," Scott said while looking over the welts on his lower legs.

"Damn, I didn't tell you about the fall I had out here last week," said Josh.

"No, what happened?"

"I don't even know. I went down hard just before the pond. It was so fast, I didn't even get a hand up," Josh said.

"At night?" Scott asked.

"No. It was right after the sun came up. It was a sand section and I think I tripped over the only rock within a hundred yards."

"At least it was sand."

"That's what I thought but it still hurt. I must have landed wrong. Anyway, I was sore most of the week from it."

"You really need to run at night more often too get used to it. There are sections out here that are bad but it's nothing compared to what you'll get in the mountains," Scott said.

Josh knew Scott had more experience on trails and was usually eager to ask questions. "What makes it so different?"

"Lot's of things. The weather, the footing, the speed you can run."

"Slow up and fast down?"

"Yeah. But at night, it's the downs that you need to worry about."

"Sure, I imagine the downhills are really steep and can be treacherous," Josh said.

"Absolutely. You have to be careful and aggressive at the same time. It's a tough thing to do."

Josh had always been fast on downhills but he had never tried to fly down a trail covered by rocks. "I think I can handle it."

"You probably can, but don't go too fast and get out of control."

"Why?"

"When the hill is really steep you can go so fast that you'll outrun your light."

Josh was confused. "What do you mean I'll outrun my light?"

"You'll see an obstacle or a turn but you'll be going too fast to make a maneuver to avoid running into or off of it." The tone had turned serious so Josh was paying attention.

"That does not sound like a lot of fun."

"It's not fun if it's a cliff," Scott said as he sprayed a heavy dose of cancerous chemicals on his arms and legs to ward off the massive deerflies that would accompany the sunrise. "Let's get going, I want as many miles as possible behind us when the evil sun rises into the sky."

Leaving the cooler concealed in its hiding spot, they re-adjusted their headlamps and vanished back into the woods.

Although the temperature was still reasonable, the humidity was not. Typical of the season, the humidity was over 90 percent and they were already drenched with sweat. At times the air was so thick that it looked like a light rain being illuminated by their lights. It certainly wasn't fog, but the heavy mist still reduced visibility as it reflected the light back at them. The runners accepted it as part of the landscape, made bad jokes, told stories, and continued to run.

As they made their way along the trail it gradually became hillier. The ground was less firm and the sandy sections increased in length and frequency. Like a couple of human metronomes, they continued at the same pace never deviating by more than a few seconds per mile. Their inner clocks calibrated by thousands of miles worth of training. Ninety minutes into the run they bounded up the largest hill on the loop. Josh knew this spot very well. It was one of the many checkpoints where he would glance at his watch and make a quick comparison to the previous loops he had run. By these checks he could tell you five miles into the loop, within a minute, what his time would be at fifteen miles when he returned to the parking area. By comparison, Scott never looked at his splits on the trail, always relying on feel to judge his pace.

"It feels a little fast to me," Scott said as they crested the hill.

Josh clicked the light on his GPS equipped watch and checked the time. "Nope. We're all right. Maybe you're just getting old."

"I am old, but so are you. Let's slow it down over these hills. We need to keep our heart rates down."

"Ok, ok. I get it. You set the pace and I'll follow obediently."

The next twenty minutes took them over the most difficult portion of the 15-mile loop. The hills really start to roll at you, one right after another, and the ground gets soft with lots of loose sugar sand. Finally, just as you think it's over, the last mile is predominately uphill and the ground is heavily strewn with rocks and roots. The old oak forest is beautiful but you don't dare take your eyes off the trail to admire it. The road to the parking area appears unexpectedly as you round one of many corners in the thick woods.

Today they returned to the cars just as the sky was starting to lighten up. The plan would be to refill supplies, change into dry shoes, and head back out within five minutes. Twenty minutes after that, by the time they were able to see well enough to turn off their headlamps, and regular folk were considering rolling out of bed, they would have 18-miles of trail running behind them.

"I love days like this," Scott said as he opened the back of the truck.

"Really?" Josh rolled his eyes and started digging through his bag for a dry pair of socks. "Someday I'm going to have to teach you how to play golf."

"No thanks. I think that game would drive me crazy," Scott laughed. "Besides, I can't afford a whole new wardrobe."

"Golf is like a good education that you can rely on," Josh explained. "It will be there for you long after your knees and ankles can't continue with these gentle Saturday morning five hour runs."

"There's gotta be something else I can do," he moaned. "Maybe five-hours of good solid lawn care would keep me satisfied."

"Not a chance. It's going to be golf," Josh sounded serious. "Don't worry. I'll help you. You know, get you good instruction, nice equipment. I'll make sure that, by the time you get on the course, you can hold your own against any great grandmother they pair you with."

"It's comforting to know you'll be there for me Josh. But in the meantime, let's get these last 20 miles in and then treat ourselves to a couple of ice cold beers."

"Deal. I'll lead for a while so that we stay on the correct trail," Josh chided.

"Fine with me. Let's go."

They made the slow jog back to the trailhead and began a repeat of the same loop they had started on two hours earlier. The relentless pace of 7:30 per mile would continue for the next hour and then, as the heat builds, it would start to get tougher to maintain the cadence, but they would still do it as long as their heart rates didn't elevate too much.

The second loop always started a little faster than the first since they were fully warmed up but Josh fought his desire to go even quicker. This was the point in the run where he wanted to feel like he was floating. Every instinct told him to speed up, that he should be covering ground effortlessly.

Today he was really feeling strong. You can never predict how your body will react to the stress of exercising for hours on end. A bad meal the night before or a missed water stop can be the dagger that kills a long training run. But sometimes, when you don't even expect it, your training comes together and you're treated to a great day. An *I can do this forever* kind of day. Josh was having one.

"Josh?"

"Yeah?"

"Take it easy. We need to stay on pace and keep aerobic."

Josh had heard the physiological reasons for the long run a hundred times but he just didn't see why Scott insisted that they run them so slow. "Fine, but why? It doesn't make sense."

"What doesn't make sense? You need the long run to build capillarization which increases blood volume in the muscles and that lets you move more oxygen," Scott explained before reminding himself that Josh was new to ultras but not distance running.

"Of course. I know that. Don't forget, I've done long runs with Salazar, DeCastella and even Grete. All when they were in their prime. I'm talking world record type of form. I know why I did long runs back then and I know why they did them," Josh sounded annoyed.

"Then what's the question?"

"Ok, look, I've trained for marathons and ultras by incorporating long runs into my schedule and I agree with the blood volume thing. Obviously, you have to get oxygen to the muscle and you have to increase the amount of glycogen that the muscle can store."

Scott nodded his head but Josh couldn't see it. "Right, you want as much energy as possible to be available during the race."

"Ok, so we agree again. Here's where you lose me," Josh said. "Why so slow? When I trained for marathons, I always did my long runs, which were 15 to 20 miles, at close to race pace and it worked great."

"That's fine for a marathon but it doesn't work very well for a 50 or a 100 mile trail race."

Josh was still arguing. "Why not? I'm still burning more fat than carbs. I'm just forcing myself to do it at a faster pace by increasing my anaerobic threshold."

They dropped onto a narrow trail into another old sinkhole as Scott continued his explanation. "You're right, we want to teach our bodies to burn fat not carbs so that we can run longer distances without bonking but you're missing a critical part of the equation."

"What?"

"The reason that we're out here running for 5 hours. That's not something you'd do while training for a marathon. Agreed?"

"No, it isn't. I figured it's more of a mental thing. Not physical. You know, learning the pace and getting used to being out there for a long time. Simulating race conditions."

"That's a big part of it, but there's more," Scott said.

"What?"

"The endocrine system."

"OK, you got me. What the hell is the endocrine system and why do we care," Josh asked.

"Well, it's probably the single most important reason that we're doing long runs. It's a series of glands that produce hormones in response to stress." They ran hard back out of the sinkhole. "We're putting our bodies through a state of prolonged stress. Much longer than the two and a half hours of the marathons that you've run and the endocrine system has to adapt to maintaining its function for those longer periods of time. During an ultra marathon, we could be out on the course for anywhere from seven to 30 hours, depending on the race that you're attempting."

"So, a couple of long runs at a slow pace will do that?"

"Not really, it's a gradual process that can take months or years but you can't really see the gains unless you do it right. If you don't run for more than three hours it won't stress the system long enough to trigger a response. So, getting back to your original question. We run aerobically so that we minimize the amount of carbs we burn, that way we can go longer and, hopefully, stress the endocrine system which allows us to go even further the next time. It's a problem marathoners don't have to deal with."

"And if we don't deal with it?"

"Simple. Then you're going to get beat badly by a bunch of less talented guys that did."

They ran in silence for a few minutes.

"Great, so how long do we build up for Hellgate?" Josh finally asked.

"That's the good news. We've been doing our buildup all through the spring and summer. I just never explained it to you. That's why you can run 35 miles today and not be a wreck in the morning but if you go too fast and stop burning fat for fuel you'll screw it up. So slow down," Scott insisted.

Josh didn't reply, he responded by a slight reduction in the cadence he had been hammering out for the past two miles. Scott seemed satisfied and, as the sky lightened enough to turn off their lights, they continued on silently.

By the time they arrived at their water stop the sun was at the treetops and the temperature was climbing fast.

"Fun's over, grab an extra water bottle for the hills, it's gonna get hot."

Josh, who had lived in Florida for most of the last 25 years, was a good runner in the heat. Some never became acclimatized to it but he had adapted pretty well for a guy who had grown up in the cold of Nebraska and Minnesota. Today, they had started early and avoided it for a long time, but the last 12-miles would be hot and humid.

Every clothing company that manufactures outdoor gear has a line of high tech fabrics that wick moisture away from your body to help keep you cool and dry. During the Florida summer, they are absolutely useless. The air is heavy and feels thick in your lungs, making you labor for each breath. Staying dry is impossible and when the sun comes up the humidity causes a haze that stretches to the horizon. Shoes, socks and clothes are soaked within minutes and add considerable unwelcome weight.

When Marty Liquori was the best middle distance runner in America he trained through a Florida summer. At one point he was struggling to run 10 miles in an hour, which should have been easy for him, and even considered skipping a planned trip overseas to race Kip Keino. At the last minute, he decided to make the trip even though he felt unprepared. Much to his surprise, he beat Keino and broke the American Record for the 5,000 meters.

There's no way to perform at a high level in that type of climate but you can adapt and train hard. That's what Josh and Scott were trying to do.

This time around they could actually see the hills and sinkholes that the trail traverses and Josh enjoyed the view as Scott led them through the marsh area that leads up to the old pine covered sand dunes. When they passed one of the trails landmarks, a peace sign, which was made of an arrangement of colored rocks and sticks just off the side of the trail, Josh was getting antsy.

They'd covered about 26 miles, a full marathon, and had nine hot miles remaining. Scott was maintaining the pace but feeling it while Josh was cruising. Sure, Josh's legs weren't as good as they'd been an hour earlier, but he still felt strong on the hills and could switch to a higher gear if needed. In fact, he had convinced himself that the pace was too slow and the cause of the tightness that he was developing in his knees. He thought that going a little bit faster might loosen his joints back up and make him feel even better. He knew that Scott would complain but, despite Scott's scientific explanation of the endocrine system he had received earlier, Josh wanted to run. He passed Scott on the long uphill and noticeably picked up the pace.

"Josh. Don't do it. We're going fast enough."

He didn't back off this time. "I just want to stretch my legs a little. We've been running that same pace for three and a half hours."

"If you go much faster, you'll start to burn carbs and that's not what we're here for."

"I know. I know. Don't worry. I'll just do it for a couple of miles."

Scott just shook his head as Josh powered up the next hill. Within a minute he had lost contact. Scott knew that Josh could run that pace for the rest of the workout without much difficulty but, once again, he had not figured out a way to make him under-stand that he didn't *need* to. The training that you have to do for a race that takes 15 hours is very different even from marathon training. Josh apparently still didn't get that and it showed this morning. Someday he'd learn the hard way.

It wasn't all fun and games for Josh. Even though he was having a good day, 35 miles is 35 miles. There's no way to run that far without discomfort. For Josh it came in the form of a deep ache that slowly built in intensity over the last hour of the run. It didn't affect his pace, but the floating feeling he'd enjoyed early in the day was replaced by a somewhat stiff legged gait that sent shockwaves through his knees and hips. The ache gradually escalated and would require ice and time to fully remove from his system. This is the way long runs go. It feels so easy for a long time but the inevitable will always happen. The pain comes. The only way to effectively delay this disintegration is to mix in a lot of walking and that's not in Josh's nature. If the terrain dictates walking, then he complies, but in general, Josh is a runner, not a walker.

An hour and a half later, they were back together in the parking lot, sitting in lawn chairs with ice on their knees and drinking cold beers from plastic cups. Hellgate was still three months away so they had some time to come up with a race plan but today's run had been a great confidence builder. Scott had admonished Josh for his lack of discipline, but Josh hadn't really listened.

"There is a reason for everything," Scott explained, "even the long slow run."

Josh nodded his head and pretended to agree but, the truth was, he felt great and didn't see any reason to run slower than he was capable of especially to benefit some invisible hormonal system that he'd never heard of before.

Despite Josh's abandonment of Scott, this morning's run had gone very smoothly. Josh and Scott had refilled their supplies at regular intervals and had stayed fueled and hydrated. As a result, they would have no trouble quickly recovering for a run the next day. Unfortunately, not every workout was as well planned as today's. When Josh started ultra running he made the mistake of heading out on a poorly planned and ill-fated solo run on the Appalachian Trail that Jill has still not forgiven him for. With Hellgate looming, he knew he'd need to be much better prepared on his next trip to the mountains.

The Appalachian Trail

"You have to imagine that training is like a bow that you
pull back as far as possible to shoot the arrow…This can be
dangerous. Sometimes you can't hold the bowstring back
any longer. Or you can overpull it."

— Uta Pippig
Winner of the Boston Marathon 3-times

July 25th, 2003, North Georgia near Springer Mountain

It all started innocently enough while they were taking an early
vacation for their 8th Anniversary.

Josh was recovering from an injury and had taken quite a bit
of time off from running. The normal procedure would be to
slowly ramp back up to the training mileage that he was running
before the injury occurred. This process, when done correctly,
should take several months. He knew how to do it the right way,
but this time around Josh decided to do something that, in hind-
sight, was uncharacteristic for a runner with his experience.

Instead of the normal build up, he decided to quickly
increase the length of his weekend runs. The reason was simple.
In July, he was preparing to take Jill on vacation in North Georgia,
very near the southern terminus of the Appalachian Trail. How
could he be that close to the greatest trail on the east coast and not
include a portion of it on a training run? It wasn't unusual for
Josh to overdo things. Given that character trait, of course, four or
five miles would not be adequate. He wanted to do a long run and
see as much of the trail as possible.

This blunder wasn't the classic "Hold my beer and watch this" variety but, although he had good intentions, it was amazing how few precautions he took.

First, he did no research on the trail. What is the elevation profile? Where can you get water? Is there access for a car anywhere? How is it marked? What's the weather like that time of year?

Second, he overestimated his abilities and the amount of time it would take to cover the selected section of the Appalachian Trail. He did not take into account the drop in his fitness level that occurred during his layoff. That mistake combined with a lack of trail knowledge caused him to start the run with an insufficient amount of food and water.

Third, there were no intermediate checkpoints setup to monitor his progress and he had no crew or method to contact anyone should he need help.

As a result, what should have been nothing more than a simple morning run the day before Jill and Josh drove back to Florida escalated into a near disaster.

The Southern Terminus of the Appalachian Trail, or AT as many hikers refer to it, is located at the top of Springer Mountain in North Georgia. There are several ways to get there but one of the most common is to hike up on an approach trail from Amicalola Falls State Park. Josh had never been on the AT or the approach trail but, without adequate information, he made the decision to run into Amicalola Falls from the North. He decided that Jill should drive him to "Woody Gap" on Hwy 60. This location was selected only because it was a point where the AT crossed a paved road. It was a choice of convenience, not based on trail knowledge. With very little sophistication, he used a road map instead of a trail map to estimate that it would be about 22 miles from his starting point to Amicalola Falls. The hastily formed plan was to drop him off at sunrise so that he could be done early and they could still have time to go for a short canoe trip on a nearby river that afternoon.

The next morning, Josh stood at the edge of the parking area where the AT crossed "Woody Gap" trying to figure out how to carry five water bottles when all he had was a single bottle fanny pack. "Well, I guess I can just loop the belt through the two hand strap bottles and then carry two regular bottles of water."

"That looks uncomfortable," Jill said.

"It is, but I'll drink the regular bottles first and toss them at the first campsite I pass. Then, I'll carry the bottles with the hand straps the rest of the way. It won't be too bad."

Jill was still not warming up to the idea of spending the morning alone. "It looks like a hassle to me but ... whatever. So what do you want me to do?"

"Go wherever you want for the next few hours. You can go back to the cabin if you want. Just be in the parking lot at the top of Amicalola Falls in four hours to pick me up," Josh said as he did a few token stretches.

Jill looked uncertain. "Are you sure you know where you're going Josh?"

He pointed a few yards ahead to the trail. "Sure, look at that tree. Do you see the white rectangle that's painted on it?"

"Yes."

"That blaze marks the Appalachian Trail for its entire length. Hikers pass through here all summer long. I'm sure that it's well marked all the way. There's nothing to worry about."

She looked skeptical but gave him a quick kiss and headed for the car. "All right, I'll see you in four hours at the falls. Don't be late."

"I won't be, it's only 22 miles."

As Josh started down the trail, he looked back to see Jill leaving the parking area and wondered if he should have given himself a little more leeway on the time. *No, I've never taken more than three hours to run 22 miles in my life. I've given myself an extra hour, that's conservative enough. Shoot, I'll probably have to wait for Jill to show up. Four hours is plenty of time,* he thought.

The early section of the run was breathtaking. He had started at one of the highest elevations on the Georgia portion of the trail and was gradually working his way to the valley. As he had explained to Jill, the trail was well marked and he was able to enjoy the spectacular scenery without paying an overt amount of attention to staying on course. The hard-packed dirt trail skirted the edge of a high cliff and through the tree line he was able to see for at least 20 miles. The sunrise was amazing and he had a hard time looking away long enough to watch where he put his feet.

There was no expectation that the footing would be great, just that it would be runnable and so far it had been. He took advantage of that and, for a while, he just seemed to float effortlessly down the trail. It was one of the reasons he had switched to trail running. You never had this feeling on the road where cars were always ready to choke you with fumes or end your career by proving they were bigger than you. No, this was very different from the roads and Josh was really starting to enjoy it. There was something very comforting about trail running, especially in remote areas where you couldn't hear cars or people, just birds, water, the wind through the trees and your own breathing.

Josh did the food and water calculation in his head as he ran. *OK, if I run this in four hours, I can drink a bottle of water every 45 minutes, which should be about right with the temperature today. So, that's a third of a bottle every 15 minutes, and I'll eat an energy gel each time I switch to a new bottle. Did I put electrolyte tablets in my pack? They must be in there from last weeks run. I'm sure I had some left.* The mild bit of concern he felt was swiftly dismissed. *It doesn't matter. I don't really need it for a four hour run anyway. Everything's fine.*

Josh was pleased that the first two miles had been rather tame and allowed for fast running but, soon after, it began to get tougher. It started with a gradual change in the trail conditions. As he ran further away from the heavily traveled area around "Woody Gap", the packed dirt gave way to rocks, lots of rocks, and Josh had to slow down to avoid twisting an ankle. At about the same time, the incline changed from a gentle downhill to a steep uphill. The increase in grade was a shock to his system and that, along with the change in footing, quickly combined to cut his pace in half. When he briefly became worried about losing time, he charged hard up the trail but, inevitably, reality overcame his enthusiasm and his pace started to slow again. The hill was short, only a quarter of a mile, but it got his attention as did the steep descent that followed. He struggled to recover and get his heart rate back under control. He was getting there but as soon as Josh hit the bottom of what turned out to be "Jacks Gap" the trail turned skyward again. For a flatlander, the terrain was intimidating. He was grinding away at it, but the climb to the top of "Liss Gap" was longer than any hill he had ever run and, not knowing the trail, once again he started to think that he was losing too much time. So, he tried to compensate by pushing as hard as he could up the incline and putting himself into race mode. The next two miles rolled through some ups and downs but it was predominately downhill. Josh hoped to have a chance to recover and make up some of the lost time. Unfortunately, the rocks were more frequent and the footing wouldn't allow him to run fast. He still felt decent but, when he arrived at the dirt road that signified he had reached "Gooch Gap", he was not on schedule and no longer felt in control of the run.

With his first bottle of water already gone, Josh started the climb out of "Gooch Gap". By this point, he realized that the trail was probably going to remain very rocky the rest of the way, hampering his ability to run at his planned pace. He was still trying though and, since his legs still felt strong, he kept up a hard effort past Blackwell and Justis Creeks. *I wish I knew how far I have to go.*

If Josh had taken the time to research the Appalachian Trail, he would have known that the four miles after Justis Creek were going to be extremely difficult. He started with a long climb to the top of "Phyliss Spur" and after a short but steep descent he continued up to the peak of "Justis Mountain". The second climb was intense and slow. By the time he reached the top, he was already working on the third bottle of water and wondering again where he was in relation to Springer Mountain. The strength he had earlier was diminishing and his legs were getting tight. Reluctantly, he took the time to sit for a few minutes and tried to admire the view, but he knew he couldn't stay long. He was losing too much time on the hills and had to keep moving.

The severe drop from the top of "Justis Mountain" to the road in the valley of "Cooper Gap" is very technical and steep but Josh attacked it anyway. When he hit the dirt road at the bottom his quads were really beginning to complain. In fact, they were screaming. He was sweating hard by then and had confirmed that his pack did not contain any electrolyte tablets. It was becoming clear that he did not have enough water and the brisk pace was destroying his legs. He would have bailed out but, without a planned intermediate stop, he had no choice but to continue toward Springer Mountain.

As Josh slowed to cross the road he nearly ran straight into a group of backpackers who were hiking in the opposite direction.

"Hey guys, what's up?" Josh asked tiredly.

"Not much. Where are you running to?" the first one in line asked.

Josh was out of breath as he stopped to chat. "I'm going to Amicalola Falls."

"Oh, cool, that's were we started from yesterday."

Josh was very interested now. "Really, do you happen to know how far it is from here?"

The hikers looked at each other and one in the middle spoke up. "Not in miles, but we hiked over 9 hours yesterday and had set up camp only a few minutes from here. So, it's pretty far."

Josh had no idea how that translated into miles either, but he agreed, it did sound like a long way. "Well, if it's that far, I'm in trouble. I guess I'd better get moving. Enjoy the trail guys."

Josh started to walk away but then he thought of one more question. "Oh, wait. Did you guys see any camping areas with drinking water between here and the Falls?"

The hikers shook their heads. "No, all the water has to be filtered. Either from a stream or from one of the water sources at the shelters. We'd give you some but we dumped the last of ours on the fire this morning. We were planning on refilling at the shelter on "Justis Mountain". Do you have a filter?"

"No, I didn't think about that. I thought I could carry enough to make it all the way to the Falls."

The hikers were starting to split off and walk towards the trail that Josh had just run down. "Sorry dude, just don't drink from the streams, you'll get sick," one of them said.

"Thanks," Josh said.

"Good luck with your run," he heard as he turned away.

With very little enthusiasm, Josh left "Cooper Gap" for the long, steep climb to the top of "Sassafrass Mountain". It was a torturous climb and when he finally emerged at the peak he once again took a few deep breaths and paused for the view. He wanted to spend 15 or 20 minutes to recover from the ascent but, unfortunately, there was no time to linger and he painfully jogged over the top and into another seemingly endless downhill that dropped him all the way back to the valley at Horse Gap. With his mood darkening, Josh was no longer certain that he could make it to Amicalola Falls in four hours. *Oh my god, it can't be 22 miles to Amicolola, I must have made a mistake.* His thoughts were all negative. *Maybe I read the map wrong. I can't believe that my legs are already this bad. This isn't good.*

At a point where he needed something positive to happen, Josh was fortunate that the next several miles were again fairly mundane. The trail was still rocky but the grade was milder and he was even able to run quite a few sections. But there was no stopping the inevitable. Josh was running out of water and, since his meeting with the hikers, he knew that there was none to be found on the trail. In a desperate attempt to stretch his supply, he quit drinking on his every 15 minutes schedule and started to conserve, but it was way too late. In fact, if he had known how far off he was on his estimate of the length of this run, he would never have left "Woody Gap". Because the truth was that, even if he had known how much he needed, he could not carry enough water for this run. It was simply too far, and the conditions too difficult.

Trying to stretch his remaining water worked for a while, but Josh ran out while making the relentless, quadricep pounding, three mile long descent from the crest of "Hawk Mountain" to the valley floor at "Three Forks". The only good thing about arriving at "Three Forks" was that he finally knew where he was. As he passed through the abandoned campground, he saw a small sign that said "Springer Mountain – 4 miles" which reassured him that at least he was on the right trail. But it didn't make up for all of the bad news. He had already been on the trail for well over four hours, he was out of water and he had a long way to go yet. Jill would already be at Amicalola Falls waiting for him and he had no way to contact her and let her know that he was going to be late. Drinking water without any electrolyte replacement had left him tired and sore but, if his legs didn't cramp too bad, at least he still felt that he had enough strength to get to the falls.

It's probably best that Josh didn't know about the severity of the climb to the top of Springer Mountain. It would be a shock when he discovered that the entire four miles was uphill and the elevation gain was almost 2000 feet but, at this point, not knowing may have been better. Josh left the campground and worked up the incline at a steady pace mixing short runs with power hiking and, after well over an hour, he finally made it to the plaque that indicated the Southern Terminus of the trail. It was five hours and 30 minutes since he had left "Woody Gap". He stood on the rock right next to the plaque and enjoyed the view, happy with his accomplishment, even though it was clear that his conservative estimate of four hours had been pure fantasy. Despite being very late and tired, Josh's spirits rose because he thought he was past the worst part and that the rest would be easy. *It has to be downhill from here to the falls. I should be there in less than an hour. Wow, over 2 hours late. Sorry Jill. I wish I could let you know I'm Ok.*

After resting for ten minutes, and reading the plaque several times, he climbed off of the rock face and started looking for the white rectangles that he thought would lead him to Amicalola Falls. That's when Josh realized his biggest mistake of the day may not have been miscalculating the distance and time. It may have been running south toward the falls. He hadn't even considered that at Springer Mountain the AT was finished. The white rectangles, which Josh had been following all day, ended at the plaque! When hikers leave the falls heading north, the approach trail to Springer Mountain is marked by signs that lead you to the trail and show you the identifying blazes to follow, but heading south from the mountain there were no signs! He had to pick from three other trails that led down from the mountain without knowing which one went to the falls. *This is a major screw-up. How do I choose? Maybe the one that looks the most used? What if I'm wrong? How far will I go before deciding to turn back?*

He was alone on the mountain and even if he had spoken out loud there was no one to answer. The completely dejected and beaten runner simply picked a trail at random and started a painful, spastic run down the mountain. He chose a trail with a similar blaze to the Appalachian Trail's white rectangle. With some luck, the white diamond he was following would lead him to Amicalola State Park. As could be expected, the descent was steep and rocky. After about 30 minutes, he reached the valley where the trail fell in along a creek. *Maybe this is the creek that feeds the falls,* he thought. Another agonizing 15 minutes went by and he came to a cross roads with another trail. Briefly, he wondered what this new trail was and if he should continue or turn. As he was looking left and right, trying to make a decision, he saw a mark on one of the trees. It was a white rectangle. *It can't be! That's the marking for the AT. Why would another trail use the same marking?* At first, he wasn't thinking clearly, but as soon as he headed toward the marking he connected the dots. He realized that he had chosen the wrong trail and backtracked almost all the way down the mountain to the AT. He was running in circles. Long, excruciating and demoralizing circles.

There was absolutely nothing he could do but make his way back to the top of Springer Mountain and try again. The energy that had barely been available in his legs the first time up the mountain was gone and, this time, it was a real grind back up to the top. After a strenuous 45 minute hike, he was once again staring at the AT Southern Terminus plaque, but this time, instead of enjoying the view, he sat down next to it and he cried. He had now been out for over seven hours and he still didn't know how to get to the falls. The sun was high in the sky. It was getting into the early afternoon and he was starting to feel weak and very, very thirsty. It had now been almost three hours since he finished his last bottle of water. He could feel the devastating effects of dehydration on his body and his moral.

As hard as he tried, he could not think of any solution to his problem except to pick another trail and run. There was no other way to get back, but the thought of choosing the wrong trail again terrified him. What if the last trail hadn't crossed the AT? He could have gone for hours before realizing his mistake. Or even worse, this time he might get within a mile of the falls and turn around thinking he had made the wrong choice.

As Josh stood on Springer Mountain, contemplating which trail to take, Jill was at Amicalola Falls going into full panic mode. Her husband was almost three hours late on a run he had assured her would take less than four hours and she was angry. She had waited at the top of the falls for an hour before deciding that she must have misunderstood him. He must have said "Meet me at the parking lot at the bottom of the falls." So she drove the road back to the bottom. There was still no sign of Josh. *Maybe he's on the trail in between the parking lots? I should walk it and make sure,* she thought. After hiking to the top of the falls she was sure that he was not in the state park and she went from pissed off to scared. She immediately thought of several things that could have gone wrong. He's hurt from a fall, he's lost and wandering in the wilderness, or he was attacked by a wild animal. While in the lower parking area, she had noticed the Park Ranger Headquarters and she thought they could help. She had totally lost her composure by the time she walked into the office to tell her story to the rangers.

Luckily, Josh had a moment of clear thought before blindly plummeting down another trail. *All right. Think. I took the center trail and it connected back to the AT. I turned left on the AT to get back up to Springer Mountain. That means the trail to the left of the one I already tried can't be the trail to Amicalola Falls, unless I missed seeing them cross at some point, which is possible, but not likely.* He thought through it again and couldn't find any fault in the logic. So, with some reluctance, he started a slow jog downhill on the right hand trail.

The rocky path was well marked with a blue blaze and worked downward through a series of switchbacks until it reached the valley floor. The underbrush was thicker here and it disoriented Josh who, up to that point, thought he was heading south. He slowly ran through the woods looking for anything that would indicate he was going in the right direction. For a while, the terrain was predominately flat but soon he saw a large hill looming in front of him and he realized that the path back to Amicalola Falls may not be easy after all. With his energy stores depleted and his legs screaming with each step, he slogged up the long, brutal hill. When he reached the top he found a large campground with picnic tables and cooking fires but no hikers or trail markings. As he walked around the campsite looking for the continuation of the trail, he noticed a small sign nearly toppled on its side. He was incredibly relieved when he pushed away a branch and saw that the sign showed "Springer Mountain - 2 miles" behind him and "Amicalola Falls - 7 miles" ahead. *Does that say seven miles? How can it possibly be that far? I didn't know the Approach Trail was nine miles long?* Once again, the lack of research was adding to the agony, but at least he had confirmation that he was, once again, on the right trail. The last seven miles seemed to last a lifetime and there is no way that Josh ever wants to hurt like that again. The hills were steep and, in his dehydrated condition, Josh's legs were cramping and shooting pain through his body with each step. His heart raced at even the slightest incline and the thirst was indescribable. Running was no longer an option so he just tried to keep moving. Two hours later, after leaving the AT for the second time, Josh stumbled into the upper parking lot of Amicalola Falls State Park. He'd been on the trail for nine hours.

This is it! I'm done. Where's Jill? I have to find something to drink. As Josh slowly moved across the parking lot towards the lights coming from a cluster of vending machines, he could only form simple thoughts. He pulled a couple of crumpled dollars from his pack and slipped them into the machine. Even his hands had lost their dexterity and it was difficult to open the cans. He knew, if he sat down to drink, he'd stay down. It didn't matter anymore. He sat to drink his Cokes and had just started to pull the shoes off of his blistered feet when a man walked up behind him.

"Are you Josh Stanton?" the man asked.

Josh looked up at the uniformed man and realized it was a park ranger. *How does he know my name?* "Yes" was the only reply he could muster.

"Thank God you made it here. Are you all right?"

Josh was listless and his speech was slow. "Yeah, I guess."

"Let me help you to my jeep, I need to take you to see your wife. She's at the ranger headquarters and she is quite convinced that you're dead." The ranger was already on his radio spreading the word that he had found the missing hiker.

Josh looked across the parking lot at the Jeep but his mind was too unclear to understand that they were looking for him. "My wife? What are you talking about?" he asked.

"She told us that you were running here from "Woody Gap" and that you were long overdue. She was sure that you had been attacked by a bear or were injured. For the past 45 minutes, we've been in the process of organizing a search and rescue effort."

"You're kidding right?" Josh was stunned.

"No, five hours late in these mountains always gets our attention."

"Yeah, I told her it would take me four hours but I was way off. I'm really sorry about the confusion."

Josh was having a meltdown and just wanted to get Jill and head back to the cabin as soon possible.

The ranger helped Josh to the Jeep and carried his drinks for him. "Did you really start at Woody Gap?" he asked as he helped Josh up and into his seat.

"Yeah, I guess I miscalculated the distance to the falls. I estimated it to be 22 miles. How far off was I?"

"22 miles? You were way off. From here, it's right at 30 miles to "Woody Gap" but as you may have found out, the trails a lot tougher than people realize." The ranger had pulled the Jeep onto the two lane road that winds down to the base of the falls where the small Ranger Headquarters was located. "I can't remember ever hearing of someone doing it in four hours. In fact, it usually takes hikers a couple of days to get there from the falls."

Oh man, did I blow it. By taking the wrong trail off the top of Springer Mountain I must have gone 36 or 37 miles. "I know, I underestimated the difficulty of the trail but the worst part was that I ran out of water 5 hours ago. I guess I didn't do enough planning. It was just a spur of the moment decision to run the trail." Josh was quiet for a minute and then summed up the day. "The whole thing was a mess from the start."

They pulled into the ranger headquarters and Jill came running out to the jeep with tears in her eyes. *She'll never let me forget this one and I don't blame her.* He apologized to the rangers for the scare and was lectured for 20 minutes before they let him go. He didn't blame them either.

The next morning, Jill drove all the way back to Florida because Josh couldn't walk.

Cross Country

"The start of a cross country event is like riding a horse in the middle of a buffalo stampede. It's a thrill if you keep up but one slip and you're nothing but hoof prints."

— Ed Eyestone
Competed in two Olympic Marathons, was a 4-time NCAA champion and 10-time All-American

Fall of 1977 to Spring 1979, Woodbury, MN

Josh's move up to the varsity cross country team put him into another level of competition, from the other teams, as well as his own. In fact, he quickly found out that he would get the toughest test from his own teammate, a junior named Sean Nichols.

Sean had qualified for the state meet as a sophomore and already held the school records for the mile and two-mile. He was only a year older than Josh but he already had a quiet confidence that the rest of the team recognized. Josh would have to find a way to fit in with everyone, but at least he wouldn't have to take the additional pressure of being the top runner, that would go to Sean.

He knew that the cross country season would be tough for him. The race distance increased to three miles and it seemed like every school had two or three runners stronger than Josh. After a full season of being one of the fastest runners in the area he was suddenly thrown into the middle of the pack. It was all right for a while but he didn't want to be in that position all year. He'd had a taste of what it's like to win and he wanted more.

The first varsity cross country meet of the fall was a reality check for Josh. It was only a small conference meet with two other schools but he only managed an eighth place finish, and even worse, he was a full two minutes slower than Sean. A week later, he had cut that time gap down to 90 seconds and felt slightly more competitive.

By the end of the fourth race, Josh had gained some experience and gradually worked his way up in the standings. His times were a little better each week and he started to adapt to the longer distance. Fortunately, he was at an age where rapid improvement was possible if a coach new how to train him properly. And now he had a real coach for the first time. Coach Feder was an avid runner himself and even did the workouts with his team. He had them running intervals twice a week and, by the time the Conference Championship rolled around, Josh had established himself as the number two runner on the team. In fact, in the last race Josh had only been 45 seconds behind Sean and had posted the fifth best time in the St. Paul Suburban Conference.

A week before the biggest race of the year, the team had just finished an interval session on the track when Coach Feder jogged over to the infield and told Josh he wanted to talk about the Conference meet. Josh was becoming more comfortable in his role as a supporting member of the team but Coach Feder was starting to think he could do more.

"How are you feeling today?" Coach Feder asked.

"Pretty good I guess," Josh answered quietly.

"You're running a lot better than last week on the intervals."

"Yeah, I did feel better today, but they still hurt."

The coach laughed. "They'll always hurt Josh. The only difference you'll ever see is that as you get stronger you'll have to go faster and faster for the same benefit. I can tell you this, if they don't hurt, you're not pushing yourself hard enough."

"There's something to look forward to," Josh said uncomfortably.

The Coach lowered his voice and looked up at his number two runner. "Look Josh, the Conference meet is next week and I wondered if you had given any thought to a strategy for the race."

"Strategy? No, I guess not. I was just going to run."

"That's fine for early season races but at this time of year it's different. You need to have a plan."

"OK, well, what do you think I should do?" Josh asked.

The Coach looked away for a moment and watched Sean jogging past the soccer field then he looked back at Josh. "I think you should run with Sean right from the start."

"What!?" He exclaimed.

"You've got to go out harder at the start of the race. You've been getting caught in the pack and it keeps you from running at the front where you should be. I want you to run with Sean for the first mile so you can get into the clear. You'll hurt a lot earlier than you're used to, but I think you can handle it. Besides, by the time it happens, everyone else will hurt just as bad as you do."

Josh was already feeling the pressure and they were only talking about the race. "I'll die during the third mile and everyone will pass me." *I'll be humiliated,* he thought.

"No. Let me tell you a simple rule of thumb that the majority of runners never learn about cross country races." The Coach had Josh's attention. "Whatever place you're in at the end of the first half of the race is approximately where you'll finish. If you get out fast and in good position, you'll hold that place to the end. Sure, you may move up or down a few spots but, generally, you'll stay in the same place."

"What if I can't hold the place?"

"I think you can, but even if I'm wrong, it doesn't matter. What matters is trying. If you want to get better, you have to be bold. I think you can do it."

Josh just sat looking at the ground. He didn't think it was a good idea to try and run that aggressively but the Coach seemed to believe in him.

"Think about it," the Coach said as he got up and headed toward the locker rooms.

"Sure," Josh said.

For the next week, Josh watched his teammate during workouts and wondered if it was possible to stay with him at the Conference Championships. The more he watched the more certain he was that Coach Feder was making a mistake, and yet, now that he was thinking about it, he couldn't force the image out of his head.

The following Saturday, he waited until the end of his warm-up on the Goodrich Golf Course, site of the conference meet, to make his decision.

He jogged up to Coach Feder. "All right, I'm going to do it."

The Coach just smiled and nodded his head.

It was a beautiful sunny morning. Winter was just around the corner and Josh took a few deep breaths of the cool crisp air. He followed Sean for a short 50 yard acceleration to prepare himself for the feeling he'd have on the first straightaway. A few minutes later, the ten teams that make up the St. Paul Suburban Conference were lined up across the fifth fairway, waiting for the starter to send them off. Josh was incredibly nervous and, when the gun finally sounded, he stumbled for a couple of steps. Like all mass starts, it was a madhouse and he nearly got trampled by his own team.

Sean was out cleanly, as always, and everyone ran at the usual out of control speed towards the first turn where the course narrowed considerably. If Josh was going to stay with his teammate, he'd have to get to the turn in good position. Coach Feder had told him to be in the top third of the field. He was too far back so, to get there, he threw in a hard surge and also dished out his share of elbows. Up ahead he saw the leaders make the turn and briefly saw Sean in a small pack just behind them. He was starting to think that this was really a huge mistake, but he was committed. He made it through the turn and, as he ran the next downhill, he moved out into a clear space and gave it all he had for 30 seconds. Within about 200 yards he had passed a large pack of runners and moved into position just behind Sean who glanced back to see who had joined his group. He seemed more curious than concerned when he saw Josh just off of his shoulder.

"Nice work Josh, now stay with us," Sean said between breaths. "We need you up here for the team score."

Josh was going too hard to say anything to Sean so he just tried to clear his mind of negative thoughts and hang in there.

The five runners in the lead group were all seniors and juniors and Josh also thought he was the only sophomore in this chase group. The older and stronger runners were cruising while Josh was struggling with all he had to stay with them but he was still there. As they passed the mile mark, he heard five minutes called out and instantly panicked. He had not run the first mile of any race that year faster than 5:30 and the thought of going two more miles scared him. *What am I doing?* He thought. *This is crazy. I can't run with these guys.*

As they rounded the next turn, he saw his coach and decided that had to keep pushing. He had to try to stay close to Sean. There was no point in trying to slow down and, since it was too late to do anything else, he tried to suppress the panic and focus on the jersey in front of him.

It worked for a while and, as they passed the halfway point, from out of nowhere, he heard his coach yell. "Ninth place Josh! Perfect!"

He watched Sean break, almost effortlessly, from his group and close the gap on the leaders who had strung out in front of them. Josh just let him go and tried to hold his position. The two-mile mark passed and he was still ninth. *Maybe the coach is right. We're all spread out now and it's a long way back to the next runner. Everyone's suffering now. Hang on for another mile.*

He tried to funnel his energy into running and kept his mind from wandering by focusing on a tree and running hard all the way to it. Then, he picked another and another. As he ran the last mile, he lost contact with a couple of runners that he had kept close but, with only 100 yards to go, he was still in ninth place. He was spent but, just as the coach had predicted, no one had passed him in the last half of the race.

Two weeks later, at the regional meet, Sean qualified for the State Championships while Josh was close but missed by just a few places. He had solidly established himself as the teams number two runner but, when Sean placed fifth in the state meet, it was clear that a move past him into the number one slot appeared to be unlikely.

A runner in Minnesota has limited options during the winter. He can try to run but the conditions outside make it nearly impossible to do much more than easy jogging. Some days you can't even get out the door. The best option is cross country skiing.

The Nordic sport is great for cardiovascular fitness and makes the transition to the indoor track season much easier. Josh went out for the team and found out that he wasn't a great skier but he didn't really care. He just wanted to stay in shape for track and working hard at skiing was the best way to accomplish his goal. So, Josh skied the entire season while eagerly awaiting the first indoor meet of the year.

Once it arrived, Josh's first high school track season was both successful and uneventful. He ran in Sean's shadow the entire year. If Sean ran the two-mile, then Josh ran the mile. They were never in the same event and yet they provided the coaches a strong one-two punch. On several occasions, Sean broke school records that had stood for years only to have Josh also better the old marks within a few weeks. By then, of course, no one cared and Sean continued to garner the bulk of the attention.

Still, it was good for Josh and he gained a considerable amount of valuable experience. By the end of the season, he had improved his mile time to 4:38 and had run a respectable 10:03 in his favorite event, the two mile.

Like the previous year, he had big plans when he left school for summer vacation. He wanted to train hard over the next three months to be ready to meet the expectations that he and Sean would face during cross country. It wasn't hard to stay motivated and Coach Feder made it even easier by organizing several special running events over the summer.

Everyone on the team participated in those summer events and several, including Josh, also worked on Coach Feder's farm in Wisconsin, bailing hay and doing various chores. It was hard work, but being out there with his friends was fun and the time went by quickly. They did a lot of running and when school started back up, Josh, Sean, and the rest of the team, were in shape and ready for cross country.

It was Sean's senior season and after his fifth place finish at State the year before he was a favorite to win every time they competed. Josh was amazed at how well Sean handled the stress. He ran like a machine and it seemed like he actually became more relaxed as the pressure intensified. Josh, on the other hand, was still learning to deal with the expectations of his team. He wasn't as talented as Sean and, after a couple of sub-par performances early in the year, he began to question his ability. His mental state was eroding and it was Sean, not his coach, who finally came to his rescue.

They had just finished running a three mile loop through the woods on the north end of the school property and Sean had pushed the pace pretty hard. Josh, in typical fashion, had been the only one that was able to stay with him. Afterward, they started to run a warm-down together.

"What's going on Josh?" Sean asked.

"What do you mean?"

"Well, you're killing everyone in practice, including me, but in the first few meets you're back in the pack. After the way you ran over the summer, I thought you'd be on my ass all year. What's the deal?"

That was a question Josh had already been asking himself lately. "I don't know. I just seem to feel like crap on race day. Sometimes I feel great out here during the week and wish it was Saturday."

They ran along silently, taking a woodchip path down to the creek. Sean was the leader of the team and really wanted Josh to run better, but as confident as he was in his own abilities, he was not a coach and wasn't sure what to say. Still, he felt like he needed to offer some type of advice to the younger runner.

"Maybe you're just running too hard during the weekday training sessions. Why don't you back off a little bit next week and try to be more rested for the meet?" Sean suggested.

It sounded like a good idea to Josh. "I'll try it. I sure can't run any worse than I did last weekend. I placed terrible."

By now, they were running alongside the creek and Sean stopped running to face Josh. "Look Josh, don't worry so much about your place. You need to just get out there and run hard because you want to, not because someone else expects you to. You need to love the feeling of flying down the trail and not care at all about how much it hurts. It has to make you happy. If you can do that, if you can get that feeling, then your race position and the times will just take care of themselves."

"You really love this?" Josh asked. "Is that your secret?"

"No! It's not any secret," Sean laughed. "It's just how I feel when I run. I never think about running a certain time or trying to win. I just do the best I can and try to enjoy everything about the race. I try to stay in the moment."

"Are you saying that you don't have a race plan?" Josh was confused.

Sean started jogging again and Josh followed him. "No, I don't really have a race plan. I have a few basic thoughts that I try to remember at the line, like getting out clean so I don't get trapped if the course narrows. I don't want to waste energy trying to pass a lot of people to get back to the front but, most of the time, I'm just trying to feel connected to the trail or wherever I'm running. It's like I'm alone out there, just me and the elements. Of course, I want to go as hard as possible, but I don't really think about the other guys in the race."

"Well, it sure works for you. How do you deal with everyone expecting you to win?"

"I don't even think about that. You can't run fast, week after week, if you let the pressure of winning become the driving force to your running. You have to trust your training, love what you're doing and just let it happen. Again, you have to be doing it for yourself not someone else."

They were coming back out of the woods and could see the school on the hill in front of them. "I'll try to think that way. It seems like coach expects me to run great every week and I just don't handle it as well as you."

Sean looked right at Josh to make his next point. "Hey, remember that he doesn't know everything. He's a high school biology teacher not the coach of the Olympic Team."

"Right, I hadn't thought of it that way."

"Look, you just have to figure out if you're doing this for the right reasons. If you're only doing it because you want to win and get the money and the chicks, then believe me, you've picked the wrong sport. You've got to do this because you love it. It has to be personal."

Josh nodded his head in agreement. "Ok, I think I get it. I'll back off and try to run how I feel instead of killing myself everyday. Maybe I'll make it to raceday with more in the tank."

"And what else?" Sean asked.

"I'll try to worry less about everyone else's expectations?"

"That's all I'm saying," Sean said.

"Thanks Sean."

"Hey, this can be fun if you let it be."

They had come back around the small duck pond and were jogging along the building toward the locker room when Sean stopped to talk to a couple of teammates who had cut the workout short. Josh wondered if they needed the talk as much as he had. It was Josh's first glimpse into the psyche of a state champion caliber runner. Unfortunately, some people aren't able to run free of worry no matter how hard they try. Josh really hadn't grasped the meaning of the lesson. If he had, he would have enjoyed the next six years of competition a lot more.

He didn't know if it was the talk with Sean that got him going but Josh did start to run better. Within two weeks, he placed second to Sean in a three team conference meet and then he actually gave Sean a scare in a dual meet a week later. He never actually caught Sean during the race but he did get within 50 yards at the two mile mark and he maintained the gap for the final mile, finishing only eight seconds back.

Confidence has as much influence on a race performance as anything else. It doesn't matter how great your training has been if you fold when someone passes you or when you start to hurt. It's true that not everyone has what it takes to race hard once the pain gets intense. For those that can, having confidence is what allows them to push past the barriers and attain higher levels of performance. It was coming back slowly, but Josh was starting to regain that confidence.

The Conference meet turned out to be a dream race for Josh, while the State Regional Qualifier was very nearly a nightmare.

According to their plan, Sean took the lead immediately at the Conference meet while Josh laid back in the chase group and waited. He hoped that the five runners that went with Sean would overextend themselves and crash and burn. Josh would then run them down on the last mile. So, he stayed close, running only 10 to 15 seconds back and watching the lead group.

For Josh, this was like being in the chair at the dentist. He was expecting to be in pain soon and the anticipation was the worst part of it. When Sean finally surged at the two mile mark, all of his competitors cracked and on queue Josh made his move. It was beautiful. Sean ran strong to the finish while Josh picked off the few runners who had dared to run with him in the lead group. When he hit the final straight and started to sprint, he was in second place and his second All-Conference selection was assured. On top of that, their one-two finish also gave the team the boost it needed to jump to a second place finish in the team championship.

Everyone was ecstatic and the idea that the entire team might have a chance to qualify for state, unthinkable at the start of the season, seemed less remote. To accomplish that goal, the team would have to place in the top two at the 32 team regional qualifier. It would be a large race with well over 200 entrants and the top 5 individuals would also be rewarded with a trip to the state meet. It was a longshot, but they thought they had a chance.

On race day, high hopes weren't enough. Sean was stellar again and ran away from the field for the medalist honors but the rest of the team ran below their capabilities and their seventh place finish left them a long way from making the big show. Individually Josh still had a chance but a top five finish would be tough and might require a little bit of good fortune. As difficult as it was going to be, it was made worse during the first mile when Josh was elbowed in the stomach and had the wind knocked out of him. For 30 seconds, he ran clutching his abdomen and gasping for air. By the time he had recovered, he was well back in the pack. As soon as he was able, he shook it off and ran. His adrenaline level was surging as he passed runners and moved up through the field. Over the last two miles, he ran great and wasn't passed by a single competitor but, when he saw his eleventh place finish, he figured he was done for the year.

There was only one chance. The runners that are on the two teams that qualify aren't counted in the top five for individuals since they're already in the meet. Coach Feder, Sean and Josh watched the board anxiously as the results were posted. The first place team had three runners in front of Josh. They were second, fourth and seventh overall while the second place team had taken third, ninth and tenth. They counted it a second time to make sure but Josh was in the state meet. Six finishers in front of Josh wouldn't count and that made him the final qualifier. Sean had a big smile on his face as he walked past and slapped Josh on the back.

"We're going to State!" He said as he started to jog. "Come on, let's do a warm-down."

For ten days, Josh basked in the attention that he finally shared with Sean. Qualifying for the State meet had surprised a lot of people, including Coach Feder, but the race itself would raise even more eyebrows.

The meet was held on a hilly course near the University of Minnesota. The start was wide open, the curves were gentle, and the hills were nicely spaced and rolling. It was setup to be fast. With only two teams from each of the ten regional qualifiers, it was actually a smaller field than the last race but the talent pool was much deeper.

After a textbook warm-up, Sean and Josh got out to a clean start and ran together for the first half mile, then, Sean just took off. Once he was dropped by Sean, Josh was left to battle the pack for position. He was a much stronger and more confidant runner than he had been a year ago. When he hit the hills that were sprinkled over the final mile, he was ready to make a bold move. He poured everything he had into the last five minutes of the race and was totally spent when he staggered across the finish line. Sean was already there waiting.

"All right Josh!" he yelled.

Josh had crossed the line but was in no condition to talk yet. He was bent over clutching his knees and struggling to recover. After a couple of aborted attempts, he was finally able to straighten up and join his teammate.

"Did you win?" Josh stammered.

"Nah, I was second. I got out leaned at the tape." He didn't sound very upset for having just lost the State Championship by a step.

"By who?" Josh asked. He couldn't believe that anyone in Minnesota could beat Sean.

"That guy from Lakeville that moved here last spring. Morrison. The kids got wheels. I threw in a hard surge 400 yards out and thought I had him but he came back on me. The last 100 yards was side by side and he got me with a good lean." He looked thoughtful not angry. "That guy's got some talent *and* he's only a junior so you're gonna be stuck with him next year."

Josh felt bad for Sean and didn't understand why he was taking it so calmly. "Are you all right?" he asked.

"Oh yeah, sure. It was a great race and I had a chance to win. There's nothing wrong with getting beat as long as you do the best you can and can walk away proud of the effort you made," Sean said.

Josh just thought that if it had been him, he'd be pissed off after losing such a close race. Looking back at it years later, Josh realized that Sean had been a very enlightened 17 year old. Josh's friend Scott would have recruited Sean to be an ultra runner.

Sean smiled at Josh and continued. "Speaking of being proud. How's it feel to be All-State?"

Again, Josh was confused. "What are you talking about?"

"I counted them up at the finish. The results aren't posted yet but, unless they disqualify you for some grievous act during the race, I had you in 14th place. The top 15 make All-State."

"No shit," Josh said excitedly.

Sean nodded his head. "No shit. Next year you'll be back and you can take your shot at this thing. Just make sure you work on your kick because Morrison will be back to."

Josh left the University campus with visions of a future State Championship dancing in his head.

The lessons that Josh learned about racing from Coach Feder and Sean were reinforced over the years by other runners and by his own experimentation. Josh firmly believed that if you wanted to be competitive, you could not let anyone get away from you during the early part of the race. It was a strategy that he would use over and over successfully for the next 30 years. Scott would have a hard time ever convincing Josh that it was a bad strategy for trail ultra marathons. Like a lot of things, Josh would have to learn that the hard way.

Strategy Session

"The idea that you can't lose contact with the leaders has cut more throats than it has saved."

— Arthur Lydiard

Runner and world renowned coach of several of New Zealand's Olympic champions

November 2005, Tin Cup Tavern, Central Florida
Countdown to Hellgate – 4 weeks

Scott came through the front door and immediately looked for his friends in their usual spot. He saw that Josh was already there and he also saw Jill putting money into the jukebox. In front of Josh, he noticed they were already set up with a pitcher of beer, an appetizer, and that a few pint glasses were spread across the table. The bar was quiet this afternoon and they'd be able to talk comfortably about the race without interruption. It had to be done today since Josh had a hectic travel schedule approaching and would be on the road almost every day in the final three weeks before Hellgate.

Scott weaved through the other tables and grabbed a chair across from Josh. "Hey dude, how's your golf game?" he smiled.

"It sucks and you know it. I can't even get time on the driving range between work and this training schedule," Josh moaned.

"Poor baby, you spend every Saturday covered in dirt, blood and spiders while all your golf buddies are smoking cigars and drinking beer out on the course."

Josh pushed a glass towards Scott. "Sounds like I've made a bad career decision and you're my manager. Maybe I should fire you."

"You can't. It's a permanent position, and besides, I'm also moonlighting as your shrink and that's something you can't do without."

Josh laughed. "No doubt about that. No doubt."

Finished at the Jukebox, Jill pushed a couple of chairs aside to get to Scott and give him a hug. "Hey loser, glad you could make it," she said affectionately. Despite the stupid stuff he was continuously talking her husband into doing, she liked Scott. He had a harmless, easy going manner that let him get away with all sorts of mischief.

"Hey sweetheart. Are you sure you're up for this crewing operation?" Scott asked. "It's going to be a long night out there."

"I'm not letting the two of you run up there unsupervised!" She exclaimed. "Neither of you can be trusted to do the smart thing when you're racing. I'm going to be the voice of reason that you clearly don't have in your own heads anymore."

"Yeah, I lost my voice of reason when I was a shy, innocent 18 year old," Josh said sadly.

Scott acted concerned. "That's awful, where'd it happen?"

"The Jacksonville Marathon," Josh pretended to be in anguish just thinking about it.

"Shut up Josh," Jill said as she punched him in the arm.

Josh rubbed his hands together. "Ok Scott, what's the brilliant plan to conquer Hellgate?"

"I don't know about conquering, but if you spread that map out we'll at least try to figure out a way to survive to the finish."

After two months of following Scott's training routine, Josh was ready for some details on the race course itself. They had been running 90 to 100 miles a week since September and had been extremely consistent on their long runs. They had done 35 miles, without fail, every third Saturday and 20 to 25 miles on the Saturdays in between. Plus, at Josh's insistence, they'd done another mid week trail run of 2 hours at a harder pace. Though he'd tried, Josh hadn't been able to convince Scott to go to the track and run intervals but they did do a hard tempo run each

Tuesday and some light turnover work on Thursday. As a result, they felt like they were strong enough to run a decent marathon and somewhat hopeful that the long runs would serve them well at Hellgate.

Jill moved the beers around as Josh spread the map out on the table. It was a detailed topographical map of the Jefferson National Forest complete with fire roads and trail markings. Meanwhile, Scott handed them copies of the course description that the race director had emailed to everyone.

"We'll read the description and follow it on the map. You have to know where you're at and where you're going at all times. We don't want any surprises out there. It's something you should have done before you ran on the Appalachian Trail."

Jill glared at Josh.

"Thanks for bringing that up buddy," Josh said to Scott.

"I'm sorry, but it's true."

"Fine, let's do something useful like turning this topo map into a rough cut elevation profile," Josh said.

They spent the next hour and a half reading numbers off of the contours and estimating distances. The result was a reasonably accurate graph that showed the major climbs and descents. After they finished, they seriously questioned whether or not it had been a good idea in the first place. They might have been better off not knowing. The profile showed nothing but steep lines moving up and down. There were hardly any flat spots to be found. It seemed that they would spend the entire race going up or down and the length of the climbs was pretty intimidating as well.

"What the hell is that at the end!" Jill exclaimed.

Scott peered at the map. "That, my friends, is the Blue Ridge Parkway. It would appear that the final aid station is in the valley on one side while the finish is on the other side."

"Oh, that's a nice touch," Josh said. "It looks like we hit that, what is it? About a 2,000 foot climb? At around 60 miles. Very sweet."

"Yeah, in light of that news, maybe we should discuss some strategy," Scott suggested.

Josh sat back with his beer and took a drink. "It's all you buddy, the floor is yours."

Scott leaned in and in a conspiratorial tone started to lay out the plan. "First, we need to be clear on a basic premise for running Hellgate, which is to be conservative. I'm basing that on a vast amount of research conducted at my own expense."

Jill started laughing. "You mean you finally figured out how to Goggle something on the internet?"

"Exactly!" Scott exclaimed as Josh, with a wave of his hand, ordered another round from the bartender.

Scott continued. "The usual deal with a 100 kilometer race is run it like a 50 mile and just hang on for another 12 miles. There's not much difference, but that won't work at Hellgate."

"Why not?" Jill asked while Josh dug in his pocket for some money to pay for the drinks.

"It won't work because this race is not a run-of-the-mill 100k."

"Pay attention Josh," said Jill.

"Look at the times that have been run there the past two years. A lot of good trail runners, guys that can run 50 miles in six and a half hours, have run Hellgate. Based on their 50 mile times, they should be able to run 100k in under 8 hours but most of them have run between 12 and 15 hours at Hellgate. What's going on out there? What's happening to them on this trail?" He had their attention. "Obviously, those extra 4 to 7 hours concern me. Look, we all know that it's a tough race, that's a given. But how tough is it really? I think those times tell the story. There's a lot more to this race than just running 60 miles. Take a look at this. The course record is only a couple of hours faster than the winning times of most 100 mile trail races around the country."

"So, what do we do? Treat it like its a hundred mile race?" Josh asked.

"Right," Scott responded. "We have to respect the distance, the midnight start and the terrain. We run the first 30 miles while pretending that its 50 miles. Then, we do it again. We can't get caught up racing people during the first four hours."

Josh was thoughtful. "So, just so I understand, we don't try to win, we just let everyone go?"

"You'll catch a lot of people during the second half of the race if you run this the right way. If you go for it at the start, you're going to be toast," Scott said firmly.

Josh didn't say anything but he was clearly bothered by this strategy. It was a part of running ultras that he had never gotten comfortable with. His strategy in road races was simple. Never let anyone get away. In ultras, it was always a mess since everyone starts at completely different speeds. Anyone can run hard for 3 or 4 hours and you could never tell who is really strong. You could take a chance and follow whoever leads but experience has shown that it can be disastrous to follow the wrong person. It didn't appeal to Josh, who liked to know exactly where he stood at all times, but it was not unusual in an ultra to run alone for hours with no information at all.

"Josh? Are you ok with that? Running easy the first half?" Scott asked.

Josh, obviously disturbed, looked up from his drink. "Yeah, sure. Why not?"

Scott was skeptical. "All right, since we can, let's run the first few miles, from there we'll take what the course gives us. Obviously, run every flat you see, because there won't be many. Also, when they aren't steep enough to destroy your quads, run the downhills. Finally, whenever you encounter an uphill, and there'll be a lot of them, go by your heartrate and stay aerobic, in other words, hike fast."

"Come on Scott, are we going up there to race or birdwatch?" Josh's sarcasm and indifference was starting to piss Scott off. "Let's run the damn thing. Keep an eye on the leaders and don't let them get away."

"My advice hasn't done any good on our training runs, so I guess I shouldn't expect you to listen now," Scott said icily.

Sensing tension, Jill jumped in. "Ok, what do I do?"

Scott glared at Josh as he reoriented the map so that Jill could see it better. "There are nine aid stations. We need to pick out the ones you're going to drive to and decide what you need to bring for us. Also, we have to have some time estimates, so that you know when to leave for the next aid station."

"That's easy. I'll just leave for the next aid station as soon as you both have come through. Right?"

"Ideally, that's how it works, but with two of us it depends upon how close we are. That's why we need to figure out how long it takes to drive between them. If the gap between Josh and I is too large, you may need to leave for the next aid station before whoever's in second comes through. If that happens at one of the major checkpoints, you'll have to leave a drop bag for the slow guy," Scott explained. "You'll have to make some decisions on the fly."

"Ok, which spots do you think I can get to?" Jill asked.

Josh finally rejoined the discussion. "Well, there's no need for you to be at the first one. It's only a few miles into the race and I don't plan on stopping."

"Me either." Scott said. "The second is when the course crosses the Blue Ridge Parkway at Petite's Gap. It's a nice paved road and should be easy to get to. I think it would be a great spot for you to go and provide support for everyone, even though we won't need much that early."

"I might want to use a powdered drink mix during the race. Jill, you could have that ready for me there," Josh said.

"That's a good idea. Also, we need to have the option of adding or removing a layer of clothing whenever you're able to see us," Scott suggested.

Jill started taking notes. "Where next?" she asked.

Scott looked at the map. "Aid station three looks like it'll be hard to get to. I'd say skip three and just head for four. It's not too far off of the Parkway and won't be such a hassle to find in the dark. Station four is also Headforemost Mountain, which is a major checkpoint. It's also the highest elevation of any aid station but since it's close to the Parkway you should be all right."

"Do you need anything special there?" Jill asked.

Josh responded quickly. "No, the same as at aid station two, except we may need to refill our energy gels."

"Got it," She said as she continued to write notes. "Where next?"

"Well, we might be spread out by then, so skip Jennings Creek and go to number six which is," Scott looked at the map before answering. "Little Cove Mountain," he said.

"Little Cove Mountain," She said while writing. "Is it hard to get to?"

"It doesn't look too bad but, from this description, it does sound somewhat remote."

Josh took the description from Scott and quickly scanned through the information on aid station number six. "Look at the estimated time for the leaders to arrive."

Scott was now looking over his shoulder. "Oh yeah, it may finally be light out at the aid station. That will make it a lot easier for Jill to find."

"Great, I'll be there, then what?" she asked.

"Well, you'll definitely need to be at number seven. That's Bearwallow Gap and it's the second major checkpoint," Scott said. "Also, according to this description, the trail between six and seven is tough, so we won't be very fast. That should insure that you have time to make the drive before we get there."

"You'll have to have everything ready at Bearwallow Gap," Josh said. "There's no telling what we'll need, so have it all available."

"Right, by then we will have run for 10 hours in wet shoes, so it's very likely that we'll have some blisters to deal with and, as before, we'll need all the typical refills of gels and drinks. Anything else Josh?"

"How about making sure to offer some anti-inflammatories since we may not remember?"

"OK," Jill said.

Josh was looking at the map again. "Make sure you stay there until we both come through since we'll need your help. Afterward, I'd say you can just make your way back to the finish area."

"You don't want me at that last aid station before the Parkway climb?"

Josh sat back in his chair before responding. "Well, it's on the opposite side of the ridge from Bearwallow Gap and may take a long time to drive around to. If you think you can make it, great, but if there's a large gap between Scott and I, just skip it and head for the finish."

"A large gap?" Scott feigned shock. "I'm confused. I didn't plan on being that far ahead of you."

"Ha, ha," Josh said sarcastically. He really didn't think that Scott would be able to stay close but he also knew that 60 mile races could be unpredictable. If Josh screwed up even a little bit, Scott would be right there ready to pounce.

He had already found out that as the distance goes up, speed is less and less of a factor and that Scott would become a legitimate threat to beat Josh. Even though they're friends and training partners, Josh perceives it as a rivalry and he doesn't like to lose to Scott. He'd have to be on top of his game at Hellgate.

"Is that it?" Jill asked while scanning her notes. "I don't need to do anything else?"

"Just smile a lot and don't let us spend too much time in the aid stations," Scott said.

"That's easy. I'll just kick your butts if you overstay your welcome."

"Perfect," Scott chuckled. "I think that's about it."

Josh started to fold the map back up. "Ok, I'll pick you both up at the airport on Thursday night and we'll drive up to the mountains on Friday morning."

Everyone agreed and, with the business of Hellgate behind them, they ordered another round and let the conversation drift back to ordinary daily events. The Thanksgiving holiday was fast approaching and Christmas loomed a month later but there was still plenty of time to worry about the race. Tonight they wanted to put it out of their minds and focus on enjoying the company of more friends who were arriving at the Cup.

The golfers and volleyball players would outnumber the runners tonight. That was fine with Josh. He had been friends with Brad, Lance, and many of the others for over 20 years. It would be a lively night.

Josh looked around the table at the group that was assembling. Most of his close friends were athletes of some sort but, surprisingly, very few were runners. Years ago, in college, he'd get up early in the morning on weekends and slip away for a long training run before anyone else was awake. If he was seen leaving or returning, they'd give him the look. It was the inevitable *why the hell do you run* look. Over the years, he'd explained to each of them, to the best of his ability, what he believed were the misconceptions surrounding running. Some, like Brad and Lance, were easy to talk to and, if you could find a bit of common ground, they'd connect the dots and gain a sense of what it was all about. Others would never get it. It had been at least 15 years since Josh and Brad had had the dreaded *why do you run* talk.

Josh had dressed for his Saturday morning run and grabbed a garbage bag full of empty bottles to dump in the trash on his way out of the apartment complex. Brad heard the commotion and looked up from the couch.

"Are you going for a run?" he asked.

Josh stopped just inside the door. "Yeah, I'll be back in a couple of hours."

"Fine, you wanna do anything later?"

"If you can wake anyone else up by the time I get back, let's go to Cedar Key or something," Josh suggested.

"Sure," Brad said, "that sounds good."

"Later," said Josh as he turned back to the door.

"Can I ask you something?"

He stopped again. "Yeah, what?"

"I've been watching this for years. How the hell can you get up and run this early. You've gotta feel like shit."

There it is. Josh thought.

"It's not so bad. After a few miles, it will actually help with the hangover. Besides, training is the place to feel like shit, not racing."

"Well, I don't know why you'd want to run anytime and I certainly don't see why you can't miss a day."

"For one, as strange as it is to some people, I *like* to run. As for missing a day, the guys I have to race aren't missing any days and I don't want to get my ass kicked the next time I go up against one of them."

Brad sat up and shrugged his shoulders. "I'm sure that skipping one day wouldn't affect you that much."

"You're wrong," Josh said firmly.

"If you say so, I suppose you're right, but I don't think you've ever even tried to relax on a Saturday. You might find out that it doesn't hurt you at all."

"It's not like I've never missed a workout. I've missed plenty. That's how I know what the end result would be. I don't want to feel like crap and I don't want to lose. So, I don't skip workouts," Josh said.

"Well, more power to ya, buddy. I've tried to run a few times and it sucks. I don't understand why anyone would put themselves through it every day."

"That's a typical reaction and I understand it," Josh said, "in fact, I even agree with it a little bit."

"What do you mean?" Brad asked.

"Well, I've been injured several times and had to take extended time off to recover. Getting back in shape after a layoff is hard. It's not magic. Every time I try to come back from an injury, it's brutal. Even a couple of miles feel like crap. My legs hurt all the time. When I run, I feel like I can't get any air. I'm just like Joe Jogger sweating it out in lane five at the local high school track."

"Then why do it?"

Josh came back into the room and sat down. He looked down at the floor and paused. "Because I know," he said.

"You know what?"

"I know what's going to happen later. I know how I'm going to feel a month into the training. I know how it's going to be when I get back into race shape. That's the part the general public, even the three times a week runners, will never experience. Most people don't stick with it long enough to get a glimpse of what it's really like to be a runner. They'll never know what it's like to be in four minute mile or 30 minute 10k shape."

"What's the difference? I run and I hurt. How do you feel?"

"When I'm there? When the training has come together and it all starts to click?"

"Yeah."

Josh closed his eyes and pictured it. "It's really hard to describe. I suppose effortless would be a good word. At that level, you can run at alarmingly fast speeds without getting winded.

You can carry on conversations while blowing through 10 miles in under an hour. Nothing hurts. No matter how hard you train, you can't make yourself sore and you recover almost immediately. The landscape just flies past you and the world shrinks into a small sphere. The faster you run, the tighter the sphere and the more focused you become on the next 10 yards you're about to cover. You can go at almost any speed but your body seeks out a perfect pace that requires very little effort or concentration to maintain. The fitter you are, the faster that pace becomes. That's the zone. You feel like you can run forever in this perfect state. You can be cruising at sub six minute mile pace with no pain, no labored breathing, nothing but the breeze against your face and the feel of your feet grazing the earth. It's effortless. You can see the ground moving under you but you appear to float a few inches above it. Like a dream."

"You feel like that while running under six minute pace?" Brad asked.

"Absolutely. Imagine running on a treadmill and using the handrails to lift your weight off of your legs but keep them moving. You'll feel like you're flying but you won't feel any impact with the ground. It's sort of like that."

"You make it sound fun."

"It can be as cool as any feeling in sport. Like taking a Nolan Ryan fastball over centerfield or making a spectacular catch in the endzone."

"Well, as nice as it sounds, I could run every day for 20 years and never be in four minute mile shape. So, if that's what it takes, I guess no mere mortals, like me, will ever have a chance for that feeling."

Josh disagreed. "That's not true. I know you can't get all the way there, but you can get past the part where running feels like a task to be avoided at all costs. You, or anyone else, can train to the point where you no longer hurt while running. A point where a three mile run is invigorating and enjoyable. It can become something that you look forward to each day. So good that you schedule each morning around it."

He had Brad laughing now. "I don't think so. That's really hard to believe."

"I know. That's why so few people ever get there. For most, running five or six days is all they can handle. After that the discomfort gets the best of them. They never make it past the 30 or so days it takes to put the leg soreness and lethargy behind them. For the few that are able to break past the 30 day barrier, they are rewarded with pain free runs and improved health. They're hooked."

"You're running for a top university team. You gotta admit this is hard to relate to."

Josh thought for a moment. "Ok, how about this. How many scratch golfers are out there today? Not pros, just guys carrying there own bag."

"Scratch golfers? I don't know, but not too many."

"Exactly. You're an excellent player, you've taken lessons for years, and you play with the best amateurs in the area. And yet, you don't really know more than a couple of guys that can shoot par. Why do all these people play golf when they have no chance of shooting par?"

"Yeah, well, par's not exactly easy."

"That's my point. It's not easy or common to see anyone shoot par."

Brad was lost. "So?"

"So, the pros shoot under par all the time. Last week I saw Trevino shoot a 62 on TV. That's 10 under par for 18 holes. No amateur can relate to that."

"No, I know I can't," Brad said.

"But every time you play, you hit some great shots. Maybe a huge drive right down the middle. So sweet you didn't even feel it come off the clubface. Or, maybe, a magnificent sand shot or even a beautifully read putt."

"Sure."

"So, those shots give you a glimpse into the world of the scratch golfers. They motivate you to practice and get better. You want to have that sensation more often. The reason is simple. In golf, crisply hit shots with the proper trajectory, spin and distance make you feel good about yourself. It's cool."

"There's no doubt about that, but it's not the same as running," Brad said.

"Sure it is. Do you think anyone can just pick up a set of clubs and hit those shots?" Josh asked.

"No, of course not. It takes a lot of work."

"Right. It takes time, knowledge and commitment. How many people try golf a few times but give it up because they suck?"

"A lot of people quit, but if they give it a chance and stay with it long enough, they'll get hooked."

"You mean they'll eventually learn enough to hit a couple of those elusive great shots. They'll get a brief look into the world they see the guys on TV inhabit. It'll feel fantastic and they'll want more."

"Ok, ok, I see where you're going with this. You're saying that, if they get too frustrated before getting to the point of hitting a few of those shots, they'll quit without ever understanding what golf's all about. They won't get why so many people love it and you think the same thing happens when runners stop without breaking through your 30 day barrier. They'll quit, thinking that running is horrible, like me, without understanding what guys like you are getting out of it. They'll just give you *the look* that you hate."

"You got it," Josh said as he stood and headed for the door. "I've gotta get going. I'll see you in a couple of hours."

They never discussed the *why do you run* question again. Years later, when Josh started racing ultras, he gave up his Saturday golf game because it interfered with his long run. Brad and Lance understood.

The tables at the Tin Cup quickly filled and after a few more beers, everyone was telling stories about dumb things they did as kids. Scott asked Josh to tell the story about the airplane. Josh was reluctant to tell the story about his banishment from the State Cross Country Meet during his senior year of high school, but an offer to buy the next round by one of his notoriously cheap friends who had never heard the story spurred him on.

"It was the fall of 1979, during the Cross Country season," he began quietly, as everyone pulled chairs closer to hear.

Aerial Attack

"I'd give them a 10 for creativity and a zero for judgment."
— Principal Paul Wilke

October 1979, Woodbury, MN

E very time Josh told the story it sounded made up, but it had actually happened.

Josh's senior year was turned upside down on October 8th of 1979. It all started as a joke. A homecoming prank that snowballed out of control and, in the end, found its way to the national wire services and to the front pages of both of the Twin Cities major newspapers. Indirectly, it led to the longest run of life.

Woodbury was a small suburb on the east side of St. Paul, Minnesota. The schools in the neighboring towns were all part of the St. Paul Suburban Conference and provided intense rivalries in the sporting community. Hockey still ruled in Minnesota, but the homecoming football game was the king of the fall athletic season. Josh was having an outstanding senior season in Cross Country. Finally out of the shadow of Sean Nicols, Josh had established himself as the top runner in the Conference and one of the top five in the state. He had won most of his races that season, with only the conference and regional championships remaining. All he needed was an expected strong race at the regional and he would move on to the Minnesota State Championship.

Although it had become a large part of his life, Josh had other interests besides running. For instance, he loved airplanes. It was early in his senior year but he had already decided that he would forgo the art scholarships that had been filling his mailbox to pursue a degree in Aerospace Engineering. Where he would

94

study was still undecided. All of the schools he was considering had track teams but he was unsure if an athletic scholarship would follow after the state championships were over. He put off the school decision and waited for the big races. In the meantime, he made the study of aircraft his hobby.

As part of his interest in flying, he had joined the Civil Air Patrol during his junior year and started taking lessons in a Cessna 172. The small single engine plane was easy to fly and soon he and his friend Dave were taking their solo flights.

Once they were free from the observation of their instructors, and they became more and more comfortable with the plane, they started pushing its limits. At first it was just standard maneuvers like stalls, but it quickly escalated into barrel rolls and loops. On one occasion, they even flew the plane higher and higher, until the air was so thin that they were gasping for breathe, and the plane actually started to lose lift and fall from the sky. These, maneuvers, and others, were extremely dangerous aerobatic tricks that the Cessna was not structurally equipped to handle, but they tried them all anyway. There were a lot of close calls when they pushed the boundaries a little too far but when you're 17 you just don't think about getting hurt. With each flight, they got more confident, but they were running out of things to do.

Surprisingly, taking the plane out was as simple as signing your name on the list, completing a checkout and filling it with gas when you returned it to the hanger. This ease of access definitely contributed to their decision to use the plane for their prank.

They were about to do something that any reasonable person would have advised against. They did it anyway. Afterward, a quote from the Minneapolis Tribune, which was attributed to the principal of Josh's high school, simply said, "I'd give them a 10 for creativity and a 0 for judgment". Indeed, the judgment may have been bad but the planning was certainly not.

For weeks before homecoming, Josh and Dave had been taking the plane out for regular flights to remote areas over Northern Minnesota and Wisconsin. They had recruited Paul, a non-pilot friend, into their group and he joined them on these flights.

If they were seen on these "missions", it was only by fisherman and campers and no one ever reported what they saw. What would they say? "I saw a small plane make 20 or 30 passes over the lake I was camped next to and it looked like they were dropping things into the water". Beyond that, it was nothing. The plane flew away and never returned. Each flight was to another of Minnesota's 10,000 lakes.

At 9 p.m., while their friends formed groups in parking lots and tried to figure out where to party, Dave, Paul and Josh gathered in Dave's basement and started filling plastic sandwich bags with powdered cement. About four pounds went into each bag before they were sorted into several medium sized containers. The work was dusty and they had laid out painting tarps to keep the furniture clean. When they had 50 bags in each container, they carefully carried them out to Dave's car and headed for the airport.

The South St. Paul airport was a small, uncontrolled strip about 15 miles from the Twin Cities International Airport. There was no tower, so each plane communicated its intention to take-off or land by radio to nearby aircraft. This would be their home base. The Cessna 172 was kept in the next to last hanger at the end of the single landing strip.

They started work on the plane as soon as they arrived. It began with the removal of the rear doors which took the most time. Then they pulled out several rolls of black tape and worked their way around to every identifying mark. Each number was carefully covered with the tape. Finally, the containers were loaded into the back.

They had a plan. Earlier in the day, Josh had met with a couple of other friends whose participation would be crucial. They had been given handheld radios and detailed instructions on where to be and what to do. Josh was counting on them. He promised himself that, if anything unexpected happened, he and Dave would abort the plan immediately.

Once the preparations were complete, they all sat for a while and went through the checklist again. When they were satisfied that everything was ready, they pulled the car into the hanger, shut the door and waited for 2 a.m. to arrive.

Meanwhile, Josh's other friends were out partying. They were part of the plan and, after several rehearsals, they knew where they were supposed to be, and when, but as the night wore on they lost focus. One of them drank too much and started puking in a friend's downstairs bathroom. Another left to pick up his younger sister who was stranded at a party across town. The others just got involved in the myriad of things that distract teenagers late at night. They were all his friends but Josh hadn't taken into consideration that, at that age, everyone is unreliable.

At 2 a.m. the hanger door opened and a modified Cessna 172 with no identification rolled toward the runway. Twenty miles away, their friend's sister was playing with a handheld radio that she had found on the backseat of her brothers car. He was already asleep in his room.

Inside the Cessna it was cramped. Dave was flying the plane and Josh was in the back with the containers. The doors were gone and, even though he was wearing a seatbelt, Josh felt very exposed. Paul was in the co-pilot seat setting up a homemade piece of equipment which mounted by the window, just inside his door. The route they were flying would take them over the campus of the opposing school that was scheduled for this year's homecoming football game. It was nearing 3 a.m., a time when they were sure the entire school grounds would be empty. As an extra precaution, their friends had been instructed to arrive at the school at 2:30 a.m. and make a full sweep of the area on the ground. If anyone was there, the plan would be aborted. This vital information was supposed to be relayed to the plane, by radio, as it flew overhead at 3 o'clock. If any of his friends had made it to the school, the plan might have worked.

The Cessna flew steadily at an altitude of 3,000 feet, just as it had during its countless flights over the lakes of Minnesota. The purpose of those flights had been accuracy, and it had manifested itself in the form of the device that Paul was looking through. Through trial and error, they had built and calibrated a sight which could be used to accurately hit a target on the ground from 3,000 feet. All they needed was a calm night and a steady flight speed. The strange looking instrument would do the rest. With

Paul lining them up, they could hit an area the size of a basketball court every time.

It was incredibly noisy inside the plane and Josh had to unhook his seatbelt and lean partially into the front seat to monitor his small radio. As they made the first pass over the school, all he heard was static. Changing frequencies made no difference and, as they flew out of range, Josh asked Dave to turn around and make another pass over the area. As Josh worked the radio, Dave and Paul strained to see any movement on the ground. There were lights all around the school but a large portion of it was still shrouded in darkness. There was no way to be sure it was clear. They had to make radio contact with their friends.

Officer Daniels and his partner didn't pay particular attention to the small plane passing overhead even when it returned a few minutes later. It never occurred to them that it was awfully late for a private plane to be flying that low over a residential neighborhood. Besides, they were here to look for vandals on foot or in cars. There had been rumors that some students from Woodbury High School might show up this evening to do something. Officer Daniels assumed it would be the usual eggs and toilet paper routine. He and his partner would put a scare into them and run them off.

Overhead in the Cessna, it was tense. They couldn't get an answer on the radio. They made a third pass over the school and again looked for any sign of movement below them.

"Do you see anything?" Dave yelled back to Josh who had strapped back into his seat.

"Nothing, I think it's clear but I wish we could get confirmation," he shouted back.

Paul chimed in. "We have to make a decision; we can't just fly back and forth all night."

"Right. I say we just go ahead," Dave said.

Josh looked down at the ground. He was worried. This was not part of the plan. In fact, he had promised himself that he would abort if anything went wrong. This had to count as "gone wrong".

"I think we should forget it and go home," Josh said.

"No way! There's no one down there! Let's do it!" Paul was excited and had no intention of backing out now.

It was two against one and, even though it didn't feel right to Josh, he didn't have a good enough argument to convince his partners. "Ok, let's go. Make another pass from the south, right over the water tower, and we'll let 'er rip."

The aircraft banked to the right and Dave lined up on the tower. Meanwhile, Paul was busily setting up his sight and watching the ground for his target. Josh was also busy. He pulled the first container closer and loosened his seat belt to get some mobility. It didn't take long for the school lights to appear and, as they got closer, Paul started barking out orders to Josh. On queue, Dave let the plane tilt slightly as Josh dumped the first container. The force of the wind immediately spread the bags out into a thin line across the sky and it was done. From the plane you couldn't tell where the bags went, they simply disappeared into the darkness.

Officer Daniels had parked his car away from the lights but in a position to see a majority of the school grounds. He and his partner were quietly talking and laughing when the bags hit the parking lot in front of the school. They struck with unexpected force. Each bag sounded like a shotgun blast and there were a lot of them. A completely confused Officer Daniels dove for cover near the squad car, while his partner hit the ground with his gun drawn.

It lasted less than 10 seconds and then the silence returned. The parking lot was full of dust, which lit up under the streetlights. The plane, which had been overhead 30 seconds earlier, slipped away unnoticed.

"Did we hit it?" Dave hollered.

"There's no way to tell, but I'm sure we did." Josh was confident that Paul's device would work perfectly and it had.

Officer Daniels was also breaking the silence. "What the hell was that?! Sven! Are you all right?"

"I'm fine except for my shorts which may need laundered!" He was already up and scanning the woods around him. "Where did that come from?"

"I have no idea but that wasn't eggs and toilet paper. I'm getting some backup out here NOW!"

Oblivious to the flurry of activity below, Dave followed the plan. He slowly banked the Cessna to the left and lined up for a pass coming in from the west. They wanted to make four runs as quickly as possible and then get back to the airport. By the time anyone arrived at the school to see the damage, they would be home in bed.

By this time, Officer Daniels was wide awake and he noticed the lights of the plane approaching from the west. He hadn't made the connection yet but it seemed "off" to him. *Didn't I see a plane earlier?* Within a minute he got his answer, as a second barrage of bombs hit the school. This set was further away from his position and nailed the bleachers and press box of the football stadium. Again the plane was gone. *Oh my God, they're bombing the school from an airplane!* The plane continued on a vector away from the school. Behind them, Josh and his friends didn't see the lights that signaled the arrival of the other police cars.

"Turn your lights off!" Officer Daniels yelled. The backup forces were as confused as he had been a few minutes earlier. After he quickly filled them in, they decided on a plan. While they turned off all the lights and waited for the plane to return, the ranking officer placed a few calls and started waking people up. He wanted the tower at Twin Cities International Airport to track this aircraft. When it returned they would all hit their emergency lights at the same time. In addition, they would shine every spotlight they had at the plane. Two officers watched intently with binoculars and would try to get a tail number.

When Dave completed his latest turn and setup another approach to the school, it was already plunged back into darkness. It was very loud in the plane but now it made no difference. Since the plan was already in motion, they had stopped talking. Soon, they saw the lights of the school and, for the third time, Josh moved a canister of bags into position.

When they were almost to the target, Dave once again gave the plane a slight tilt and Josh let the bags go. This time, before the bags had a chance to hit their mark, the campus below them lit up like a battleground and bright spotlights searched them out.

Dave reacted instinctively by throwing the plane into a dive and turning away from the lights. By the time the bags thundered into the ground, the plane was gone again. It wouldn't return, but the police didn't need it to come back. They had it. The small plane was now on the radar screen at the international airport and they would easily catch up to it as soon as it tried to land.

Josh held on tightly to the seat in front of him as the plane moved violently into a steep banked dive. "Where did the cops come from? They weren't there a few minutes ago!"

"I don't know but we need to get this plane on the ground fast before they figure out who we are," Dave said.

Paul had an idea and started hollering to get Dave and Josh's attention. "We can't fly all the way back to South St. Paul, it will give them too much time to get a track on us. Dave, where's the nearest uncontrolled landing strip?"

"White Bear Lake has one."

"Let's get there fast and then sit tight until morning. They may not have a way to follow us yet. If we can we should try to hide the plane from view."

"Done. Everyone hold on I'm going to fly low all the way there."

It only took ten minutes to reach White Bear Lake and Dave quickly set up an approach and brought the plane in for a smooth landing. They had started to taxi back and were just about to the other end when, to their dismay, police cars started pouring through the front gate of the tiny airport.

No one said a word as Dave immediately turned the plane back onto the runway and hit the throttle. The police cars roared onto the runway and briefly pulled alongside with their spotlights blazing before the Cessna lifted off and flew back into the night. It didn't take a genius to figure out that they might be in a bit of a bind. Josh leaned back into his seat and closed his eyes. *How did this happen? We planned everything. Someone must have talked. Of course that's what happened. Way too many people knew about the plan. Damn, we should have aborted when the radios didn't work.* His mind was processing information at high speed, looking for options, but he couldn't think of any way out of this mess. He certainly knew that flying the plane away from the

White Bear Lake airport was just digging a deeper hole but he wasn't ready to concede just yet, and neither were his friends.

"They're tracking us on radar from the International Airport," Paul said.

Dave gave him an incredulous look. "No shit."

Josh leaned forward to hear the conversation. "Well, what are we going to do now? They're just going to be waiting wherever we land."

"We have to avoid the radar. Since it's so flat around here, there's only one good spot to do that." Dave looked back and saw Josh slowly nodding. He knew the spot Dave was referring to but didn't like it at all.

Josh sat back again and yelled above the noise. "Be careful Dave, that's very tricky flying."

Dave nodded and turned the plane toward the St. Croix River. High banks flank the river that divides Minnesota from Wisconsin and in the area near the twin cities it's also very wide. They flew through the night at treetop level as they approached the bluffs. As soon as they were over the river, Dave descended to within 50 feet of the water and leveled out. In the dark it was terrifying. They flew under the large utility lines that crossed from one side to the other, all the while, on the lookout for large boats and barges. They even flew under a couple of bridges. It was scary but, after a while, they were certain that they had beaten the radar.

By now they were about 50 miles north of the cities and it was becoming remote. They finally banked away from the river and, staying low, started looking for a place to land. It didn't take long to find a straight, secluded dirt road. For a relative novice, Dave was a pretty good pilot and he had no trouble landing the Cessna on the road. The aircraft rolled to a stop and, after just sitting for a while, they quietly climbed out and started pulling the tape off of the planes wings and fuselage.

The plane itself had become an albatross around their necks. They tried to come up with a way to disassociate themselves from it but there were too many connections. Eventually, the plane would be found and it would easily be traced back to them. Hours of discussion proved pointless. In the end, they couldn't think of any way to avoid getting caught. It had just never occurred to any of them that they would be unable to return the plane to it's hanger without detection. Sure, they knew someone might talk after the fact, but they figured they could always just deny involvement. To actually be caught red-handed had been inconceivable.

Fours hours passed as they argued over what to do. It was early in the morning and, luckily, they had still not seen a single car on the remote road but they knew they couldn't stay here indefinitely. They had to make a run for the hanger.

They loaded back into the Cessna and made a perfect short field take-off. Dave really tried to enjoy the flight since he didn't expect to keep his license after this was over. They took a long meandering route back to the cities. Desperate to avoid being recognized as the missing plane from the night before, they finally approached South St Paul airport from the opposite direction. There were no other planes on approach so they quickly slipped in and landed the plane. They bypassed the re-fueling area and headed straight for the hanger. Unexpectedly, as they arrived at the hanger, there was no one there to stop them and they excitedly started cranking the door up. For a moment they thought they had pulled it off. Then, without its lights or sirens operating a single police car came around the corner and headed for the plane. Within seconds, three more came around the corner and fell into line right behind the lead car and the boys solemnly quit working on the door.

The first car stopped and an officer got out and walked towards them. "Hey guys, you've had quite a night. We didn't know if you were going to come back or not. Step over here to the car," he said as he pulled out the first of three sets of handcuffs.

The story was front page news in the Minneapolis and St Paul newspapers and, once the wire services picked it up, there was a lot of explaining to do. From Josh's high school, the repercussions were quick. They were all suspended until further notice. The police had so many things to choose from they couldn't figure out where to stop charging them with crimes. It seemed like every day they thought of another one to add. They were all 17 years old and charged as juveniles but that all ended when the Feds arrived. The Federal Aviation Administration came in hard and fast with its own set of charges and one of the things Josh found out right away is that the F.A.A. has absolutely no sense of humor.

Through the first few days, Josh thought this might all blow over and he'd get back into school in time for the Conference Championships. After all, the three of them were at the top of their class academically and had never been in trouble with the law before. It was just a homecoming prank, not a bank robbery. But after a week went by, the story was still picking up steam and he knew his season was over. The question now was would he finish school at all or would he spend his senior year in a juvenile detention center answering questions about ink blots to a staff shrink.

It was touch and go for a long time. Lawyers battled, deals were made and, in the end, the charges were reduced, fines were levied, and community service was doled out in massive doses. Much too late to save Josh's cross country season, everyone went back to school. The F.A.A. handed out lifetime revocations of Dave and Josh's pilot's licenses and eventually the story faded out of public awareness.

Still, for Josh it was a personal disaster. All of his plans for college were in shambles. He had missed all the championship races included the State Championship. The scholarships he expected to compete for would go to other hopefuls. Unless he went to a small school, he would have to walk-on to compete. He'd looked at a few, but Josh had no interest in a small school. He wanted to race at the NCAA Division 1 level. The frustration built to a crescendo in late November when Josh received a polite rejection letter from the University of Southern California. Just like the letters from Villanova, L.S.U. and Arizona, it said he was welcome to try and walk-on but, unfortunately, no scholarship was available. Over and over, he was reminded of how much missing the State Meet had cost him.

He mopped around the house that evening and tried to figure out what to do about college. The pent up energy began to build and, as usual, he went for his training shoes. The sun had just set, and the streetlights were coming on around the neighborhood, when he left the house by the back door. It had snowed a few days earlier but it didn't stick for long and now it was wet and muddy everywhere. He cut across the backyard and ran down the bike trail behind his parent's house. It was a cold, clear night and the moon was just becoming visible on the horizon. Josh felt the crisp air in his lungs and on his hands but he knew he'd be warm in a few minutes. There were a lot of cars on the road, so he elected to take a route out of town that had a nice wide shoulder. Although he knew the road well, he had never run it before. It would take him to the bluffs and then downhill to the Mississippi River. He started running, committed to the direction, but with no idea of where he would go once he reached the river.

Josh ran hard right from the start, burning energy and calming his anger. It was late, but the moon illuminated the gravel shoulder just enough that he didn't need to worry about falling. As he ran away from town, the traffic diminished and soon he heard only his own footsteps and hard breathing. He continued at a steady pace but, by the time he arrived on the downhill that led to the river, he was no longer running with the same aggressiveness that he'd had earlier.

The bluffs over the Mississippi gave him a fantastic view of the city lights, which he kept glancing at as he ran the winding road down to the riverbank. Once there, he stopped briefly to catch his breath and figure out where to go next. As he did some light stretching, he looked around and started to enjoy the feeling of freedom that this unplanned night run was providing. At that moment, he felt like he could run until sunrise. It was unrealistic, but that's how he felt.

Josh continued running south along the river and, little by little, the euphoria he felt earlier wore off. Several miles later, Josh really started to feel the effects of his earlier effort and quickly selected a route that would get him back home. Unfortunately, there was no way back that avoided running the long hill up to the treeless ridge at the top of the bluff. He lowered his head and focused on a spot 15 yards ahead of him as he powered up the incline. It was a long, tough hill, and he wanted to walk, but he didn't. Instead, he stayed with it all the way to the top and then jogged slowly as he tried to regain control of his breathing.

The rest of the run was uneventful. Josh was tired, but satisfied, when he jogged back into the driveway of his parent's home.

The next day, he drove the loop, curious about the distance. When he saw the odometer pass 20 miles, he knew he had never run that far before. A mile later he was back at home. As he suspected, it had been the longest run of his life. He felt a slight boost to his pride for having completed the long run but, even so, it had not eased the disappointment and frustration of missing the State Meet.

The weather was already getting cold and he was going to face a long Minnesota winter before he could seek redemption during his final outdoor track season.

Sick as a Dog

"Once you're beat mentally, you might as well not even go
to the starting line."

— Todd Williams

Top Ranked US 10,000 meter runner of the 1990's

November 2005, Boone, North Carolina
Countdown to Hellgate – 3 weeks

Josh woke up at 5 a.m. for his morning run and, without
waking Jill, he immediately called Scott.

"You're not going to believe this but I'm sick," he said.

Scott was already awake and preparing for his own workout.
"Are you sure?" he asked.

"Yeah, I'm sure."

He didn't sound good but Scott knew it was too soon to
panic. "Maybe it's just allergies. Sometimes that happens to me
after a long run in the woods. It can feel like the same thing, but it
clears up pretty fast."

"I don't think so, but I'll pick up some over the counter
allergy medicine on the way to work," Josh said.

"All right, call me later and let me know how you're feeling."

"Sure, later."

"Later," Scott said as he hung up the phone.

Josh walked around the house for a few minutes getting more
and more agitated. Finally, he went back into the bedroom and
woke Jill up from a sound sleep.

"What is it?" she asked while rubbing her eyes and looking
for the clock.

"You're not going to believe this but I'm sick!" he whined.

Jill groggily looked up at him and as the realization that he had woken her up just to tell her that he was sick sunk in, her expression changed noticeably. *Maybe I should have told her later after she was already awake,* he thought. It was not long before he had affirmation that he should have waited. *Wow, can my wife swear.*

The day before he got sick, Josh had completed his final long, long run in preparation for Hellgate. He and Scott had gone to the Citrus Hiking Trails for a 35 mile jaunt. After that run, it was supposed to be a nice enjoyable three week taper leading up to the race. He'd still do a couple of long runs but they'd be in the 15 to 22 mile range. Nothing that would be considered very taxing compared to the training he had done over the previous two months.

This was not the first time Josh had gotten sick during the taper phase of his training. In fact, it seemed to be an ugly trend. The last four races he had entered, he either ran while ill or was sick within a week of the race. Maybe it was just the body's way of slowing him down after weeks or even months of hard work. You could call it a forced recovery. Whatever the reason, it made no difference at all to Josh. He didn't want to lie in bed and rest. He wanted to run and getting sick really made him angry.

That night, Scott called to check up on him. "How are you doin'?"

"Like shit. I'm so pissed off right now. Why do I get sick before every race? I hate it."

"I know. Maybe it'll work out for the best," Scott offered optimistically.

"How could it be for the best?"

"Well, the last couple of times it lasted two weeks and that went right into the race. This time you're three weeks out. That almost guarantees that you won't be sick anymore when race day rolls around."

"Yeah, maybe," Josh said.

"You know the drill. Take your vitamins and drink lots of fluids. And unless you want to miss the race entirely, please, take a few days off from running. Give yourself a chance to recover."

"Ok, I'll take all my medicine and play it smart. You're probably right. I won't lose much fitness by taking a few days off but it goes against my nature."

Scott was a bit surprised that Josh had, sort of, agreed to take some time off. Feeling like he had accomplished the goal for his call, Scott quickly got off of the line. "Great, get better and call if you need anything."

"See ya Scott," Josh said as he set the phone down.

The next two weeks were difficult for Jill as Josh moved between hope and depression. His mood swings were fast and furious, causing more than a little marital stress. Jill had seen it all before. Josh was an extremely easy person to deal with while sick, if, and only if, he did not have an upcoming race. But if he had even an inconsequential time trial planned or just a long training run that he viewed as crucial to some upcoming event, he became unbearable. Everything was a disaster. He claimed that after a week off he had, in effect, "wasted all the gains" it had taken him six months to achieve. He was, of course, insane.

The first few days went by as expected. Josh became increasingly agitated as the illness took a firm grip on him. He waited expectantly for the day that it would turn around and he would start to improve. Since it was "just a cold' he never went to the doctor for advice or medicine, he just tried to fight it off with vitamins and rest. He stubbornly continued to go to work and, after the fifth day, he couldn't stand the inactivity anymore and went for a short run.

He ran over the weekend and tried to convince himself that he was getting better. He told Jill that his head felt better and that he would be fine in a couple of days. It might have worked out except for the business trips.

After struggling with the illness for 10 days, Josh left for a business trip to Austin, Texas. It just happened that Austin was one of his favorite cities and he didn't want to cancel the trip. Several days of eating too much Mexican food at Chuy's, staying up late drinking beer at the pubs on sixth street, mixed in with some hard training runs, caused his health to slip backward. When he returned to Florida on Friday night, the illness had turned for the worse. His head was congested and he had a cough, deep in his chest, that even frightened his normally optimistic wife.

"You've got to go to the doctor and get some antibiotics," Jill told him. "Are you trying to kill yourself?"

"No I'm not, but I can't get a prescription over the weekend and I'm not going to the emergency room for a cold," he responded. "I'll go Monday."

"You can't. You have another trip Monday, right?" she asked.

"Damn, you're right. I'm flying out early for North Carolina."

"So that's it. You won't be back before the race. Is your plan still to drive to Roanoke on Friday morning and pick me up at the airport?" she asked.

"Yes. But I don't think I need a doctor. I don't have a fever and, other than the cough, I feel all right," he said.

"Well, you don't sound all right." She looked concerned. "Maybe you should just skip this race."

"No way, I've trained too hard. I'm going," he said firmly.

She knew that there was no way to change his mind when it came to running. At least she would be there to keep an eye on him.

On Monday, Josh flew to North Carolina and made the two hour drive to his hotel in Boone. Long before he arrived, he knew he had blown it over the weekend. He should have gone to the emergency room. The recurring illness had established itself solidly in his chest and he couldn't take a deep breath without inducing a long series of painful coughs. There was no way that he could run like this. On Monday night he called his sister, a Registered Nurse, under the guise of finding out what type of over the counter medicine he should try. In reality, he wanted to talk through the symptoms and see how bad it was. He was afraid of missing the race, or even of having a doctor tell him he had to miss it. They don't understand running in the first place. He knew his sister would tell him the truth. *I guess Scott was wrong about being better in two weeks. I'm definitely going to be in bad shape when we toe the line.*

Josh was sitting up in the bed with several pillows piled behind him for support. If he tried to lie down and talk he had bad coughing attacks. He opened his cell phone and speed dialed his sister.

"Hello?" she said.

"Hey Jen, what ya doin?" he asked.

"Hey big brother! Nothing much. Just hanging out with the kids watching a movie. Where are you?"

"I'm at a lovely hotel in Boone, North Carolina," he answered.

"I figured you were out of town. You don't sound good. Are you sick?"

"Yeah, that's one of the things I wanted to talk to you about. I got this thing a couple of weeks ago and it's really hanging on. I can't seem to shake the cough," he explained.

"There have been a lot of people at the hospital with that lately. Did you go to the doctor?"

"No, not yet."

"Of course not! You never do. Well, you better go as soon as you're back in town cause that does not sound good. It could be working its way towards pneumonia."

Josh hesitated. "Actually, I'm signed up for a race this weekend in Virgina and I'm not going to be back in town before then."

"You're kidding. A race! I don't think that's a very good idea." Jennie was familiar with her brother's recent race selection and knew it would be an ultra.

"How long is it?" she asked.

"It's a trail race. Somewhere in the neighborhood of 66 miles."

"Oh perfect. I suppose it'll be cold?"

"Yeah, it starts at midnight and it's in the mountains so I don't expect it to get above freezing," he answered.

"Ok, I've heard enough. Skip work tomorrow and go to either the hospital or a critical care facility. You absolutely have to get on some medication tomorrow and, even then, I don't see any way for you to run by Friday night."

"I was afraid you'd say that but I'd rather hear it from you than a doctor," he said. "I'll try to find a walk-in place in the morning."

"Good, call me and let me know how bad they think it is and what they prescribe," she instructed.

"Fine," Josh was getting depressed again, "I'll call you as soon as I know what's going on."

The call to his sister just confirmed what he already knew. He could feel the way his chest rattled when he took a deep breath and he expected that any medical professional who listened to it would be unmoved by his pleas to race on the weekend.

The next morning, Josh cancelled his meetings and drove his rental car around Boone looking for an urgent care center. Once he found one that had an opening, he planted himself into a chair and waited. It would be a long morning and he was prepared to be there for a few hours.

Josh hated doctors. They don't understand runners. On the rare occasion that he has to see a doctor, he always tries to find one that's an athlete. Any type of athlete will do but it's always a big plus to find a doctor that runs. Naturally, he didn't have any chance of doing his normal screening process in this situation so he just took whoever they had available. In a rare display of full disclosure, he was going to tell them everything. If he had pneumonia, he wanted to know.

Dr Larkin, as it turned out, was not a runner. However, as luck would have it, she was sympathetic to his situation and willing to help. He explained the timeline and detailed all the symptoms that he was suffering through. She thought that he might have pneumonia so blood was drawn and tests were conducted. Ultimately, she concluded that Josh's cough was due to a bad case of bronchitis and, as expected, she advised against running Hellgate.

Dr. Larkin was writing notes on a clipboard as Josh digested the news. "Is there any way to treat this quickly?" he asked hopefully.

"The best I can do is give you a prescription for a steroid and an antibiotic," she answered looking up. "I can also give you an injection of steroids to try and stop the coughing. I doubt that it will get rid of it but it should help some."

"I'll try anything."

"Well, it's Tuesday, I don't see how you can possibly do this race of yours three days from now, but I'll have the nurse come back and give you the shot. Everyone reacts differently but maybe it'll work for you," she said.

As she left the room, Josh thanked her again and waited fitfully for the nurse to return.

He didn't feel any different after the shot but hoped that it would speed up his recovery. Immediately after his appointment, he drove to the pharmacy and filled his prescriptions. With the Doctor's visit complete, he decided that he was to wired to go back to the hotel and sleep. So, he informed his customers that he felt fine, and went back to work. He wanted to keep his mind off of the race but he quickly found out that nobody wanted him around. As soon as they heard his cough, they told him to get out of their offices and come back when he wasn't contagious.

He wanted to go back to work on Wednesday but there was still no improvement. With a lack of progress, he became desperate and started taking multiple over the counter medicines, along with the prescriptions. All that got him was nausea along with a headache and sinus pressure. He slept poorly and, by Thursday morning, he knew he was going to run out of time. Then, just to show him that things could get worse, the diarrhea started. It's a common side effect of antibiotics, but he wasn't ready for it. All of the mental preparation that he had done in the months leading up to the race was disintegrating.

Despite the fact that Thursday was a carbon copy of Wednesday, he knew he had to make a decision. He had been sitting quietly in his hotel room in Boone at 10 p.m. Thursday night when, without saying a word, he went to his luggage and started to assemble the clothes he expected to wear during Hellgate. It was 20 degrees outside which would be a perfect opportunity to see how he was going to feel 24 hours later at the starting line.

As he walked out of the hotel, the cold air hit his lungs and he fought the urge to cough. Afraid to take a deep breath, he cautiously jogged out of the parking lot towards a dimly lit side street. For ten minutes, he silently weaved through the neighbor-hood. When his legs had loosened up, he made a half hearted attempt to pick up the pace. Within a hundred yards, he was running at under seven minute mile pace and feeling pretty good. He held the pace for about three minutes and then pulled back and floated to a stop. As soon as he started walking, he was overcome by a furious bout of coughing. It came from deep in his chest and caused him to bend over and clutch his stomach. *No way,* he thought. *I can't possibly run like this.* For the first time, he was considering the possibility that he may not make the race, when a lone car came around the corner. Josh moved to the edge of the street just as the lights blinded him. As the car passed, he stepped a few inches too far off of the road and slipped on a small patch of ice. He hit the ground before he could even put his hands up. The impact on his knee made him angry more than anything. What was he doing out here? He should be in the hotel resting, not out on these dark streets making an already bad situation worse. He walked back to the hotel, changed clothes and tried to get some sleep.

Rejection

"I ran to get a letter jacket, a girlfriend. I ran because I was cut from the basketball and baseball teams. I ran to be accepted, to be part of a group."

— Jim Ryun

First high school sub 4-minute miler, and later, the World Record holder at multiple distances

1980, Woodbury, Minnesota and Gainesville, Florida

The Minnesota winter had done as much damage to Josh's racing as his suspension from school the previous fall. By the time he was back in class and training normally, he'd lost the momentum he had built through his sophomore and junior years. In an attempt to make up ground, for the first time in three years, he skipped the cross country skiing season and just tried to run. It didn't work out as he had hoped. The severe winter caused his training to become erratic and, when the indoor track season rolled around, he was uncharacteristically sluggish.

The University of Minnesota field house is the venue for high school runners to test their fitness during the long, arctic-like winters that plague St. Paul. The old windowless structure houses a 220 yard dirt track and a variety of areas dedicated to the field events. Other than the discus and javelin, all outdoor track and field events are contested there. It was the only place you could race indoors during the winter, so he tried to get there once a week for some speed work and, after a full season of cross country, to get the feel for the track again.

Traditionally, Josh had run there several times each year beginning in January. He loved going to the field house. It was

115

always surrounded by huge mounds of snow that had been plowed from the neighboring streets and it felt like a refuge when he walked through the door. He even loved the smell of the place. The predominate thing that he noticed when entering was dust. It was, after all, a dirt track and dust was expected, but there was another odor mixed in with it. They sprayed a layer of oil into the dirt, to try and keep it from becoming airborne, and it was that combination of oil and dust that Josh remembered season to season. To him, the strange smell would always be associated with indoor racing at the fieldhouse.

Previous winters he had used the indoor races to build confidence and to gain experience before the outdoor season, but this year was different. After his junior year, he was considered one of the elite in Minnesota high school track, which meant that he was now a target. He couldn't just cruise through these races for fun anymore. This year he would have to really put out an effort because there were guys all around the twin cities that wanted nothing more than to beat Josh Stanton. The fact that he showed up, even though he knew that he was not in great shape, wouldn't matter.

He almost always ran the mile. Occasionally, he would run the half but this week one of his cross country rivals, a half mile specialist, was there to race. Enjoying competition is one thing but Josh didn't want an early season beating. So, a few hours after arriving, Josh walked to the makeshift starting line for the mile run. He started slow and drifted in the middle of the pack for the first quarter. Then he began to methodically move through the fast starters. The field events were taking place at the same time on the infield and they used a large net hung from the rafters to keep them separated. From the inside lane, it was so close that you could brush your shoulder against the net as you ran and it gave you the impression that you were really flying, even if you weren't. By the end of the third quarter Josh had worked his way through the mass of runners up to second place, but the leader was not coming back to him. He pushed hard the last 300 yards but didn't close the gap. It was the first race of the year but, even so, Josh's time of 4:52 wasn't great and he got beat by someone he'd never heard of before. *I ran faster in the 9th grade.* He replayed the race in his head and chastised himself for his lack of preparation as he jogged back to get his warmups.

The next week was more of the same. Josh ran decent but not great. He was certainly consistent, which he had lacked during his sophomore and junior years, but he hadn't run very fast yet and it bothered him. By the end of February, he had entered six races, five of them in the mile run, and his fastest time was only a 4:41, which was still much slower than his best. More disturbingly, he lost several times. He searched for positives and found a few. The most important news was that he was stronger. He could run hard and recover quicker than before. He tried to keep the lack of success early in the season from discouraging him too much and continued to work hard. Coach Feder seemed unconcerned and told him to be patient. He just needed to work on his speed and that would happen once they got outdoors.

The snow and ice eventually melted and the early season dual meets began. Josh ran well but an honest assessment would have been that he was steady but not spectacular. Going into the season, he had high individual expectations, but after he was voted in as the team's "Captain", he changed his plans. The team needed the points that Josh could provide and, at most meets, he would run anywhere from two to four events. At most meets, he would double in the mile and two-mile and maybe anchor a couple of relays. As a result, he led the team in scoring, a role traditionally held by a sprinter or jumper. By the end of the season, it would lead to Josh being voted as the teams "Most Valuable" runner. Twenty five years later, of the hundreds of awards Josh has earned, the small trophy that he received from his high school teammates is the only one that he still has.

The season went by quickly, and Josh did run some good times, but he always felt tired. He had gradually run better and better and, by mid-season, his mile time was down to 4:31, and he finally had run a decent two-mile, clocking a 9:35 at the Burnsville Relays. But the writing was on the wall. The championship races were approaching and too many meets, combined with too many events, had made his performances lackluster. He knew it. Still, if he could qualify, he thought he could make a good run at the State Meet.

First, he had to get through the St. Paul Suburban Conference Meet. This meet was all about points. His coach had entered Josh in the mile and two-mile runs. He was also scheduled to anchor the distance medley and two-mile relays. He knew that it was going to be a difficult day and he would have to pace himself. So, when the leaders went out hard in the mile, he held back to conserve energy. During the second half of the race, he flew past almost everyone. He felt good but on the final straight, seeing that the leader was too far ahead, he backed off and settled for second place. An hour later he ran a personal best in the half mile while anchoring the two-mile relay to a third place finish. Afterward, his legs felt like rubber. It was a hectic day, and Josh tried to slip away to rest when he could, but it seemed like he was always warming up, racing or practicing handoffs with the relay team. When the distance medley was called to the line, he was still tired from the first two races. That didn't stop him from running hard and his anchor mile run provided the edge as they moved from 5th to 2nd during his final leg. At the end of a very long day they called the two-mile, which is always one of the last events of the meet.

He was physically beat up but this was a race that Josh wanted to win very badly and he showed it by starting with the leaders who had set a brisk pace right from the gun. Just after they passed the mile mark, Josh went hard for 600 yards and broke away. The rest of the runners were demoralized and almost gave up, figuring that Josh would continue to hold the pace the rest of the way. As he approached the bell for the final lap, he knew he was in trouble but continued to mask his fatigue. He was simply worn out. His reputation as a strong finisher was all that saved him. If they had known how awful he felt, they would have gone after him. They missed their chance because if anyone had been close, they would have crushed him. Luckily, he was alone and able to hang on for the win in one of his slowest times of the year.

Only four days later, without nearly enough rest, Josh was running in the State Regional Meet. Anyone finishing in the top two, in an individual event, would qualify for the State Championship.

Josh was entered in the mile and two-mile, but he really thought his best chance at state was in the longer race. It wouldn't take long to make the decision of which race to concentrate on as Josh was tripped, and fell hard, on the second lap of the mile run. By the time he got untangled and back on his feet the leaders were gone. He did finish the race but he was now only thinking about the two-mile.

Fortunately, the two-mile went totally according to plan. Josh ran side by side with his friend and rival Bill Field whom he'd been battling with since the ninth grade. They dropped everyone early and ran together until the final lap where a relieved Josh pulled away and got his State Meet qualifier.

The pressure to win the State meet intensified during the next week as Josh continued to train as he had all year. His coach, who had helped Josh immensely during the past three years, was now in over his head. Josh needed to peak for this race but the coach didn't know how to help him do that. Instead, he kept pushing Josh hard all the way up to a couple of days before the meet. He was severely over trained and the result was the same uninspired type of performance that he'd had all season.

The race went out fast and, not knowing how he was going to feel, Josh jumped right in with the leader. He wasn't about to let anyone go in his final high school race. He tried to stay positive but, as they passed the half mile, Josh was already worried. His legs felt tired even though they were running at a pace he should be able to handle. By the time the mile marker flashed by, Josh and the defending champion from Lakeville High School had gone through in 4:35, nearly on meet record pace, and put a gap on the rest of the field. He was in perfect position but Josh was already hurting bad. On the fifth lap he lost contact and soon he was being passed. He didn't give up, but when he dug down for more, he was greeted with an all too familiar feeling, there was absolutely nothing there. He watched helplessly as runner after runner passed him. By the time it was over, he had dropped to 10th place and run his slowest two-mile since his sophomore year. Afterward, he walked off of the track and threw his spikes into a trash can.

Later, his coach retrieved the shoes and returned them, apologizing for his role in Josh's poor race. It was a nice gesture but it didn't make Josh feel any better. He blamed the coach's lack of knowledge for his failure to achieve the performance he knew was inside of him. He had no idea that a week later the coach would make up for everything in the best way possible. Coach Feder had managed to get Josh into the mile run at the *Meet of Champions*.

The *Meet of Champions* was an annual track meet held at the University of Wisconsin at River Falls that featured the finest track and field athletes from Minnesota and Wisconsin. Normally, it was limited to the first four or five finishers from the respective state meets but Coach Feder had pulled some strings. He knew that Josh's chances at state were sidetracked by the fall he had during the mile run and he used that to get Josh into the meet. Josh would have one more chance to end his senior season with the race he knew he was capable of.

During the week between the state meet and the announcement that Josh was in the *Meet of Champions*, he did very little running. He was physically beat from the long season and mentally dejected because of the state meet. So, he had taken the time off and it was exactly what his legs needed.

A few days later, as his coach drove him to Wisconsin, they decided on a strategy for the race. Once they arrived, and Josh began his warmup, he knew it would be a different story than the state meet. He felt rested and strong. He accelerated down the backstretch in lane eight, just bringing himself to race pace and then quickly backing off. The burning and aching was gone, as if by magic, and he felt quick and powerful again.

Twenty minutes later, when they were called to the line, Josh greeted the other Minnesota runners. He knew them all, but the Wisconsin runners would be wildcards. He had seen the qualifying times but he didn't know their strengths and weaknesses. That unknown influenced his strategy. He didn't want this race to come down to a mass sprint at the finish only to find out that one of the Wisconsin guys had 50 second quarter speed. He had to hurt them earlier than that.

The gun sounded and, amid a flurry of elbows and spikes, Josh fought for position. They jostled through the first turn but by the time they reached the back straight, it had all sorted itself out. Josh ran easily in lane two to avoid getting boxed in and waited.

After a week of rest, Josh was amazed at the difference in his leg speed. He held his spot through the turn and when he heard the quarter mile split of 66 seconds he almost smiled. Even this soon, the pack had thinned enough for him to slip over to the inside rail. Once there, he watched the leaders carefully as they ran the turn. He expected a move to be made on the back straight and, since his strategy required that he be with the leaders at the half mile, he was prepared to react quickly. As often happens, the leaders slowed slightly as they ran the first turn on the second lap. Not surprisingly, as soon as they exited the turn a Wisconsin runner moved into the lead and increased the pace. Josh was ready for it and immediately went after him, along with five others. The group reassembled on the second turn and then ran together into the front straight.

The pace was fast and Josh had perfect position just off of the Wisconsin runner's right shoulder. As they passed the clock, Josh heard the split called out and was, again, right on pace. The second lap had taken another 66 seconds. Like everyone else, Josh was feeling the effects of the first two laps. It was fast enough to hurt anyone with good finishing speed, but still not fast enough to drop the contenders. That was about to change as Josh attacked going into the turn.

It almost looked like he had miscounted the laps and it caused the runners behind him to hesitate. When they realized it was a real attack, a couple of them broke from the pack and started to chase him. Josh had told himself to forget the final lap and to pretend this was it. He'd have no choice but to run hard all the way to the finish.

The chase group was determined and got close on the second turn, but they fell back when Josh continued to hold the pace down the front straight. He could see Coach Feder jumping around on the infield, as he heard the bell ring for the final lap. He glanced at the clock on the way by and saw a 3:15 displayed.

He'd thrown a 63 second third lap at them and was still going strong. *That should get everyone's attention,* he thought.

Behind him the race was fragmenting into small groups. The sprinters, hurt by Josh's surge, had fallen back. Meanwhile, the strength runners were trying to grind it out and hoping he would falter.

As Coach Feder had instructed him, once the third lap was over, Josh picked a new target. He visualized the finish line as the end of the back straight and tried to hold his pace all through the turn. It worked for a while but by the time he started down the back straight he was tightening up and slowing down. He was still 250 yards out but it was already too late for the chase group. Josh had enough of a gap to stay away to the finish.

He ran the final straight in pain but with a huge smile building. He was going to beat the state champions from Minnesota and Wisconsin in the same race, a feat that had been unthinkable only a week earlier. He cruised the last 50 yards and really enjoyed the moment. His time of 4:21 was a personal best by 10 seconds but it was the way he did it and who he beat that caused him the most joy. He'd beaten two arguably better runners by having a plan, sticking to it and then, gutting it out when it got tough.

High school was over and college was on the horizon. He'd gone out in style.

Looking back, the number of events he competed in certainly had a negative effect on his individual performances. On the other hand, despite being tired, he was able to improve his personal best in the mile to a respectable 4:21 and lowered his 2 mile time to 9:35. But, when he ran poorly at the State Championship meet, he knew that no Division 1 scholarships were coming his way.

Even though he still wanted to run for a team, Josh decided to forget about choosing a school based on track and pick based on academics. The F.A.A. had taken his pilots license but that didn't change his goal of becoming an Aerospace Engineer. The University of Florida had a solid engineering program and it was only 40 miles from his parent's new home in Ocala. After some soul searching, the decision was made to move to Gainesville and attend the University of Florida in the fall.

Josh had not contacted the universities cross country coach but he really wanted to make the team as a walk-on in the fall. He didn't really care about the scholarship anymore. Sure, the extra money would have been great but he qualified for student loans and would be able to pay for his classes without it. Like most of the guys that ran cross country, he'd do it with or without a scholarship. He just wanted to compete at the highest level.

Head Coach John Randolph was a former coach at the U.S. Naval Academy in Annapolis, MD. He came to Florida and began recruiting an excellent group of young talented runners for his team. He was very gracious and accommodating when Josh finally got up the nerve to ask him for an interview.

The office was located on the fourth floor of the Athletic Department compound next to the football stadium. Coach Randolph's large desk was the predominate feature in the room but, from the leather chair across from the coach, you couldn't help but be intimidated by the awards and memorabilia that covered all the walls. This wasn't a locker room office at some small high school in Minnesota. It was NCAA Division 1, the big leagues, and Josh was slightly overwhelmed.

The coach walked confidently into the room and smiled at Josh. "Good Morning Josh, I'm glad you could come by."

Josh stood to shake his hand. "Thanks for seeing me Coach Randolph."

"No problem at all. As I understand it, you're interested in competing for us in cross country and track."

Josh nervously started to state his case. "Yes sir, I was hoping that you would let me join the team and, with your help, I'm sure I could improve my times and eventually be an asset."

"Well, I'm glad that you're interested. After you called, I did a little research and I found that you ran pretty well in track your senior year. It looked like low 4:20's for the mile and the 9:30 range for the deuce. Does that sound right?" Coach Randolph asked while looking at some numbers on a notepad.

Josh shifted anxiously in his seat. "Yes, that sounds right. I also ran a 15:20 for 3 miles in cross country."

"Those are all good times for a high school runner but things are a lot different here."

"What do you mean Coach?" Josh asked.

"For one, we run over 6 miles for our cross country races and that means you need to run faster for 3 miles than you ran your senior year *and* you have to keep that pace up for twice as long." The coach had come around to Josh's side of the desk and was now sitting on the edge while talking to him. "In track, you're not quite fast enough yet to run the mile so you'd have to move up to the 5k and 10k, which are extremely difficult events to run on the track. Have you ever run a 10k?"

"No, the longest race I've ever run was 3 miles during cross country season but I'd like to try it as soon as possible."

The coach paused to think. Clasping his hands together behind his back he returned to his side of the desk. "Look Josh, it's obvious that you have talent and desire. I just don't know if you're ready for this level yet."

"Ok, what should I do?"

"I'd like you to get out and run some road races. Get a little more experience. Unlike some schools, we don't carry an unlimited roster. You only make this team if we're confident that you have a shot at our top seven, a chance to score in a meet."

"You want me to run some road races. Then what?" Josh asked clearly disappointed.

"Then you ask to see me again and we'll talk some more," he answered.

The interview was over. He wasn't rushed out but there was no indication given that any more negotiation would take place. Coach Randolph was happy to talk about training theories, goals for the team, anything at all, but Josh was not on the team. That was decided.

After another ten minutes of small talk, Josh stood to shake the coach's hand again. "Thanks for your time coach."

"My pleasure Josh. Keep working hard and you'll find a place here. Remember, I'll be watching."

"I will coach. Thanks again."

Josh stood outside the old brick building and looked back up at the coach's office. *I'll call him again next year and, if I have to, the next.* He walked back to his dorm room, determined to make the team, someday.

Winter Storm

"Big occasions and races which have been eagerly
anticipated almost to the point of dread, are where great
deeds can be accomplished."

— Jack Lovelock
Former World Record holder, Mile run

Dec 9th, 2005, 6 a.m., Roanoke, VA
Countdown to Hellgate – 16 hours

A storm was coming.
It had been all they talked about on the news for the past
two days. There were severe winter storm warnings up
and down the east coast but, so far, nothing had happened. Josh
watched and waited, wondering if it would hit before he had a
chance to get out of North Carolina. Finally, he couldn't stand it
any longer. He jumped in the car and headed down the deserted
backroads for Virginia. He arrived ahead of the storm, as did Jill
and Scott's flight.

When he picked them up at the airport, he was starting to
think that maybe the bad weather would slip past to the north and
miss them completely. Even after they checked into the hotel and
settled in after dinner there was no sign of the storm.

It was with more than a small amount of optimism that they
went to sleep late Thursday night; but by morning everything had
changed.

Jill woke to see Josh standing at the window of their hotel
room, at the Marriott in Roanoke, with the shades pulled back.

"Jill, come take a look at this," he said.

"What is it?" she asked.

"Snow and ice. We got hammered last night."

She quickly came over to the window. Everything was covered with a beautiful six inch deep layer of pure white snow and it was still coming down. "No way. Now what?"

"I don't know. Right now I doubt we can even get the car out of the parking lot and there's no telling what the roads are like in the mountains."

"Will they run the race?" It didn't sound like Jill would be upset if the race was canceled. Josh's voice sounded terrible and he was still fighting the diarrhea the antibiotics were causing.

"Let's buzz Scott's room and see what he thinks," Josh said, "this kinda stuff probably happens to him all the time."

Scott had already seen the storm's aftermath from his room and, surprisingly, he had *not* been in this situation before.

"Sure, I've run in some snow before in the mountains, but I've never been on ice like this and I've definitely never had to worry about whether or not I could get to the starting line in one piece," he said after coming up to their room. "Did you both forget? I live in Florida too!"

"All those ultras and you've never had conditions like this?" Jill was shocked.

"Nope, never have," he answered.

"Well, what do we do then?" she asked the two men.

They all looked at each other and, finally, Scott spoke. "Well, first, let's get some breakfast. Then, I'd suggest a nice Jacuzzi and some stretching. Maybe run a mile or two on the treadmill. You know, treat it like a normal morning."

"Business as usual. Don't even worry about what you can't change," Josh said.

"Right," Scott walked back to the window to look at the parking lot and continued, "later, after the plows have been through, we'll head up the Interstate and see how it looks in the mountains."

"Sounds like as good a plan as I've heard so far," Josh said. "I'm going to change clothes. Let's meet downstairs in 15 minutes."

Josh's bout with diarrhea wasn't over yet, and he had no intention of eating, but he would go with them anyway. With the race nearing he had to get some calories into his body, so he had already decided that he would just drink Boost meal replacements instead of eating solid food. With some luck, he might make it past his problem before Midnight.

They were bored but the morning went by as they had planned and, by noon, once the salt had done its job, the Interstate appeared to be open. They got in the car and drove a few miles north of Roanoke and exited the highway to check on the back roads. At first, they thought it would be fine, but when they moved onto the less traveled road, and finally to the dirt roads, they found them to be impassable.

"You can't drive on these roads up to the Parkway Jill, especially at night." Josh left no room for debate.

"No way." Scott agreed.

"Ok, so, what do I do? Should I just drop you off at the start tonight and drive back to the hotel?" she asked.

"That might be best. That is if they still have the race," Josh replied.

"Don't worry about that. I'm telling you with 100 percent certainty that this race will happen," Scott said confidently.

Josh looked at his friend like he was crazy. "What makes you so certain?"

"Two words. *David Horton.* Trust me, it'll happen on schedule."

"Fine," Josh said, "let's assume it's happening. If that's the case, let's take a few minutes to walk down this road and see what we're in for when we move higher up the ridge."

"Good idea," Scott said.

Jill stayed with the car as Scott and Josh made a short trip up the nearby hill. They were only gone twenty minutes and when they returned they looked concerned.

"Well?" Jill asked.

"Not to good. Not to good," Josh muttered. "I think we need to revise your crewing plans. Do you have your notes with you?"

"Of course, right here," she said as she opened a notebook and started searching for a pen.

Josh took the top page and started reading. "Let's just try for the two major checkpoints. Headforemost Mountain may be hard to get to but Bearwallow Gap is in the valley and on a main road so it should be a snap."

"I agree," Scott said, "just try for those two and forget about the rest. Also, let's send drop bags to Headforemost Mountain just in case Jill can't get there."

"Yeah, redundancy is good," Josh said, still looking at the notes.

Jill took the page back and started scribbling some changes onto it. "All right, that's what I'll do."

They were all quiet for a moment and each of them stared out into the woods. The ice on the trees glistened in the sunlight and it looked very serene and beautiful but they all knew that at Midnight it would become a monster.

"Are you guys sure you want to run tonight?" Jill asked.

"Of course," Scott replied.

Josh looked at her like she was the crazy one, not them. "That's a ridiculous question," he said.

Scott headed for the passenger seat. "Well, we're not doing ourselves any good here. Let's just go back to the hotel and chill for a while."

Josh opened the driver's door. "Yeah, let's go."

Jill lagged behind, looking down the icy road and scanning the woods. She climbed into the backseat and stared, for a moment, at the grown men who were chatting in the front seat and then just shook her head. *They're both mental cases,* she thought.

The Marathon

"To describe the agony of a marathon to someone who's never run it is like trying to explain color to someone who was born blind."

— Jerome Drayton
Winner of the 1977 Boston Marathon

January 1981, Jacksonville, Florida

The meeting with Coach Randolph gave Josh a purpose through the fall. As he had been advised to do, he trained on his own and started running local 5k road races. Every now and then, he would have a really good day and lower his personal best by a few more seconds. It didn't seem like much, but the time, eventually, started to add up into significant performance gains. He hoped that the coach was true to his word and watching him.

Although he trained alone, Josh had traveled to quite a few 5k's with some runners he'd met in Ocala. They gave him a lot of information about the local race scene. On one of the many early morning drives, they told him about the Jacksonville Marathon. It was to be run in January and Josh thought it might be fun to use it for motivation over the holidays. Even after he entered, for some reason, he wasn't intimidated by the fact that his longest race had been three miles and now he was going to jump up to 26.2 miles. He knew he could run the distance. The problem was that he didn't have a strategy for the marathon. He had nothing to use as a guide. So far, he only knew how to run one way and that was all out from the start.

So, when Josh found himself on the starting line that January, he was unprepared. He would have to gain the much needed experience while on the course.

The runners milled around nervously, waiting for the start. Some, like Josh, ran sprints and tried to get loose, treating it like any other road race. Others merely waited in groups talking. When the gun finally went off, showing his inexperience, Josh bolted into the lead. It was a warm, overcast day but a slight breeze made it feel cooler than it really was. He had no idea how fast he should go so he just ran.

By three miles, which he passed within a few seconds of his personal best, he was clear of the field. Only one runner stayed close. They continued on and, soon, the other runner began to very gradually close the gap. He pulled even with Josh as they approached the five mile mark.

The other runner was older than Josh by about 10 years and seemed to be floating across the pavement with no effort at all. "Hey, what's your name?" he asked.

Josh was running too hard to talk in anything but short choppy sentences but he tried to act like it didn't hurt. "Josh," he responded.

"I'm Frank. This course is supposed to be pretty fast but I've never run it before. How about you?"

Josh couldn't believe how casual this guy was. They were still moving at a sub six minute per mile pace and this guy was talking to him like they were in line at the bank. "First time. Here," he managed to get out.

"Cool, how many marathons have you run before this?"

Josh had to stop talking it was putting him into oxygen debt but he still tried, unsuccessfully to hide it. "None. First marathon. Longest race. Was. Three miles," he said between breaths.

"Wow! This is quite a jump in distance. Well, why don't we just run together for a while and try to get a good lead on everyone else?"

"Great," Josh said, hoping it was the end of this very one sided conversation.

As the miles passed, Josh decided that Frank was a machine. Listening to his breathing and hearing the balanced sound of his feet striking the ground in a steady unchanging rhythm was almost hypnotic. Josh tried to be cool and stay just off his shoulder, but he was already starting to suffer and knew there was a long way to go. The smart choice at that point would have been to back off and let Frank go on alone, but Josh just didn't think that way. It was all or nothing.

They were still together as they passed through the 10 mile checkpoint, but Josh was in trouble. He was tired and his feet were starting to throb. He had only run a handful of road races and, at this point, didn't know much about racing shoes. A few weeks earlier, he had bought a pair of light Nike shoes that were new on the market. It was a great shoe for the 5k's he had been running but it was not a marathoning shoe. For that matter, he didn't have marathoning feet yet either. They were just not tough enough.

He felt the heat starting to build on his heels and on the balls of his feet. He had very little experience with blisters but it was obvious he was about to have serious problems. Naturally, he ignored the signs and continued to run a half step behind Frank. While they passed the halfway point of the loop course and starting working their way back along the St. Johns River towards the finish line, Josh's feet were literally falling apart. Thankfully, Frank hadn't spoken to him for several miles so he was able to keep his distress to himself.

The pain was becoming severe and, as he rounded a corner, he thought that he felt something tear loose. He was committed to the pace and kept running quietly behind Frank as the skin peeled back from the bottoms of his feet and started to ball up under his toes. It hurt, but by now, so did a lot of other things. His legs were starting to give out and he thought he might have lost a couple of toenails. There was a definite squishing sound with each step and, when he glanced down, he thought his shoes looked red, even though he knew they had started off as white and blue.

Josh tried to focus and let the miles flow by. Through the haze that the pain caused, he saw mile markers passing and he knew Frank was still there as well. If he'd had more experience or known anything about the marathon he would have been scared.

Ten miles is a long way to run while things are falling apart that badly.

The man with the experience was Frank. He could see that the youngster was in trouble but, up until now, he had been content to run without any surges. He felt that he could break away at any time but he didn't want to run alone from any further out than necessary. So he calmly bided his time.

Meanwhile, Josh's parents were anxiously waiting at the 20 mile mark. They had not been to very many races while Josh was in high school, but they were always supportive of their son's running. They came to races when work allowed, or when it was a special event. This first marathon had qualified in Josh's mind as a special event, and they had recognized it by driving their motorhome to Jacksonville, which gave him a comfortable place to rest the night before. Neither of them had ever run a road race but, when they had seen Josh at 15 miles, they had no trouble recognizing that their son was struggling to keep up with the leader.

Josh didn't know what to do. Every step caused shooting pain and, after 18 miles of hanging on by a thread, Frank had just opened a gap on him. When he tried to dig into his reserves and respond he found nothing but pain. He watched helplessly as Frank slipped away. There was no way he intended to give up the chase and he continued to push hard but, with each passing mile, Frank became smaller and smaller in the distance. When he saw the 20 mile mark coming up, and saw his parents waiting, he made a snap decision to get out of the torture chamber that his shoes had become and switch to another pair. He started yelling to his mother to get his training shoes from the motorhome and, while she did as he asked, he sat down on the curb and tried to remove his racing shoes. Just as he finished carefully taking them off, his mother ran up with the training shoes.

She stopped a couple of feet away and held them out to Josh. The look on her face told the story. Josh's socks were soaked with blood.

"Oh my God. Do you need another pair of socks?" she asked.

Josh was grabbing the shoes from her. "No, I can't risk taking these off."

"What's going on? I've never seen this happen to you before."

He pulled the laces as loose as possible to make room for his feet. "I don't know. Wrong type of shoe I guess. How far behind am I?" he asked.

His father stood to the side stoically watching the scene.

"A couple of minutes at the most," she said.

He stuffed his swollen, bloody feet into the shoes and laced them up. He expected relief when he stood by was shocked that the pain had actually increased. The shoes applied pressure in different spots than the racing shoes and those spots weren't numb.

"I've gotta go," he said.

There was nothing he could do. Three minutes had already been wasted. He got to his feet and started to shuffle down the street. Soon, the shuffle turned into a slow jog and eventually a hobble that resembled running. There was no way to dull the throbbing so he just continued toward the finish line as fast as he could. Behind him, his parents watched, wondering if he'd make it the last six miles.

His enthusiasm for reaching the finish line lasted about three miles. That's when another runner caught and passed him. Emotionally it was devastating. He had been clinging to the idea that he could hang on for second place but now that carrot was gone and his body was crashing in ways that he had never felt before. A hundred yards further down the street, he stopped running and sat down in the middle of the road. He was done. He had left everything on the course and it had beaten him.

One by one, runners passed Josh as he sat in the road. He had no idea what he was waiting for but he just sat there as they went by. Every single one asked if he was all right, and he responded to each that he was fine. Then, when he was convinced that anytime the familiar sight of the motorhome would come around the corner to give him a ride home, a runner stopped.

The expected question came. "Are you all right?"

"Yeah, I'm fine," Josh answered. But this one didn't run away like the others.

He reached down and grabbed Josh under each arm and started lifting him. "Then get up and run," he said.

"What are you doing? Leave me alone," Josh stammered.

"No way. If you're not hurt, get up and run with me. It's less than three miles to the finish. Come on."

Josh didn't say anything but, when the unknown runner started jogging, Josh went with him. He wasn't able to stay with him long but, once he was back on his feet, he did keep shuffling down the street.

Josh hadn't run any races that required he take fluids while running. So, on this warm day, he had run past the aid stations with barely a glance at the assortment of drinks and snacks. He was paying the price with dehydration and a near complete depletion of the carbohydrate stores in his muscles. There was no way to make up for it now so, as he rounded the final turn to the finish, he was in an awful state. He saw the motorhome and knew his parents were here. *Where's the finish?* he wondered.

His father saw Josh jog to toward the group of people that were cheering and realized Josh was confused. He immediately ran towards his son to help.

"Where's the finish?" Josh yelled at the group.

"Through the gate and once around the track," someone answered.

It might has well have been on the moon because he wasn't going any further.

Josh stopped and turned towards the motorhome. *A lap around the track. No way. I'm done.* He took a couple of steps in the direction of the air conditioned shelter only to see his father running towards him. *I've never seen dad run before. What's he doing?*

"Josh, it's once around the track. You need to finish."

"No," Josh said as he continued towards the refuge of the motorhome.

"Turn around son. You've come this far. You have to finish."

"I can't."

"Yes you can! I'll run with you," his voice was firm and he was clearly becoming emotional on the subject of Josh finishing.

He grabbed Josh's arm and started pulling him toward the track. "All right," Josh said as he started shuffling again.

He was a complete wreck by now, but it didn't matter. He ran a lap around the track with his father who stepped aside as Josh crossed the line. Frank had gone on the win in 2:27:12 and Josh had made his marathon debut with a ninth place finish and a time of 2:58:24

Later, as he crashed on the bed in the motorhome, he realized that he didn't even know enough about marathoning to know what he had done wrong. Certainly he had made more than one mistake but allowing himself to become so dehydrated was devastating to his performance and the shoe choice had been debilitating. All in all, it had been an extremely tough day. Looking for positives, he had pushed the boundaries a little further out. The Jacksonville Marathon had been the longest run of his life and, when he thought about it in those terms, he took pride in the fact that, with his father's urging, he had finished.

Pre-Race Meeting

"When the meal was over we all had a quiet rest in our rooms and I meditated on the race. This is the time when an athlete feels all alone in the big world. Any runner who denies having fears, nerves or some kind of disposition is a bad athlete, or a liar."

— Gordon Pirie
1956 Olympic 5,000 meter Silver Medalist

Dec 9th, 2005, 8:00 p.m., Jefferson National Forest
Countdown to Hellgate – 4 hours

The ice covered parking lot was full of cars and they could see light streaming through the window of the large building at the far end. As they approached, they could here muffled voices that turned slowly into a wall of sound.

"Well, at least we're not the only idiots to risk our lives driving through the snow to the pre-race meal," Josh said.

Scott just laughed. "Are you kidding? There are a hundred people signed up for this race. I think that, by definition, makes them all idiots and I expect to see every one of them here tonight."

"I suppose you're right."

"Damn right I am. In fact, don't be surprised when they start riding up on horses, skis and snowmobiles. They'll use whatever they can get their hands on to make it to the starting line."

Jill was smiling as she baby stepped her way across the parking lot. "Try and remember that the two of you were idiots even before you signed up."

"I love you too, dear," Josh said as he slipped trying to catch up to Jill. "Wow, this ice is really bad. If this is on the course we're screwed. These shoes are going to be useless."

Scott was also staring at the ground and walking with tiny, cautious steps. "Let's not worry about what we can't control and do something productive, like getting our asses out of this cold."

As they opened the door to the dining hall, they were hit with a welcome blast of warm air. The front room was set up with a few sofas and chairs, arranged around a large fireplace. Some of the runners were already forming a makeshift line into the dining hall.

"Let's let them know the Floridians have arrived and get our numbers," Scott said as he moved across the room towards the registration table.

Their entries were quickly found and, as they walked away from the friendly ladies who had helped them sign in, towards the dining hall, Jill unfolded Josh's complimentary race T-shirt. "I was right! You're both nuts," she said.

"What are you talking about now?" Josh asked.

"Look at this shirt, I think it says everything you need to know about Dr. Horton's little race through the woods."

She had Scott's attention, as well, and he stopped to unfold his shirt. He looked it over and his smile was followed by laughter. It was a nice long sleeve shirt with a picture of a wall and a gate. Behind the gate there were flames. Above the picture, it just said "Hellgate 100km" and the starting time "12:01 am, December 10, 2005". But it was the quote under the picture that had gotten Scott and Jill going. It was a quote from Dante's "Inferno" that referenced the gates of hell. It simply said "Abandon all hope ye who enter here".

"Not a bad sentiment and probably pretty accurate. Let's mingle and eat," Scott said.

The pasta dinner looked fantastic but Josh was too scared to eat any of it. The antibiotics were already threatening to ruin his night and he didn't want to make things worse. Jill and Scott did not have the same reservations and moved down the buffet line like it was their last meal. Just like every other ultra on the east coast, the majority of runners appeared to know Scott and he spent most of the next hour catching up and talking about everyone's most recent races. Meanwhile, Josh sat quietly at the corner table brooding. His cough had lessened in frequency but not in severity. When it hit him, it rattled his chest and caused concerned looks from the adjacent tables. The concern wasn't for Josh, it was for themselves. They didn't want to get sick by sitting next to some fool who came to the race with what sounded like a case of pneumonia.

Dr. David Horton, runner, race director and teacher, moved through the crowd greeting runners like he had known them his whole life. It didn't seem to matter if you had met him at a race a week before or if you had spent a month crewing for him on one of his epic adventures. He's just the type of guy that makes you feel welcome.

There were a hundred conversations happening around the room but when he raised his arms everyone turned and focused their attention on the enigmatic founder of Hellgate.

"Thanks for coming. I hope everyone is enjoying the dinner and I want to thank our hosts for allowing us to use the dining hall and for providing such a great meal.

"I want to take a minute to say a few things about this adventure that you've all signed up for and maybe to offer some advice to the first timers.

"I suppose the first thing we should talk about is the weather. As you can all see, it's not good. We've had some volunteers out there this evening marking the course with streamers and chem-lights. From what they've reported, the entire single track trail has about six inches of snow covering it which means you cannot see the rocks. Also, there's a thick, icy crust on top that isn't strong enough to hold your weight so you're going to fall through and break the crust into lots of slippery, sharp pieces that will dig into your ankles. It will be hard to keep your balance or to get a solid footplant anywhere on the trail sections.

"The fire roads are worse. There's a continuous sheet of ice across all of the roads that's at least an inch thick. It's extremely slick. In the spots that are protected from the wind, there may be some snow to give you a little bit of traction but, at higher elevations, where the road is exposed, I expect it to be treacherous.

When we start, it's going to be about 15 degrees and it won't get above 25 degrees all day. So, don't expect any of the snow to melt."

A lot of side conversations were breaking out. "What about the aid stations?" someone asked.

"What about the aid stations? That's a good question," he paused briefly, "well, I'm concerned. We don't know if we can even get to the higher elevations. I'll try to let you know, as you pass through aid stations, if you should take extra food and water for possible missing aid stations ahead. We just don't know what's going to happen."

The murmur was slowly building as the crowd continued to talk amongst themselves. Finally another entrant spoke up. "What about our crews?" he asked, "are they going to be able to get to the aid stations to meet us?"

Dr. Horton paced back and forth at the front of the room. "I wouldn't recommend that anyone try to get to the higher elevations unless they have a four wheel drive. Even then, it may be too dangerous. If you have crews with you, you should consider changing your plans. The routes that they would normally take between aid stations are going to be closed. Even the Blue Ridge Parkway may be closed. That means, even if they can get to each location, it will require significant detours and lots of time driving at night on unfamiliar roads."

"What about the cutoffs?" a runner near the back of the room asked.

"That's another good question, thanks for reminding me. There are two major checkpoints on the course. One is at about 22 miles and another is at about 42 miles. We have strict time limits for reaching both of these locations. The first time limit is 6 hours and 30 minutes and then you'll have another 6 hours to get to the second checkpoint. I know for you first timers, these time limits sound easy. I can assure you that they are not. Even under ideal conditions they're tough. You must arrive at these aid stations by the appointed times to be allowed to continue on the course. Don't ask for exceptions! If you don't get to these aid stations by these times, data from the previous two years demonstrates that you can't finish in less than 18 hours, which is the time limit to be listed as an *official* finisher."

Some of the runners at Josh's table were concerned and one of them spoke up. "Are you going to extend the cutoffs and allow us more time due to the weather and the conditions of the trail?"

Dr. Horton looked straight at them and responded loudly. "NO! We are not changing the time limits!" He looked back at the group and added seriously. "I know this is going to be very difficult, but the cutoffs are going to remain as planned. If you miss either cutoff, you'll be pulled from the race. I'm sorry, but that's the way it's going to be.

"What am I missing? Oh, another point is that, as you are all aware, this race is held in the national forest. What you may not know is this is deer and bear season, so there will be lots of hunters out there. Please be nice and friendly to the hunters, THEY HAVE GUNS!!! Because of this, you may want to consider wearing some very bright colors."

That information prompted a loud murmur to fill the room as everyone started talking amongst themselves.

"Please remember, above all, that we're in this together. This is going to be a great adventure for all of you but you'll need to be smart to get through it. Help each other! If you see someone going off the trail in the wrong direction, help them! Don't let them go. If a course marking is damaged, or moved, and you know it's wrong, fix it! These are basic things that we have to do to help each other make it through.

"Most important of all, have fun!" He paused. "This is a great course. I think it's one of the best events you'll ever be involved in and I hope you take some great memories home with you.

"Now, we have about and hour before we're going to load the cars and drive over to the starting line. I'll be in the lead car, just follow the caravan. It's only about 40 minutes from here so we'll leave at 11 p.m. We'll have a final check in once we're at the start.

"So, you can relax for the next hour and then we'll be ready to go. Thanks again for coming!"

As the meeting broke up, the runners split into groups and started to socialize and prepare their clothing and equipment for the start.

Josh had been in hundreds of races but there was a different feeling in this room tonight. Maybe it was just the weather that added a sense of dread to the event, but the feeling was there. The runners were not just nervous, an emotion that he always saw before races, this time they seemed to actually be frightened. He saw it here and there around the room, and more importantly, he felt it himself. He'd had a bad couple of weeks leading up to Hellgate and, for the first time in his life, he actually felt fear before a race. It was a fear of the unknown, the dark, the weather and of failure.

The Walk-On

"It is true that speed kills. In distance running, it kills
everyone that does not have it."

— **Brooks Johnson**
Coach of the 1984 U.S. Olympic Team

August 1982, University of Florida, Gainesville, Florida

For two years, Josh concentrated on school but he still
trained and raced regularly. He became fairly well known
by the local road race crowd and even started winning
occasionally. He hadn't given up on his dream of running for UF,
but he hadn't heard from Coach Randolph in all the time since their
last meeting. When it happened, it was completely unexpected.

Josh received very little mail, so the letter with a crisp UF
Athletic Department logo in the corner really got his attention. He
tore it open and eagerly unfolded the single sheet of paper. The
note was short and to the point.

Josh,

*As I told you to expect, I've been keeping an eye on you
over the past two years. You've shown a tremendous
amount of improvement over that time. You may not have
seen me, but I have watched you run in several road races
and I was impressed with your tenacity. On a couple of
occasions I watched you come back, after being passed late
in the race, to win over runners that I know are very
talented.*

142

I believe that this years Florida Cross Country Team will be one of the strongest ever and I'd like you to be a part of it. We'll be running a four mile time trial on the course that we use for our home meets on Saturday the 10th of August. I'd like to see you come out and join the select group of runners that I've invited to run this race as potential "Walk-On's". I think you may have what it takes to be a part of this special team that we're assembling.

We'll meet on the east side of the Univ. of Florida Golf Course clubhouse at 8 a.m. on the tenth. I'll look forward to seeing you there.

Best Regards

Coach Randolph
UF Track & Cross Country

The tenth of August. That was only a week away. There was no way to do any additional preparation, he'd have to do his best and hope that he was good enough to make the team. After two years of running alone and coaching himself, he was ecstatic to finally have a chance at making a Division 1 team.

He treated the time trial as if it was the most important race of his life because, to him, it was. For the next week, he waited nervously for the chance to take another step forward towards his goal of racing in an NCAA Championship. By the time his alarm rang on Saturday morning, he had already been up for hours. During the week, he had tried to run on the University golf course but he was not exactly certain of the route the cross country course took. He'd have to wait for the time trial to see it all.

He arrived first and, when he realized he was alone, became worried that he had the wrong day, or worse, he was in the wrong location. Ten minutes later some runners in Florida track sweats came jogging up and his anxiety reduced considerably. He went over to introduce himself just as a second group arrived. It didn't take long to figure out that he was in a different league than he was accustomed to. He was introduced to Keith who had won the

Penn Relays and SEC Championship at 10,000 meters the previous year, while running a national collegiate best time of 28:02. A friendly sophomore named Jack, whom Josh discovered had won nine state high school individual titles in Tennessee, introduced himself. There were two runners who had run sub four minutes in the mile, an NCAA Championship finalist in the steeplechase and various other runners with credentials that made Josh's 32:14 personal best in the 10,000 meters seem very puny indeed.

He was very distressed and started to think that he had made a terrible mistake coming to the tryout. He might have left if Coach Randolph hadn't walked up and called him by name.

"Morning fellas," the coach said. "I'd like you all to say hello to Josh. He's going to be running our little time trial today so make him feel welcome."

He was stuck. *This could turn out to be very embarrassing,* he realized.

The coach ran through a few details and got everyone organized for the start, which would be on the golf course down near the lake. Josh felt like he was the only one that was concerned. The rest of the guys were joking around and didn't seem to be warming up nearly enough. He was in over his head and he felt like everyone knew it, including Coach Randolph.

Just run your ass off. Don't give up no matter what happens, he thought.

They were all spread out in a line when the coach rode up on the back of a golf cart. "Everyone ready?" he yelled. "Great, let's run together as a team." He looked down at his watch and hollered again. "Go!"

The first hundred yards felt like a full sprint to Josh as the faster runners jockeyed for position going into the first turn. He fell into line near the back and tried to hang on. He would have been even more demoralized had he known that the strongest individuals were holding back according to Coach Randolph's instructions. They would encourage the next few in line to stay with them and keep a team of at least five together the entire distance. Josh was doing everything he could to stay with the pack but, by the time he saw the golf cart stop and the Coach jump off with his watch, he was in last place out of 15 runners.

He heard times being yelled out in front of him and, as he passed, he saw the coach look him in the eye and calmly say, "four forty six, hang in there Josh". He felt a shot of adrenaline as he passed and, for a moment, the pain dulled.

He was starting to lose the leaders but a second pack had split off and he was still hanging on to the back of their group when they hit the first long hill. The race was on a golf course and the final hole leading into the club house was a nearly 550 yard uphill par 5. Josh was disheartened when he learned that they would run the hill during the second mile and again at the finish of the fourth mile but the reality of it was even worse. It was intimidating to see how quickly the lead group vanished up this hill while he suffered all the way to the top. When he crested the top and started back down the other side, his lungs were on fire and his legs were wobbly. *Just hang on to the two mile. Come on. Run.*

Once again, the coach was waiting with his watch. Josh had moved ahead of a couple of guys but he was definitely slowing down and he knew the time would not be good. The coach made eye contact again as he went by. "Nine fifty. Don't give up Josh."

The third mile was almost flat and Josh started to gut it out. He caught a couple of more runners and was actually closing back on the second pack when he saw the now familiar sight of the coach waiting along the trail. He heard the crystal clear voice calling out numbers as he approached. "Fourteen fifty eight. Last mile. Stay with it Josh."

Fourteen fifty eight! That's my fastest 3 mile ever! He was amazed that he had run a personal best as a split and was still being crushed by at least 10 runners on this team. *How can they do this? It looks like they're not even working hard.*

He stopped looking around the course and focused on a spot 10 yards in front of him. He broke it down into time segments just trying to hold the pace for 30 seconds and, when he was done, he would go for another 30 seconds. It worked until he hit the hill for the second time, then it just disintegrated into a wall of pain.

He had run hard in road races before, and in high school, but he had never hurt as bad as this and kept running. It was a different pain than the marathon or even the pain of blisters or of an injury. This was a deep pain that engulfed his legs from hip to ankle. The cells were screaming for oxygen but the blood couldn't keep up anymore. With each step, it got worse.

He thought he heard the coach yelling but he couldn't understand him anymore. He kept his head down and gave it everything he had as he climbed toward the finish. When he crossed the line, it was as if he was in a vacuum. He couldn't get any air and had to steady himself against a tree while his lungs fought to force life back into his muscles.

That's it. I'm out. He thought. *I fell apart at the end and lost a couple of spots. That leaves me almost last and there's no way he's going to take me.*

Once he was able to breathe again, Josh slowly walked over to the large oak tree that several of the other runners were sitting under. He didn't say anything to them as he found a place to sit. They were quiet as well. He assumed that they thought there was no use talking to a guy that's about to get cut. There was some hushed conversation but it stopped when the coach strode confidently up to the assembled runners.

He was looking at notes on a clipboard. "Nice work guys. I had Keith at 19:08. Ted, Mike and Mark at 19:21. Let's see, Bart and Ray at 19:28 and then David finished out the top seven at 19:35. That's a nice close group for early in the year and I liked the way you all stayed together for the first three miles. Once we get into the season, our first few races will be five miles and then we'll bump up to 10,000 meters for the rest of the year. We'll have to work on our strength, but today you all looked great. Go for a short warm-down, and I'll see you at the track at 6 a.m. tomorrow and we'll get a long run in."

Everyone started to gather their gear up and head out for a warm-down but Josh didn't know what to do. Coach Randolph noticed him staring at the ground and walked over.

"Josh, nice run today."

"Thanks coach, but you know I got killed by those guys."

Coach Randolph chuckled at Josh's concern. "Of course you did, they're one of the best teams in the nation." He looked at his clip board again. "It looks like you ran 20:23, which isn't bad, but what really interests me is that, even when you were dropped, you never gave up. That's something we can work with. Go for a warm-down and I'll see you at six."

"What? I'm on the team?" Josh was shocked.

"You always were, I've already got a locker set up for you. I've seen you race enough to know you wouldn't fold today. You'll have to work hard to do it, but I think you have a chance to crack this team's top seven before your time here is done."

"Thanks Coach. I won't let you down."

The coach watched Josh run down the trail after the rest of the team and shook his head. In what other sport would a guy work so hard to make a team when he knows he'll never get a scholarship. He'll endure twice a day practices, travel, fatigue and injuries, all while trying to get a college degree, whether you pay him or not. Runners. As a coach, you gotta love them.

Midnight Start

"Jogging through the forest is pleasant, as is relaxing by the fire with a glass of gentle Bordeaux. Racing is another matter. The runner's mind is filled with an anguished fearfulness, a panic, which drives into pain."

— **Kenny Moore**
2-time Olympic Marathoner who finished 4th at Munich

Dec 10th, 2005, 12:01 a.m., Hellgate Creek, Jefferson National Forest, VA

Had anyone in the area surrounding Hellgate Creek Park been looking out their window at 11:30 p.m. they would have seen a strange procession of cars making their way toward the small, snow covered, gravel parking area near the Glenwood Horse Trail. The cars and vans slipped and slid down the narrow road, all following Dr. Horton's lead vehicle. They filed into the parking area and, within minutes, the recently deserted trailhead was surrounded by a collection of oddly dressed runners all bouncing around trying to keep warm. The headlamps gathered briefly around the race director's car for a second checkin and then dispersed, as each runner began their own pre-race rituals.

After checking in, Josh and Scott got together and walked down to the start line to see what condition the trail was in. It was snowing lightly and, in the valley, it was deathly calm. The trees were incredibly beautiful as each was coated with a thin layer of ice and sparkled as the headlamps lit them up. It didn't take long to get away from everyone else and, as they became more isolated, the beautiful trees suddenly started to look a bit spooky.

Josh tried to ignore the feeling, preferring to focus on positive thoughts. They found the trail head and very cautiously started a slow jog away from the parking area. At first, it seemed like it would be all right. The snow felt firm under their feet and their shoes were getting enough grip for them to run at a comfortable pace. The good feeling lasted all of a hundred yards, at that point the trail dropped down to cross an area that appeared to be a normally dry creekbed.

"What do you think?" Josh asked.

"It looks like its runnable, but this may not be representative of what we'll see once we're out of the valley."

Josh's clicked on his high intensity handheld light as they approached the shallow drop-off. "Watch it here Scott."

"Whoa!" Scott yelled as his feet slid on the ice. He was momentarily out of control but managed to regain his balance without falling. "That's not good," he said, while looking down and scraping the ground with his shoe.

Josh was also looking at the ground. "Nope. Not good at all," he agreed.

They turned together to continue jogging down the trail but were unable to make progress up the gradual incline. Their feet were sliding backward with each step and they had to put their hands away from their bodies to try and keep their balance. It was like watching a couple of tightrope walkers perform.

"Were screwed," Josh said dejectedly.

"Maybe not. It might not be like this everywhere."

"Yeah, right. I'm going back to get my bottles. You coming?" he asked.

Scott paused and looked down the trail. He had run in tough conditions before and knew that he could deal with it, but he was worried about Josh, whose confidence had already been ruined by his illness. This would make it even worse. He looked at Josh and wondered if his friend would make it through the night.

"Yeah, I'm coming," Scott said.

They walked back to the car and made their final preparations for the start. It was cold, about 15 degrees, and a big part of the discussion was how much to wear. If you misjudged and didn't wear enough, you would get cold and that would reduce your leg power and endurance. If you *really* miss the mark, it could cause hypothermia and death. Conversely, if you wear too much, you'll sweat and that means you'll risk dehydration and even in sub-freezing temperatures the results are cramps and worse. Both are bad, so you have to get it right. Scott always told Josh that he should be somewhat cold standing at the start line. Then, as your body heat builds up during the race, you would feel great. As long as you're running, or at least moving hard enough to keep your heart rate up, you'll stay warm, but not sweat. Unfortunately, if you get hurt and can't run, you'll feel warm for a while, but it won't take long to go back into the hypothermia zone. Josh decided to wear an extra light jacket that he could dump at the first drop bag area if the weather warmed at all.

When Dr. Horton headed for the trailhead they all moved as a group behind him. It was so different from a road race where everyone is busy stretching and running several warmup miles. Here, there were a few token stretches of chronic problem areas but, other than that, there wasn't much reason to warmup for a 66 mile race. Just run real easy for the first mile to loosen up and you'll still have 65 miles to catch anyone that got away.

Everyone was guided to a van that was parked at the trailhead and, once the group had assembled, a few runners led them through a nice rendition of the national anthem. After some final instructions by the race director, the countdown began. A horn signaled the start of the race and everyone was off and running. Josh was loaded down with two water bottles, one in a pack and one handheld. He was also carrying a few energy gels, extra batteries and a handful of electrolyte tablets. The headlamps all around him lit up the trail so he didn't even need his flashlight, but he carried it anyway.

Josh had gotten a good position near the front so that he could avoid being stuck behind slower runners on the single track trail. However, he didn't take into account the bad footing and, almost immediately, he realized that he was caught in a group that was going faster than he really wanted to go. He ran recklessly over the same section of ice he and Scott had slipped on 15 minutes earlier. It seemed like everyone around him was running much faster than he could and, afraid of falling, he was unable to get into a rhythm and relax.

His first impression of the race was that the entire field had lost their minds and were running too fast. He had expected the start to be laid back, with everyone showing the proper respect for the distance, and conditions. Surprisingly, it was more like the frantic start of a road race complete with flying elbows. After getting cut off for the third time in less than a mile, Josh was frustrated. *What are they doing!* After three months of preparation, and a lot of anticipation, it wasn't anything like what he had pictured in his mind.

He felt like he needed to slow down, but he was in line on the single track and could hear the footsteps behind him. Although Scott had been working on this part of Josh's mental training, it was still incredibly difficult for Josh to let someone pass him. His high school and college cross country brainwashing was still in effect. *This isn't the same,* he reminded himself as he slowed and moved slightly to the side to let a few runners past him. *There's a long way to go. I'll see them again.* He thought briefly about the short conversation he'd had with Scott as they were lining up.

Scott had tapped him on the shoulder only a minute before the horn sounded to start the race. "Josh? You all right?"

He turned to look at his friend. "Yeah, I'm fine. I just feel like I've forgotten something and I'll remember about the time I'm in the middle of the forest."

"That's typical. Don't worry about it, you have everything you need," Scott chuckled. "Just remember, the place you're in at the first aid station doesn't matter at all in a race like this."

"Right."

"Stick to your plan and don't get caught up in the craziness at the start."

"I will. You don't think I can show even a little restraint, do you?" Josh sounded hurt.

"I know you can't!" Scott slapped him on the back and laughed. "Just try to have fun, all right?"

"All right, You too."

He could show restraint. He just didn't do it very often and there was no reason to think that this would be the night. But he had told Scott he'd try, so he backed off the pace a little more and let a couple more of the eager runners pass. That seemed to take the pressure off and he was finally able to settle into a comfortable pace. There was such a long way to go that it was perilous to let thoughts of the distance into your head so early. So, all Josh did was concentrate on what was in front of him. He wanted to make it to the first aid station in good shape.

The first couple of miles were predominately flat. There was a slight uphill grade, but nothing that caused any stress, and the rolling hills and turns masked the overall incline. He was already struggling with the snow that covered the trail and, according to the latest reports, it would be much worse at the higher elevations. Still, he was running at a decent pace and the coughing, which had been so vicious all week, appeared, for the moment, to be under control.

The first aid station was only three and a half miles into the race but it came immediately after crossing a wide, frigid stream. They had been told it was too wide to jump, and that the rocks weren't really spaced properly to step on in an attempt to stay dry. The advice was simple. Just run right through the water and don't worry about it.

Josh's body heat was building and he was just beginning to feel comfortable when he saw the lights of the aid station. The creek appeared out of the darkness and he plowed straight into the calf deep water. It was shockingly cold and he high stepped through as fast as he could, thinking incorrectly, that he might stay somewhat dry. The rocks on the bottom were slick and what he found out was that speed means danger. He nearly went down, but managed to regain his balance with only his hand touching the water. He slowed down, letting the icy water penetrate his shoes and socks, as he carefully worked his way up the opposite bank. Only when he was clear of the wet bank did he resumed jogging into the lights of the aid station.

The aid station was a blur of activity but Josh, who had enough water to make it another hour, had no intention of stopping this early. So, he sloshed through with a couple of short *thank you*'s and looked for the next course marker.

The frenzy of the first few miles was abruptly gone. When Josh turned uphill from the aid station, on what would have normally been a dirt road, the field quickly started to string out. But tonight the road isn't dirt. It's covered with a thick layer of ice that feels solid under Josh's feet. His headlamp doesn't illuminate the road very far in front of him but he looks left and right for snow. After a hundred yards, he's already determined that the light snow cover over portions of the ice is the only way to get any traction. He seeks it out.

The road leading away from the aid station will carry them continuously uphill from the valley floor for nearly four miles to the top of the ridge, where they'll cross over the Blue Ridge Parkway at an altitude of nearly 2,300 feet. The grade is steady but early in the race, while they're still full of energy, some of the leaders elect to run all the way to the top. The elevation change is significant but Josh is so focused on the small area that is lit up in front of him that he doesn't notice the magnitude of the climb. The cold air is invigorating, and he was actually beginning to think that maybe he should run all the way to the Blue Ridge Parkway. As he starts passing runners who are walking, and a few who are running, his confidence starts to build. He thinks that maybe his cough will be held at bay by the medication and that he'll have a good day.

About a mile from the ridgeline, the road turns sharply uphill and makes a hard switchback that gives Josh a view of the valley below and the road he has been running for the last half hour. It's a beautiful sight. The road, which would normally be invisible in the darkness, is lit up by a string of headlamps all the way to the valley. It gives Josh his first visual reference of the height of the ridge and, seeing how high he is already, confirms his belief that he can run to the Parkway. His legs still feel strong as the welcome sight of the aid station lights become visible in the distance.

He came in alone. It was much more subdued than the first station, but they were still very attentive and met Josh in the center of the road as he ran up with his bottles open, ready for a refill.

"Water or Conquest?" A volunteer asked.

"One of each, thanks," Josh answered slightly out of breath. "How far ahead is the leader?"

The volunteer looked surprised by the question. "I don't know for sure. Maybe, five minutes?"

Josh always wanted to know where he was in a race but had a hard time getting the information during ultra-marathons. It was almost like the volunteers at the aid stations weren't even paying attention to times as the runners past through. They recorded race numbers to keep track of everyone, in case a search and rescue was needed for a lost runner, but position in a race was not as easy to get. Josh didn't have time to wait for any additional information. He had his bottles back and was already running across the Parkway toward the chem-light that marked the entrance to the single track trail which dropped steeply down the east side of the ridge.

He made a sharp left turn at the marker and plunged into the shadows. For the first time, he felt alone on the trail. The noise of the aid station quickly faded and he didn't see any lights in front of him or behind. The trail was covered with six inches of snow and he could see the footprints of the leaders. It was much steeper than he expected and he was bombing down the path, nearly out of control. The thick crust of hard, icy snow on the top was breaking away in chucks as he passed and his shoes slid unexpectedly in random directions, twisting his legs and causing him to stumble over and over again.

Too fast! I'm going to wreck my quads. He thought as he tried to shed off some speed.

The descent was steep and technical. It was exactly the type of trail that Scott had warned him about during their long runs together. The plunge continued at breakneck speed for almost two miles and, by the time he reached the small creek at the bottom, the trail had dropped nearly 1,000 feet. Finally, it started to level out and Josh relaxed as he turned and ran parallel to a stream. The trail was still covered with snow but there were more rocks and the footing was uneven and tricky. It wasn't a good idea to relax too much but he felt good about getting to the stream unscathed and started to shine his handheld light towards the water, enjoying the view.

Then, before he could react, his foot pushed through the snow and caught between some rocks. He tried to regain his balance but seconds later, he was airborne, flying headfirst into the darkness. He hit hard, with his hands in front of him, and the impact sent his water bottle and headlamp careening onto the rocks near the stream. A quick mental inventory told him that he hadn't been injured but he could see that his light was in danger of falling into the stream and he needed to move swiftly. He hastily scrambled on all fours down the rocks and grabbed it before it slid off. He laid there for a moment, relieved to have survived the fall without any broken bones. After checking the light, and reassuring himself that there was no damage, he sat up, slipped it back over his stocking hat and readjusted the beam. Shortly, he stood up and brushed the snow off and, as he calmed down, he looked back to where he had fallen. He saw the rocks drop off sharply and he could also see where he had missed the switchback. If he had been paying attention, he wouldn't have missed the corner. At the bottom of this hill he'd learned a hard lesson. He knew that, from now on, he'd have to stay constantly alert because this trail could reach out and grab you at any time.

As he walked along the creek, adjusting his clothing and equipment, he noticed that the constant beam of light had also given him some depth perception problems. At first, he hadn't felt it too drastically, but coming down the hill had worsened the effect and contributed to his fall. Now, as he stared at the shadows cast by rocks that were briefly illuminated by the weird glow of LED's, he felt like he was watching it through someone else's eyes. It was like he was in a trance. He decided that for the rest of the night he would use his bright handheld light in addition to the headlamp. Maybe that would give him back his depth perception. So, clicking on the bigger light, he started to jog along the creek. He instantly felt better and, as the trail crossed over the stream, his coordination was good enough, with the extra light, to step rock to rock and avoid drenching his feet again.

Josh had hoped for a little bit of relief down in the valley, maybe a nice firm section, but within a few hundred yards, the trail turned back towards the parkway and a twisting climb up the ridge began. The footing was tough and Josh was glad he had made good time running the road earlier, because he was not going to be going fast on any portion of the trail. Still, he power hiked hard up the incline, fighting against the snow and rocks, for at least a mile. The blackness that surrounded him made every small change in grade seem like the end but, when he focused the bright light further up the trail, he couldn't see the top. Even when the trail abruptly dropped away from him, he wasn't sure if it was going to be the anticipated long run back to the bottom, or just a brief drop, followed by miles of additional climbing. He had studied the map but now, when he needed to, he couldn't bring a mental image of the course profile into focus. The uncertainty made the distance seem longer than it really was and he constantly had to convince himself that he wasn't off the trail.

Once he finally crested the ridge, the path quickly vanished and Josh had to adjust the angle of his headlamp to make it useful again. The descent was shorter than the first one, but just as treacherous, and all the way down Josh fought to stay focused and upright. Sticking with his new plan, he used the bright handheld light to his advantage as he barreled down the mountain, weaving between trees and quick stepping through the rocks as if they were hot coals. He crashed through the infinite number of small branch that criss-crossed the trail and, behind him, he could hear the sound of shattering glass as the ice fell away and created a mini-avalanche in his wake. He was cruising and could even see the light of another runner coming into view.

Josh had almost caught up to the other light when he reached the end of the single track section. Up ahead, near the glow of a chem-light, he could see the road that would take him to the next aid station. Josh came off the trail fast and hit the small drop to the road with too much speed. Once again, he had no time to react as his feet went out from under him. This time, however, it was ice, not rocks, that did the damage.

Josh went done hard on his hip and shoulder and slid the rest of the way to the road. Cursing, he frantically looked for his water bottles, which had both gone flying when he hit the ice. They had rolled downhill 20 yards, but with his bright light he was able to find them. Once again, he was lucky to avoid injury. He'd be bruised and sore the next day but, as quickly as possible, he started back up the hill towards the next chem-light.

He wanted to keep working hard and resumed a steady jog up the incline. After only a few minutes, he realized that, unlike the first hill, which he had been able to run all the way to the summit, this one was much steeper. When he looked ahead, he could see a few lights strung out in front of him further up the road. *They're walking.* He thought. *This is a good chance to make up some ground.* Josh continued to run the hill and, sooner than he expected, he was passing the walkers. He wanted to make up time, but he could feel the effort causing his heart rate to elevate too much. Scott had repeatedly warned him about going too hard early and blowing up later in the run so, reluctantly, he started to walk.

It wasn't an easy walk. It was a power hike. His arms pumped and his head was up, not bent down staring at the ground in a death march. He wanted to make good time even if he was walking and it worked. He continued to catch and pass runners who just couldn't match his pace.

Josh thought about the map again, as he alternated between short runs and power hikes, and was sure that it was uphill, on this road, until just past the third aid station. It was hard to estimate distance, but he thought he had gone at least a mile since he came off the trail, and that would mean he has another two miles until he gets there. He was determined to continue pushing himself, while everyone else seemed content to walk at a slower pace and save their energy.

When the aid station appeared, he moved methodically through his water bottle filling routine and exited with as little delay, and socializing, as possible. He immediately started to run, fueled by the news that he had reached the third aid station in 4th place. He had fallen twice but escaped both times without any injury and now he was moving through the field and gaining ground on the leaders. Miraculously, his coughing had been suppressed by the medication and, as he gained momentum, he was starting to really feel good.

A mile after the aid station, the grinding climb up the road ended and the route curved back into the woods. For a couple of miles Josh was following the bright beam down a twisting trail that dropped sharply through a heavily wooded area. He heard the usual sounds of snow and ice falling behind him but, as he once again found himself alone, he also heard the frightening sounds of animals. He was amazed at how loud a squirrel or bird could be when they're hidden behind a veil of darkness and it was impossible to avoid thinking about the bears that frequent these mountains.

At first, he was happy when he came back out of the woods and saw the road again. He'd had a few successful runs on the road already and was thinking about cutting into the gap the leaders had on him. But this road was different. As soon as he stepped onto it, he slipped badly. He didn't fall but it was enough to make him slow down to a careful jog. It was easy to see the problem. This road was too high to be concealed from the wind and the side was exposed to the elements because of a steep embankment that was devoid of vegetation.

As beautiful as the view from this elevation would have been in daylight, Josh forced himself to remember that, tonight, the road was part of a treacherous and demanding landscape. He continued his grind up the steep incline, while trying to stay in the soft snow that was relegated to the edge of the road. It worked for a while, but soon, he noticed the wind was picking up and the snow cover had started to thin out significantly.

The road was tilted. The black abyss was to Josh's left and the road tilted away from it. That tilt, as slight as it was, caused Josh a lot of trouble. After ten minutes on the slope, the road had become a sheer sheet of ice and he was no longer able to run. His hands had moved away from his body for balance and, even then, he had to slow considerably. Even though he had been reduced to walking, it was inevitable that he fall. Still, it happened fast and he couldn't soften the impact. He landed solidly on his left knee and winced from the shooting pain. He made it back to his feet and started moving again but even slower than before.

Two people, that he had worked hard to overtake earlier, passed him and he had to just grit his teeth and let them go. He was being so careful, watching every step and picking the best route possible up the slope, when he fell again. It was identical to the last fall and he struck his left knee again. It took longer to get up this time and he stood for a while, rubbing his knee and looking at the icy road. His heart rate had dropped down to a comfortable "watching TV" rate, and for the first time, he noticed the cold. Josh pulled his hat down lower over his ears and moved all the way over to the weeds before trying to continue uphill.

For the next thirty minutes, Hellgate was responsible for exacting a vicious and cruel punishment on Josh's knee and spirit. He fell again and again and again. Each time, he got up slower and felt the cold a little more. He had just told himself that he couldn't take another fall when it happened. He hit the ice firmly, as he had done six or seven times previously, but this time, he opened his hand slightly to absorb the impact and lost his grip when the butt of his flashlight slapped into the ice.

Josh is helpless as he watches his flashlight disappear over the side of the road and fall into the darkness. There is pain radiating from his knee as he scrambles across the ice covered road to the edge of the drop-off. He moans when he sees that his light has tumbled far down the steep, snow covered embankment. Any attempt to retrieve it would be foolish. As he lies on the ground looking down at the lost light, he feels the cold wind, fights against the rising feeling of anxiety and tries to force his heart rate back to normal.

Breakthrough

"A lot of people run a race to see who's the fastest. I run to see who has the most guts."

— Steve Prefontaine

At the time of his death at age 24, held every U.S. distance running record from 2,000 to 10,000 meters

Fall of 1982 to Fall of 1984, University of Florida

Being a member of the University of Florida Track and Cross Country teams, while trying to pursue an aerospace engineering degree, was an almost unmanageable task.

First, there were the scheduling conflicts caused by the two-a-day practices. Josh would be at the track at 6 a.m. everyday for a morning run and then rush across campus for some classes. He had to fit everything in, including lunch, before returning to the track for the daily 3 p.m. training session, which could last two or three hours. Then, it was time for dinner and maybe a little studying. Oddly, none of his professors seemed to have a clue that the university actually had student athletes. Trying to register for classes that fit the tight schedule would not have been possible without the influence of the Athletic Association. The second problem was racing. Travel to meets required missing classes, and sometimes tests, which put Josh at a severe disadvantage. When a test was scheduled for a Friday, he was screwed. He'd spend a couple of days arguing with professors, trying to take the test early, or make it up the following Monday. In both cases, they acted like he was doing something dishonest when, in fact, the rescheduling made it much more difficult for him compared to his fellow students. It was a juggling act that took some time to get a handle on, but Josh worked hard to get it right.

The running part of his life became so different from anything Josh had done before, that he couldn't even compare it without laughing. Under Coach Randolph, he was doing workouts that made his prior training look like a joke. What would have been a great race in high school, was nothing more than an average Tuesday night training session for Josh's new teammates. The adjustment was as much mental as physical. He had to forget about what he perceived as limits and distract himself from thinking about the clock.

Initially, his improvement was rapid. He was moving up on the depth chart with dreams of actually cracking the top seven and traveling to a meet but, until then, he was relegated to only competing in meets on UF's home course. Unfortunately, after about six weeks, he started to have problems from all the faster paced running. The pounding was causing pain in both of his legs. He expected aches but this just didn't feel right. He was reluctant to say anything but, after a few weeks, he couldn't get through the workouts anymore. He had to tell Coach Randolph what was wrong.

That was Josh's first experience with the machine that is the UF Athletic Association. He was sent, without delay, to a series of doctors for diagnosis. The examinations were accompanied by a multitude of tests, including an extremely expensive bone scan. Josh was a student and had no extra cash, and no insurance, but it made absolutely no difference. He never saw a bill for anything. Prior to that week, he didn't understand that once you're on a team, regardless of if you're on scholarship or a walk on, you're covered for everything. Top notch health care was a perk he hadn't expected.

He received the bad news within a day. He had two stress fractures. They were mirror images of each other on the inside of each tibia. It was to be a precursor to a series of injuries that would be caused by the bone structure of his feet and lower legs.

The only treatment was rest. Josh was told to quit running, cold turkey. For the next eight weeks, to maintain his cardio-vascular fitness, he spent an hour or more each day riding a stationary bike in the training room at the O'Connell Center but, by the time they let him get back outside for some easy jogging, cross country was already over. Needless to say, it was an unspectacular way to end his first season on the team.

The buildup to get back to his previous training level was done steadily throughout the off-season and by the time he went home for the holidays he was running better than ever. Josh even ran a couple of races around New Years to determine his fitness level. The results were encouraging and he was excited about the upcoming track season. Coach Randolph wrote the schedule, even in the off season. It was tough and Josh was being challenged daily by the quality of the workouts. The idea of alternating hard days and easy days was not even considered. They ran hard day in and day out. All the while, they were learning how to run while tired and trying to break through to the next level.

Months later, in early March, Josh ran another in a series of hard Tuesday night track workouts but, this time, when his teammates pressed the pace, he was able to match them stride for stride.

His big breakthrough came on a memorable night that brought out the fastest distance runners in the area, not just the university team. The occasion was a visit from former UF track team member John L. Parker, Jr., the author of the classic "Once a Runner". John was in town to write a Sports Illustrated article on Gainesville resident Barry Brown who was about to tear up the record books in the masters division. All of the locals came out in force for the photo shoot that would provide pictures to accompany the article. It was setup as a typical Tuesday interval session that the SI photographer would shoot. The idea was to show Barry training at the local track with his friends. It turned out to be a classic of its own and, even 20 years later, those who were there know it as "Tuesday Night Madness".

Barry and Mr. Parker were talking as the photographer setup lights. The other runners milled around, waiting. There were a total of twelve and Josh was excited to be included in the group. The only downside would be to get separated from the pack and be seen in an SI feature article getting his clock cleaned by eleven guys. He was determined to keep up.

They were going to run a mile, then follow that with two repeats of 800 meters and finally a couple of 400's. It sounded easy enough. Anyone that felt good could take charge of setting the pace and Barry would try to be near the front for the photos. It would be a legitimate workout not just a setup.

After an abnormally long wait between the warm-up and first interval, they were finally organized and ready to go. All twelve moved to the line and without a word they simultaneously leaned forward and accelerated into the first turn. It was calm, as a workout should be, and lacked the insanity of the first lap that goes along with racing but they were still going pretty fast. Josh settled in near the back and tried to get into the zone. It was strange to be running so fast without any surges or race tactics to worry about. Everyone was just holding position and staying at a steady pace.

As they came down in front of the main grandstands, the photographer was clicking away and Mr. Parker was actually reading off splits at the line. The entire group went past in a pack at 67 seconds with Barry right at the front. Josh was 21 years old and, like everyone else on the team, was absolutely in awe of the 39 year old who could still run a 29 flat 10,000 meter. The blob of runners moved around a little bit on the second lap but the pace didn't vary and they went through the half mile in 2:13. Josh was still at the back but he was only a second behind the front runners as they tore down the back straight. Now they were all getting into it and, since these were all fast, talented athletes, the pace quickened. As they passed John for the start of the last lap, Josh heard a split of 3:18. *Wow, 67, 66, 65.* Josh thought. *Stay with them.*

The final lap turned into a battle for position as they jostled for a prime spot in the photo. No one wanted to be seen in SI at the back of the pack! As they entered the final straight, all twelve were still together and they smoothly spread out across five lanes. They were flying. Barry was still at the front and, although several could have, no one made the etiquette mistake of passing him. As a result, the entire group, after a final lap of 63 seconds, was clocked in 4:21 and it made a great photograph. It matched the fastest mile of Josh's life and it was nothing more than the first interval of a Tuesday night workout. From there it was more of the same as they ran back to back 800's in 2:05 and a pair of quarters in 58 seconds.

Afterward, the atmosphere was electric. No one had ever been part of a group workout where twelve guys ran together at such a pace. It was perfect and Josh would never forget the feeling of running with Barry and the rest of them under the lights that night.

Being able to handle the workout gave him a tremendous amount of confidence, and his training over the next couple of weeks reflected that. When Coach Randolph entered him in the open division of the Florida Relays 10,000 meters he was sure that his personal best of 32:12 would be history afterward. He was also thrilled to find out that Barry Brown would be running the 10,000 meters as preparation for his attempt to break the American Master's Record for the marathon later in the fall.

Josh's parents, as well as a few friends, drove to Gainesville to watch the track meet. All the attention made him nervous but it was also very exciting because he knew that he was ready for a breakthrough and he wanted his family to see it happen. It was late March and, as expected that time of year, the weather would be beautiful in the evening when the race was scheduled. As the night wore on, he wandered around, killing time, and waited anxiously to be called to the track.

His warm-up went smoothly and he looked for his parents in the stands as he walked to the line with the other competitors. Everything seemed to be in slow motion as they were given instructions and moved into position for the start. Once the gun sounded, Josh ran conservatively into the turn, choosing to avoid the fight for position until they got to the first straight. Moments later, the field was bunched in front of him as he maneuvered for a position on the inside rail of the back stretch. Once he got there, he tried to settle in and conserve energy. Since he knew who was entered, he wasn't trying to win the race. That would have been totally unrealistic. He was there to lower his personal best and to establish himself as a legitimate runner on the team. He wanted to be worthy of consideration for the SEC Championships and the other season ending events. To do that, he had to impress his coach and teammates tonight. His strategy was to run a steady pace all the way, with as few surges and speed changes as possible. What that pace would end up being was one of the big unknowns. He'd have to figure it out during the first couple of miles.

The leaders were already putting pressure on the pack by the end of the first mile, which they passed in 4:41. Meanwhile, Josh passed through at 4:50 and was in a good spot in the middle of the large chase group.

Josh was beginning to suffer. He had heard, over and over, from runners that were unable to run at his pace, that faster runners just had better genetics and that they didn't hurt as much while racing and that's why they could go faster. It's absolutely not true. It really hurts to run that fast and, in fact, it starts to hurt very early in the race. It's just that they are mentally prepared for the pain and are willing and able to accept it when it arrives. That's what it takes. During every race, there comes a point where a decision has to be made. You have to decide to suffer and go for the best performance possible on that day or to coast and do the best you can without hurting too much. For the best racers, that decision has already been made a hundred times in prior races and intense training sessions so that, when that pivotal point arrives, the answer is reflexive and immediate. They always elect to suffer. It's a trait that separates the recreational runner from the hardcore racer.

Although he had run much faster for a single mile, the best Josh had averaged for a full 10,000 meters was only 5:12 per mile, so the starting pace had put him quite a bit under pace for the race. It was all right because that was also part of his plan. He wanted to break the 32 minute barrier but, more importantly, he wanted to run to his potential and that meant running a pace he felt he could maintain and, so far, he was doing just that. If he could run even a couple of miles at that pace, and then control the damage later on, he would have the cushion he needed to reach his goal. He knew he had to ignore his previous bests and just run. He would concentrate on each individual lap instead of dwelling on how many remained.

As they approached the two mile point, a group of three runners had broken from the pack and were pulling away. The amazing Barry Brown had jumped into a battle for the lead with Bill Fisher of Jacksonville and Luis Ostalazaga from New York. Meanwhile, Josh tried to hang on to the pack as Coach Randolph, running in the opposite direction on the infield, appeared over and over, leaning into lane one and yelling instructions.

Josh felt like he was in a trance as the lap count accumulated. The 10,000 meters is a 25 lap race and at some point you have to hope you feel decent enough that you can get some laps behind you. Josh tried to focus on the back of the Villanova runner in front of him and fought to maintain contact. He knew without hearing the splits that he was running close to his 5,000 meter personal best and his legs registered the concern. He tried to stay calm but the alarms really went off in his head when he heard the three mile split. His mind was in a bit of a haze but he thought he heard 14:41 called out. He had equaled the fastest three mile of his life and he was only halfway done! It was obvious that tonight he would either run his best race ever or crash hard in front of his friends and family.

On the infield, Coach Randolph was becoming extremely animated. He was screaming every time Josh came around, encouraging him to move up and start passing the faltering runners in front of him. Josh understood what his coach wanted but couldn't make his body go any faster. If they slowed, he'd catch them, but he couldn't speed up. He was already at his limit or, maybe, even well beyond it.

One of his teammates, who was very solidly established in the top seven of the cross country team, was just in front of Josh and, as they began lap 13, he began closing the gap. By the time they passed in front of the grandstands on the 14th lap, they were together. Josh wanted to settle in behind him but Coach Randolph appeared and started hollering about the Villanova runner who had pulled away over the previous mile. Although it didn't feel like it, Josh had slowed slightly during the past half mile. Without thought, he put himself back on pace by passing his teammate and charging after the Villanova jersey. He chased down the backstretch, no longer worrying about time. He was just racing as hard as he could. He knew he was going to be well under 32 minutes and now it was just a matter of by how much.

The fifth mile of a 10,000 meter race is always the most difficult. By then you've put yourself in a hole physically by running in an anaerobic state for more than 20 minutes and you're just trying to survive until the last mile where the lure of the finish pulls you home. Tonight it was exactly like that for Josh. The leaders were gone but he had followed the Villanova runner through the hellish fifth mile and, in the process, they had moved all the way through the field to 4th and 5th place. They passed the start line for the 20th time and Josh knew that he'd be able to hold on to the finish. In fact, with only five laps remaining, he started to think that he could move up to 4th place. The problem now was the lead group.

The three frontrunners had destroyed the field and were bearing down on Josh. They had already lapped everyone in the race except for Josh and the Villanova runner and, as he ran into the back straight, he glanced back and saw them. He couldn't believe that he was about to run 2 minutes faster than he had ever gone before, and yet incomprehensibly, he was actually in serious danger of being lapped. Of course, he didn't want that to happen. He tried to focus and ran hard through the pain as the leaders drew closer and closer.

For the next three laps, as he dropped the Villanova runner, he maintained the gap, but with 200 meters to the line, the leaders were in a full sprint for the win. Josh, who had another full lap to run, couldn't hold them off any longer. Etiquette required that he move out to lane three and clear a path for them and that's exactly what he did coming out of the last turn. Their faces were contorted in pain as they ran past Josh for the finish and he had the best view in the stadium for Barry's 29:15 victory. If only it had been a couple of months later, it would have crushed the Master's World Record. Josh stayed out in lane three and crossed the line a second later, wide enough to get cleanly past, and charged into his final lap. Seventy seconds later, to the screaming of Coach Randolph, his parent's and friends, Josh crossed the line in a time of 30:26. He had averaged 4:53 per mile and knocked nearly two minutes off of his personal best.

There was no longer any doubt in his mind, or his teammates, that he belonged on this team. He had taken it to the next level, now he had to find a way to stay there.

Later that night, as he was leaving the stadium for his apartment, Coach Randolph stopped him. "That was a great run Josh. Two minutes under your previous best is amazing. How do you feel about it?" he asked.

"Thanks Coach. I don't know what to think. I guess it's just hard to believe," Josh answered.

The coach was thoughtful. "I thought you might say something like that and that's why I want to talk to you."

Josh was confused. "What do you mean?" he asked.

"I mean that you absolutely *have to* believe it. This run tonight changes everything for you," he explained. "Before tonight you were a good runner who had won a few road races, but now you've gone to the next level. You're going to be thrown in with a much higher caliber of runner. They'll be faster, more talented and they'll be tough mentally. You'll need to learn tactics and have an even better mental attitude if you hope to compete."

"I can learn the tactics," Josh said. "If you think I'm ready for those guys, then throw me in and I'll give it my best."

"I know you'll give it your best and, physically, I think you're ready to be there. It's the mental side that you need to work on. You're a 30 minute 10k guy now and you'll have to run like it every week. Forget about the local road races. You're not that guy anymore. As a 30 minute runner, you're going to compete in the big events and you're going to make our traveling team."

Josh couldn't believe it. "Do you think I can make the traveling team for cross country?" he asked.

"Josh, you just beat one of our top seven guys in a race he was peaking for. Yes, I think you can make the top seven, in fact, if you continue to run like this, I think you might make the top five and score in some meets this fall."

Josh was staring at the ground as the coach spoke.

"Josh," Coach Randolph said, "you have to forget about who you were as a runner. You have to think of yourself as the runner I saw tonight. As of tonight, you've moved into the elite list of 10,000 meter runners in the southeastern United States. Believe me, there's only a handful of guys that can run 30 flat in this part of the country. You just happen to have four or five on your team, which makes it seem more common than it really is. Trust me. Always think of yourself as capable of anything and don't be scared of any runner or any pace."

"I'll try coach."

"Great, keep up the hard work and you'll continue to surprise yourself."

Josh was overwhelmed by the race and his coach's reaction. "I will. Thanks."

"All right, get out of here. I'll see you at 6 a.m. for our long run."

"OK, Thanks again coach," Josh said as he turned and walked toward his apartment.

Josh was not the most talented athlete that Coach Randolph had ever worked with. In fact, he wasn't even close, and yet, there was something about Josh that the coach had recognized early on. Something intrinsic that made him an overachiever and the coach liked that. Florida was a big school and the coach got lots of blue chip recruits. The high school state champions could come in and instantly be a factor on the team but Josh had taken a different route. He had never even placed in his high school state meet, and yet, after three years of hard work, he was running side by side with the guys that did win those championships. Although he encouraged the practice of walk-ons, the coach had never had one make his top five in cross country but, tonight, he had watched Josh carefully. Maybe, just maybe, this kid would be the first.

A week later, after a brutal interval session on the track, Coach Randolph called Josh into his office.

"Hey Josh, have a seat," he said.

Josh looked around the same office he had sat in three years earlier when he first tried to make the team. "Thanks, what's up?"

"Well, I'll just cut right to it. I'm going to run you with Keith and Mark in the 10,000 at the SEC Championships."

"You're kidding!" Josh exclaimed.

"No, I'm not," the coach laughed. "You deserve it after your run at the Florida Relays. Just remember what I told you. You have to think on another level now so don't let the times you see scare you off. Run hard and you'll be fine."

They talked for a while and, unlike three years ago, this time when Josh left the building he looked back and smiled.

For the next two weeks, Josh really tried to think of himself differently. He wanted to be the runner that Coach Randolph said he could be, but the field at the SEC meet was just too good. His teammate, Keith, had run 28 minutes flat and three, from other schools, had run under 29 minutes. Josh tried to run with them but, after starting with miles of 4:33 and 4:42, they ate him up and spit him out. He blew up and finished next to last. He had mistakenly taken them on, instead of using common sense and running his own race, but what the coach noticed was that, once again, he had not given up. Even though he was crashing, he endured the humiliation of being lapped, not once, but twice to complete the race. It wasn't the finish that he wanted and, at the time, finishing was no consolation. So, feeling he still had something to prove, Josh went home and began to prepare for the fall cross country season.

To keep his training interesting, he ran quite a few road races. He was considerably faster than the previous year and actually won every race he ran that summer, including three in one day on the fourth of July. So he trained, he raced, and before he knew it, the summer was gone and August was upon him. He returned to Gainesville for the fall semester and to meet the new batch of recruits. It would be strange to run in the same four mile time trial as a member of the team and watch the walk-ons struggle to make the cut. He vowed to talk with them and make them feel welcome.

The recruiting class was strong and would make it even a bigger challenge to make the top seven but Josh's confidence level was higher than ever. In the time trial, he was eighth. Then, in the season's first meet, with the local community college and the Florida Track Club, he moved up to seventh on the team. When he placed 13th overall in the Florida Invitational the more important statistic was that he, once again, had a seventh place team finish. When the roster was posted for the Paul Short Invitational in Lehigh, Pennsylvania, for the first time a walk-on was listed. Josh was on the traveling team while five scholarship athletes were going to be left at home.

The Lehigh meet was a preview of the NCAA championship, which would be contested on the same course at the end of the season. It was cross country at its finest. There was pushing and shoving, mud, lots of elbows and some of the best teams in the nation. Josh had a good race and actually placed sixth on his team for the first time. He was gaining the valuable experience he would need if the coach chose to take him to the SEC meet in Louisiana.

The Furman Invitational in South Carolina gave Josh another opportunity to show how much he had improved. He took advantage of it by placing sixth on the team for the second time. It seemed like it would be a foregone conclusion that Josh would be on the SEC roster but it didn't work that way. Every week, the scholarship athletes that weren't on the travel team made progress. They were all very talented runners and they could move up and take Josh's hard earned spot if he had an off day in a race or even in practice. So, he was constantly on guard, pushing himself to stay with Keith during workouts so they would have no reason to bump him from the team. He would rather over train and be selected than to get dropped from the roster. There could be no sign of weakness.

When the coach finally gathered everyone together, a week before the race, for the announcement, Josh was on pins and needles.

The first five were automatic and the coach reeled off the names quickly. "Ok, for SEC's we've got Keith, John, Bill, Oklahoma Mike and Biscayne Mike. I guess that's no surprise."

The coach fidgeted with his clipboard before continuing. "We're going to mix up the last two spots and make some changes. I think some of you guys who have been here in Gainesville working hard have earned a chance at the SEC meet." Josh couldn't believe it. After three meets in a row on the travel team, he was going to get bumped.

Coach Randolph put his clipboard down. "You've all shown a tremendous amount of improvement during the season and I wish we could reward more of you, but I can only take two more.

There's no use dragging it out. Eric and Josh, congratulations, you're going to Baton Rouge."

Josh's stomach was doing backflips. Eric had moved up but Josh was still in. Now he had to figure out a way to get ready. The race was in seven days and he didn't want to make the same mistake he had made before his high school state meet. This time, he wanted to be rested and ready on race day.

The team flew on the school jet to Baton Rouge, LA, which was unusual for the Cross Country team. The plane was typically reserved for the higher profile sports, but Coach Randolph had a very good team this year and the use of the jet was an indication that the Athletic Director recognized their accomplishments. When they touched down, the weather was nasty. There was standing water everywhere. It had been raining every day for over a week and the ground was saturated. Not even Coach Randolph knew what the course was like, but they had a trip out to the site scheduled for later in the afternoon. They'd all see it together and come up with a race strategy.

The race was going to be held about 15 miles outside of town and when the team arrived they were hopeful that the course would be firm and fast. The start area was pretty high on a hill and as they jogged the first 300 yards they were pleased that, although the long grass was wet, the footing was good. Soon, they found out the problem wasn't on the high ground. When they crested the hill and looked out over the rest of the course, they gasped. All they could see was a winding black trail of ankle deep mud.

Coach Randolph muttered something inaudible and then brought them all together. "All right men, let's jog the first couple of miles real easy and see what we've got. Then, we'll get back together and talk it over."

There was a lot of mumbling and he had to quiet them down before continuing. "I want everyone's attention! I don't care what it looks like. It doesn't matter. Everyone runs the same course and if we run the best we win. It's that simple. I don't want to hear any whining. All I want to hear is how we plan to handle it and beat everyone. Let's go."

A few hours later the strategy was in place. Everyone on the team needed to get into good position early and that's not an easy task in a cross country race of this caliber. Anyone caught in the back of the pack when they hit the first water logged section would be trapped and effectively out of contention. The consensus was that, unless the teams top five were in the first twenty at the mile mark, they had no chance at the championship. It was a bold strategy. Running the whole team at that pace early could easily backfire on them. Coach Randolph wasn't running this team for second place. He wanted to win and was willing to roll the dice.

The next afternoon, Coach Randolph paced back and forth behind the team as they lined up for the start. There were seventy entrants from ten teams in the Championship race. Josh was so nervous that his stomach was churning and he had to struggle to get his breathing and heart rate under control. He'd waited a long time for this chance. He was in the big leagues.

The sound of the starter's pistol echoed through the valley as the scantily clad runners charged across the grassy field. Josh's teammate, Keith, was the defending champion and, if the first 300 yards were any indication, he was planning to repeat. He pulled his entire team along with him as he ran hard to the first turn. When they reached the mud for the first time, all seven of them were in the top twenty five overall. The mud was deep and tried to pull their shoes off with each step. It was a shock to be moving so fast and then to suddenly have no traction at all. The long spikes in their racing shoes had little effect and, as a group, they all started to zig zag through the mud, looking for any piece of firm ground. The air was full of flying mud and the runners were quickly covered by it.

Out of nowhere, Coach Randolph appeared. He was yelling out positions and barking orders at everyone. Before the race, he'd given them one last instruction. "Don't listen to the splits. In a race like this, they don't matter. The only thing you should concern yourself with is position. Everyone knows that in this mud the times will be slower so just concentrate on your position. We need to run as a team and pack in at the top," he said.

The first mile had felt like a disaster to Josh. He had worked extremely hard and yet it seemed like there were a lot of runners in front of him. In his mind, it felt like he was in last place. Indeed, the other runners were strung out in front of him but, in reality, he was still in the top half of the field and they were even starting to come back to him a little.

He hit the hills hard, leaning in and trying to take advantage of the brief good footing. In a race like this, you could lose focus and miss opportunities. Josh was hoping that would happen to the runners around him and that they would get discouraged.

During the second mile, he could see some of his teammates in front of him and he fought tenaciously to hold his position. In fact, when he passed Coach Randolph, he heard that same clear calm voice from the time trial a year earlier. "30th place Josh. Move up."

30th place. I'm all right, he thought.

He was still running in seventh on his team but he saw Eric just in front of him. He had lost track of his location on the course but it didn't matter. All Josh cared about now was passing people. The mud was causing havoc and, although Josh had seen the mile and two mile markers, he hadn't heard any splits. He tried to clear his mind and focus. The third mile had hurt most of the runners around him and he caught a few, including Eric, who now ran alongside Josh. He quickly decided that no matter how bad it hurt, he was going all out on the fourth mile. It would be like the "Meet of Champions" a few years back and he had nothing to lose. He was the sixth man and wouldn't count in the scoring anyway so he could take some chances. He'd worry about the last mile when it arrived, but no sooner, for now, all that existed was mile four.

Josh hadn't really increased his speed but others were slowing slightly so it appeared as if he had sped up. As the runners around him started to lose it, Josh began to pick them off. Within a minute, Eric was behind him along with three others. He splashed through the muddy sections recklessly and charged the downhills like the finish was at the bottom of each one. Just as his suffering was pushing him toward a breaking point, he saw "Oklahoma" Mike. *It can't be.* He thought. *Mike's too far back. He's the fifth man and his score counts. We can't win f he's out of the top twenty.* With no hesitation, Josh passed Mike and moved into scoring position on the team. For the first time ever, his position mattered. The team needed the walk-on to close the deal.

He glanced across the field and briefly saw the leaders. Keith was battling for the win and he saw a couple more of his teams jersey's near the front. *I'm number five.* He wasn't the only one that had figured it out. Coach Randolph was no longer calm and Josh heard him long before he ran past.

"You're 22nd Josh! Move up! This is your day! We need you!" he screamed.

The pressure threatened to overwhelm Josh as the race began to fragment and gaps started to open up between the runners. He no longer had anyone close to pass and yet there was a large group right behind him. It was more the fear of losing 10 places than an attempt to catch anyone, but Josh dug in and surged toward the finish.

Over the next two minutes, Josh passed two more runners but he didn't know if that was enough for the team to win. He didn't need to wait long for an answer. The coach appeared again pointing at two runners in orange at least 50 yards in front of Josh.

"You have to beat those orange jerseys! Go! Now!" The coach was frantically running alongside just outside the markers. "Beat them and we'll win!"

Josh wasn't the fastest guy when it came to a finishing kick but the mud had been a great equalizer. Everyone legs were shot and this would come down to guts. Josh knew that he had to pass them but they probably didn't know that their place was that important. If he could surprise them, he had a chance. He lowered his head and did everything he could to muster up a sprint.

The people that were lining the course screaming were nothing but background noise as Josh closed on the orange uniforms. When he was 15 yards back, he could see the crowd and the course markers in his peripheral vision, getting closer. *I'm in the finish chute! I'm out of time!* His brain screamed. With a final agonizing surge he pulled even and then passed the orange jerseys. Within seconds, they were all across the finish line and Josh, who wanted nothing more than to be left alone until the wall of pain had a chance to subside, was engulfed by the screaming teammates who had finished in front of him. A non-scholarship athlete, who had been sent away three years earlier, had helped bring home an SEC Championship.

The coach's on the fly calculation had been dead on. They won by a single point.

Headforemost Mountain

"The body does not want you to do this. As you run, it tells you to stop but the mind must be strong. You always go too far for your body. You must handle the pain with strategy."

— Jacqueline Gareau
1980 Boston Marathon winner

Dec 10th, 2005, 5:05 a.m., Jefferson National Forest, VA

With each step, the tightness in Josh's left knee increased. He had felt the swelling begin soon after Jeff left him standing on the exposed mountain road. In the biting cold, the slower he moved the worse everything got, and there was no doubt about it, he was moving slow. In the 10 minutes since his last fall, he had walked at a snails pace, taking each step as if it was on broken glass. Jeff had been right when he told Josh that he had to keep moving and fight against the cold wind. *Relentless forward motion,* he chanted. *Just get to the next aid station.*

It took another 45 minutes, and three more falls, to reach the peak of the mountain. It was the highest point on the course, and normally, he would have been rewarded for his effort with a spectacular view, but not tonight. Since it was not even 4 a.m., it was still pitch black all around him. He wanted to go home.

He didn't pause at the top, but by the time he started running downhill, his body temperature had dropped and his hands and feet were numb from the cold. The near freefalls of the earlier descents were only memories as he slogged through the snow toward the valley. He wanted desperately to go faster, so that he could warmup and he cursed his pre-race clothing decisions.

Although he'd been passed by more than ten runners while on the long, brutal climb, he quickly felt totally alone. As he ran downhill, the only indication that there had been others on this remote mountain trail were the footprints of those who had already passed through, and the glow of the occasional chem-light. Still, there was nothing for him to do except press forward and try to stay warm. So, when the trail bottomed out near another creek bed, Josh wasted no time. He crossed over the rocks, found the trail on the other side and began a hard power hike back up the trail.

When the tree sheltered road came into view, he thought of the map and knew that he was closing in on the aid station. *Another mile, all uphill,* he said to himself. *Just keep going and get there under the cutoff.*

He hadn't looked at his watch since the last aid station but assumed that he was in danger of being pulled from the race. Had he thought more about it, he would have realized that he was well clear of the cutoff and that information would have reduced his anxiety considerably. After all, he was still in the top twenty and there was no way that 80 percent of the field was going to miss the first time check. Still, he worried and, as his knee allowed, he went hard up the snowy road.

When he saw the bright lights of the aid station, it looked like a warm oasis had miraculously appeared in the middle of the cold, dark forest. For the first time in hours he looked at his watch. He had made it in five hours and two minutes, which was an hour and a half under the cutoff but pretty far off of his planned pace.

Feeling a little embarrassed by his performance so far, he didn't run in strong. Instead, Josh walked quietly into the aid station and looked for Jill. She had made it up the dangerous road to the aid station and was setting up a mini aid station for him at the car. So far, she hadn't seen him come in.

"Hey, Jillie," he said quietly.

She turned and came toward him, eager to get him setup and back out on the trail. "Hey yourself. I thought you'd be here 30 or 40 minutes ago. How are you doing?" she asked as she took the water bottle from his hand.

"Not great," he responded. "The last five miles were really bad. I fell quite a few times on this ice. I can't believe how bad I'm doing. It feels like I'm in last place."

"Well, you're not. I think you're in the top 15 or 20 and you're ahead of Scott. Hey, what's going on? Why didn't you drink your water?" She was now holding both of Josh's bottles which were still full.

Josh was confused. *Didn't I drink any?* he wondered. "I don't know. I guess I was so preoccupied with other things that I never thought about it."

"Josh, you can't do that!" Jill was not happy at all. "You've been running for five hours and have only had two bottles of fluids. You're going to get dehydrated! You need to drink something right now before you leave and at least one more bottle before Jennings Creek."

She started to dig through the packs in the back of the car and tossed a bottle of *Boost* and a *Gatorade* at him. "You're right," he said while opening the bottles.

"I suppose this means you haven't eaten any energy gels yet either."

"Nope, not since the first two hours," he admitted while chugging the drinks.

"Great, add bonking to the list. Come on Josh. You planned this for months. What the hell is wrong with you?"

Good question, he thought. For the last hour he had convinced himself that he should drop out when he made it to this aid station, but now that he was here, he couldn't do it. He couldn't do it in front of his wife or the race director who was nearby at the tables.

"I told you, I slipped and fell, a bunch of times, and I guess it took me out of my game plan." Josh had his refills and made a snap decision to continue.

"Well, get it together," Jill admonished him, "you're the one that's supposed to know how this works, not me."

"I know, I know. I'll be fine from now on," he said as he gave her a quick kiss.

They talked for another five minutes but he was getting cold and Jill was already urging him to get back on the course.

"You're right. I've gotta go. Remember, Little Cove Mountain is out of the plan for you. Just head for Bearwallow Gap instead. OK?"

"Yeah, I'll leave as soon as Scott comes through here."

"Ok, drive carefully and I'll see you there."

"Bye," she said, as Josh walked past the campfire and back towards the road.

Josh dreaded leaving the aid station. The warm fire felt so comforting after being exposed for so long on the freezing mountainside. Besides that, the bustle of activity had brought him out of the trail induced trance that he had felt coming in.

"You're doing great Josh," Dr. Horton said as Josh walked past the table of snacks. "There's a fantastic breakfast at the Jenning's Creek aid station. You should stop and enjoy it. There's going to be a super group of people there to take care of you."

"I will thanks," Josh said as he passed. *How does he even know my name?* Josh wondered. *I've never even run in one of his races before.*

Josh walked away from the lights and infectious energy of Headforemost Mountain and, as the trees engulfed him, wondered for the first time about Scott. Jill wouldn't leave until Scott made it to this checkpoint but Josh didn't think she'd have to wait long. As bad as that last section had been for Josh, he was sure that Scott had to be close behind and was expecting him to catch up soon.

He jogged slowly away from the lights and back onto the dark trail. After 15 minutes, the cold started to reassert itself. As Josh prepared to cross the Blue Ridge Parkway for the second time, he had stopped generating the body heat that had kept him warm earlier and now his hands and feet were starting to become numb. He shook his hands to get some feeling back and began running. *I've got to go faster and warm back up,* he told himself. He leaned forward slightly and, for the first time in hours, he accelerated. At first, it felt terrible, like he had never run before. His cold muscles didn't want to respond and his knee stung him with a stabbing pain but, sooner than he expected, he started to warm up and remarkably, by the time he reached the Parkway, he was gliding down the trail with slightly more speed and just a hint of hope creeped in.

Ten minutes after he crossed the Parkway, he smiled. *I'm back,* he thought.

He set his headlamp to the brightest setting and, as the trail turned downhill, he began to take chances. He put the fear of falling out of his mind and barreled down the single track. Once again, the snow and ice cascaded down the hill in his wake as he ran at a reckless pace towards Jennings Creek.

The descent was long and relentless. From the Parkway to the creek was an elevation drop of over 2,500 feet, more than double the height of the Sears Tower in Chicago. The trail had countless switchbacks and the steep technical drops were made worse by the snow cover. Josh tried to look ahead but over and over he ran too fast into the sharp corners, always on the verge of going off trail. Still, he stayed aggressive and kept pushing hard down the mountain. With each step, he felt the force of the descent jolt through his quads and knees. Despite being out for six hours, it was still very early in the day and there were a lot of steep downhills yet to come. It might trash his quads but he tried to avoid negative thoughts and ran with total disregard for the consequences.

After losing ground to everyone for the last eight miles, unbelievably, he started to see lights below him on the trail. His kamikaze dash down from the Parkway was allowing him to close in on some of the runners that had passed him during the prior two hours. With renewed hope, one at a time, he caught and passed them, each time going by hard and without comment. It was his style, on and off the trail, to pass hard during a race, always trying to look fresh as he went past. Even though it made more sense, in a long event like Hellgate, to be more sociable and enjoy the rare opportunity to have someone to talk with on the trail, he couldn't do it. He knew this wasn't a college track meet and that his rules didn't apply, but Josh made no distinction between the two. To him, a race was a race.

After what seemed like an endless pitch black descent, Josh saw, and heard, the Jennings Creek aid station. They must have seen his light and, as he hit the last steep section of trail that led to the creek, the relatively large group began to holler and cheer. It was uplifting and, with more than a marathon and 10,000 feet of elevation change behind him, he ran up to the tables feeling great.

He couldn't believe it when he saw sausages cooking on the grill. He was craving a good breakfast, and Dr. Horton told him to try it, but it violated one of Josh's many "Rules of Racing". *Never do anything in a race that you haven't done in training.* He reminded himself. The rule applied to everything including, shoes, food, drinks, blister prevention techniques, clothing and even medications. He was absolutely certain that he had never eaten a sausage breakfast in the middle of a run.

"What can I get for you?" asked the man behind the grill.

"Nothing, I just need to refill my water bottles," Josh responded.

The man was clearly disappointed by Josh's refusal to eat the breakfast that he had prepared. "Are you sure?"

"Yeah. Hey, don't get me wrong, it looks great," Josh continued. "My stomach just couldn't take eating anything right now."

"I understand. It's not a problem at all. Enjoy yourself, you're doing great," he said.

Within a minute, another volunteer appeared and handed Josh his water bottles. "What else can we get you?" he eagerly asked.

"I guess that's all I need. Which way do I go from here?" Josh asked the volunteer.

"Straight down this road for about a hundred yards and then turn left and head up to the top of the mountain," he said. "It's marked on the road."

"Thanks everyone," he said as he jogged back down the road.

It didn't take long to reach the corner and when he made the left turn he could see the road winding uphill into the darkness. Wondering if it would be covered in ice, he cautiously started to run up the center where he saw some snow. Though it was still dark, the sky was starting to lighten up and he could see much further up than road than had been possible even 15 minutes earlier. It made it easier for him to pick out a narrow section near the edge that had some snow cover and he carefully continued towards the top. He ran for a while and then, on the steeper slopes, he started mixing in some power hiking.

The road wound up and up, with each corner promising to be the last before the summit, but instead, revealing more road, leading to yet another corner. After nearly a thousand foot climb, he was moving with unexpected speed as he neared the top and his confidence soared when he blasted past another runner.

The road ended at an ugly iron gate near the peak of the mountain and beyond that, Josh could see the footprints leading down a snow covered trail. The sky was brightening up considerably and, as Josh passed by the gate, he was thrilled to finally, after more than seven hours, turn the headlamp off for good. He wanted to crack open a beer and toast the sunrise he was witnessing but, unless the invisible hunters had a stash, there wasn't a beer within 10 miles. He had survived the night portion of the run and had made it through 30 miles of the most difficult terrain on the course but, most importantly, he was still moving forward and feeling strong. Only some occasional twinges of pain on the downhills were left as reminders of the series of falls he had endured.

He felt like a new man in the daylight and, with his confidence at an all time high, he once again ran recklessly down from the summit. The trees were flying by and Josh had his arms away from his body to provide balance as he careened down the trail. He was caught between admiring the view, which was just becoming visible, and watching the trail, when he felt his foot catch on something. It was similar to the very first fall he had taken near the creek only, this time, he was moving much faster. He sensed his body get ahead of his feet and instinctively overextended on his next stride to try and regain his balance but it was too late. To make matters worse, his right leg planted solidly into the snow and, as his weight shifted, he felt a sharp shooting pain coming from the tendons in the back of his knee. He immediately flinched and allowed himself to crash chest first into the ground, but he knew the damage had already been done. Twenty years earlier, when his tendons were flexible, it would have been nothing, but now, in his forties, it was the type of strain that would put him out of commission for a month.

The impact with the rocks under the snow knocked the wind out of him and, as he plowed to a stop, he was gasping for air and already grabbing at his injured knee. No one heard him as he rolled on the ground and howled with pain and anger. All night long he had battered his left knee and now, after less than 20 minutes in the daylight, he had taken out his right knee. He rolled to his side and gradually managed to sit up and get some air into his lungs. He swore, with no one to hear except the wind and the trees and, only after a few minutes had passed, was he able to calm himself down. Once his breathing had returned to normal, he slowly got to his feet and took a few steps. He was instantly greeted with a throbbing pain behind his knee. *I strained the tendons,* he thought. *Maybe even a small tear. This pains not going to go away without some time off and I can't do anything about it out here.*

The trail was still quite steep, so he carefully walked down trying to keep his weight off of the injured knee but, each time he slipped on the uneven chunks of snow, he was rewarded with a sharp pain that made him wince. He was still on the downhill section that everyone would be running and it didn't take long for the runner he had passed on the uphill to come back into view and overtake him. The runner offered a few words of encouragement and then disappeared down the trail. Josh was frustrated beyond belief. He still felt strong but all of the falls had left him unable to run and, as he limped down to the valley, he was sure that he was done. He'd have to drop out at the next aid station.

Springtime Relays

"Road racing is Rock n Roll. Track is Carnegie Hall."

— **Marty Liquori**
Top-Ranked miler in the world from 1969-1971

May 1985, Tallahassee, Florida

Hard falls were nothing new to Josh. He'd taken his share during cross country meets and even on the roads. By comparison, the falls on trails, though more frequent, are generally less traumatic than falls on the track or on pavement. That was another fun fact that he had learned the hard way.

The Springtime Relays are held each year in Tallahassee, Florida. The field isn't as strong as the other large events of the outdoor season, but the open division of the 10,000 meters was still expected to be quite competitive. Coach Randolph had entered Josh to see what kind of condition he was in for the upcoming Southeastern Conference Championships, but Josh had his own motivation. His collegiate career was coming to an end and he wanted to do something that he had never done before, win an open division NCAA race. This wasn't the Penn Relays but it would still be an accomplishment of some significance to win. He really wanted to have a few more good races and finish his time at UF in style.

Football and baseball games only last a couple of hours but track meets are long. There are a multitude of events, and many have a seemingly endless number of heats. It can drag on well into the night. The team had taken a bus from Gainesville to Tallahassee but Josh had driven his own car. The 10,000 meters is a long event and it would be contested at the end of the meet. The

185

schedule was set up to avoid the Florida heat, with luck, the temperature would be cooler. The rest of the team might not want to hang around that late, so he drove separately to give them the opportunity to leave early. That didn't mean that Josh would miss all of their events and arrive late. Actually, he was one of the first to arrive. He loved watching the other athletes and would spend the entire day lounging around the infield, alternating between field and track events. Of course, he tried to stay out of the sun as much as possible by sitting in the shade of the grandstands, or under the trees that lined the north side of the track.

As the start of his event drew closer, Josh began to go through his pre-race routine. As usual, the meet was running late and the 10,000 wouldn't start until almost 11 p.m. By then, most of the crowd, and Josh's teammates, had already headed for home. He stuck to his habit of running three miles easy and then he did some stretching. Afterward, he would run a little more and do some sprints.

Everything went smoothly during the warm-up and Josh really felt good about running a fast race.

In order to prepare himself for the feeling of the first lap, Josh liked to run four or five hard accelerations right before a race started. He would run a steady speed and gradually speed up until he was going as fast as he was able and hold it for a few seconds. He wanted to be breathing hard when he went to the line. That was the plan as he left the track and headed across the street to a dimly lit parking lot.

Josh looked down the narrow band of pavement between the cars and tried to judge the distance. There were only a couple of lights but it looked like it was about a hundred yards. That would be enough. As he strode confidently down the 10 yard wide passage between the cars, he heard the announcer call the competitors for the 10,000 meters to the track. He felt the excitement of the race building in his chest as he charged through the parking lot. It didn't take long to reach top speed. *Hold it, hold it, hold it,* he thought.

Josh never saw anything in his path and the violent fall into the concrete took him totally by surprise. He couldn't breathe. Gasping for air, he rolled on the ground trying to understand what had just happened. Pain was coming from everywhere. His hand had taken the hardest hit, but he could feel pain from his leg and his shoulder as well. While trying to catch his breath, he struggled to sit up and look back down the corridor between the cars. He had tripped over something solid but, unbelievingly, as he stared, he swore there was nothing there.

Josh regained his composure and slowly got back on his feet. He was groggy and in pain as he inched his way back toward his starting point, half-heartedly looking for whatever had caught his foot. The cable was virtually invisible in the poorly lit parking lot. It stretched across the darkness between the cars, about ten inches off of the pavement, to divide the student area from a private faculty parking lot. He had hit it at full speed.

The announcer called the 10,000 meter competitors to the line. Josh struggled back to the track and walked into the bright lights of the stadium. He was bleeding from his shoulder and right arm and there was also a bit of blood coming from his rapidly swelling right knee. Making matters worse, he had also struck his head on the concrete, causing him to feel tired and confused as the team trainer ran towards him.

"Josh, what happened? Are you all right?"

"I don't know. I fell," he answered dreamily.

"Your race is going to the line. Can you run?"

"I think so. I'll try."

The trainer headed for the starter. "I'll hold them for a minute so we can clean you up."

As the trainer ran the 50 yards to the starter, Josh looked down at his knee and hand. They were both swelling up. In another five minutes it would be over for him, he needed to get on the track now. There was no time for a cleanup.

Bloody and somewhat confused, Josh jogged to the line. The other competitors looked at him curiously. Who was this guy?

The sound of the starting gun was echoing in Josh's head as he rounded the first curve. There were 25 laps in this race and he wanted nothing more than to get into a rhythm and forget about the accident. Except for the pain coming from his knee, the first few laps went by in a blur and Josh couldn't separate them from the warmup he had done earlier. He heard the mile split of 4:48, but it didn't really register in his mind yet. He was running in the pack and trying to stay out of trouble when he heard Coach Randolph for the first time. The laps passed and, sooner than he expected, there was another split being yelled out. *Was that 9:35?* He wondered.

By now, the field was thinning, and he was beginning to focus on the runners in front of him. He ignored the painful throbbing that was coming from his hand and started moving up through the field. By the end of the third mile, which they had passed in 14:21, he had pulled up to the lead group of three. For the next few laps, each of them probed for weakness. One after another, they threw surges at each other to see if anyone would break. There was no change in position as the four stayed together for the next mile. Josh was now fully aware of what was happening. When he passed by the line in 19:12, it was the fastest four mile split he had ever run in a 10,000 meter race.

The pack stayed together for two more laps and, finally, on lap 18, a runner from Providence made a break. The cadence had slowed slightly on the previous lap and no one seemed inclined to take the lead and reset the pace. Then, the Providence runner went. It was a bold and confident move. The next lap was run in 69 seconds and the lead group was shredded. Josh knew it was the turning point of the race and his decision was instinctive. He accelerated into the turn, on lap 19, and began to chase the leader.

The line flashed by again and Josh heard the five mile split. *24 minutes flat! This is it, I can break 30 minutes. Don't let up!* Josh had been chasing the 30 minute barrier for years, and now, he was right there. He wasn't about to let it slip away. The stadium and the people leaning out from the infield faded into a haze as Josh focused on the Providence runner 30 yards in front of him. Step by step, he reeled him back. With one lap to go, Josh came up to the other runner's shoulder.

Josh was on full automatic. His sphere of awareness, which had been so large during the warm up, had shrunk considerably. It contained Josh, the Providence runner, and the 10 yards of Tartan surface in front of them. Everything else was gone. He heard the six mile split of 28:46 and instantly knew he needed a 73 second final lap to break 30 for the first time. The pain had been building for the entire race, and now, Josh was truly suffering, but so was his opponent. Josh leaned forward slightly and ran into the curve like it was the final lap of the Olympic Games. He slid out into lane two, glanced at the Providence runner, and threw everything he had into a kick. Josh hit the final turn with a clear lead and couldn't hear a thing as he sprinted the final 100 meters to the finish.

Josh crossed the line and cruised to a stop 20 meters later. Despite being in severe distress, he turned and looked for the stadium clock. It was there for all to see. 29 minutes and 52 seconds. He fell to his knees and sobbed as the few teammates that had stayed came over to congratulate him.

After the meet was over, he walked around the parking lot across the street and stared at the cable, wondering if it had cost him the best performance of his life or helped him achieve it. There was no answer for that one, but some questions had been cleared up. Coach Randolph now knew Josh was ready for the SEC Championship. He was absolutely certain he would be on the roster the next week.

Josh was elated about his race and excited about having a chance to redeem himself at the SEC meet. He knew he wouldn't fall apart like the year before. Unfortunately, he wouldn't get a chance to run. The injured hand, not his knee, began swelling so badly on the drive home that he had to go to the emergency room where x-rays revealed several broken bones. A day later, as he sat in Coach Randolph's office with a cast on his arm, he was informed that due to his injuries he would not be included on the select list of athlete's for the SEC's. His legs felt great, his heart and lungs were strong, but it didn't matter. His season was over.

The Springtime Relays 10,000 meter victory was Josh's final collegiate race. At least he went out in style.

Little Cove Mountain

"The great thing about athletics is that it's like poker
sometimes: you know what's in your hand and it may be a
load of rubbish, but you've got to keep up the front."

— Sebastian Coe

*Twice an Olympic Champion at 1,500 meters, he also
set 8 outdoor and 3 indoor World Records*

Dec 10th, 2005, 8:12 a.m., Jefferson National Forest, VA

J osh reached the road at the end of the single track descent and
looked for the aid station, but there was nothing in sight. He
tried to remember the markings on the map, but he couldn't
recall it clearly enough to know if he had several miles remaining,
or if it was going to appear around the next curve.

For a while, he walked down the remote road and enjoyed
the silence that engulfed him. Then, after a mile with no sign of
the aid station, he got bored with walking and tried an easy jog.
The slight uphill grade allowed him to run without straightening
his knee, which kept the pain at bay. For a few minutes, he was
actually feeling decent but when, for what seemed like for the
hundredth time, the incline became too steep to run any longer, he
went back into a power hike. As he climbed toward the ridgeline,
he grabbed his water bottle and got another surprise. It was frozen
shut. He tried to open the spout, and then the top, but they were
both solidly encased in ice. That got him thinking about his
energy gels, which he quickly retrieved from the outside pocket
of his jacket. They were also frozen solid. He moved all the gels
from his pocket to a nice warm spot under his knit cap. He hoped
the body heat escaping through the top of his head would

eventually thaw them out. There was nothing he could do with the bottle, so he stuck it back into his pack and waited for the next aid station to fix it.

Shortly, the angle of the incline reduced again and Josh resumed his easy jog up the road. He was astonished to find the pain in his knee had actually diminished and he was moving along at a decent clip when an Airstream trailer appeared in the distance. At first glance, Josh didn't even realize that it was the aid station. It was much higher up Little Cove Mountain than he expected but, when he saw that there was a nice fire burning next to a table full of treats, he knew he had made it to the sixth aid station.

"Hey," Josh said as a young couple got up from lawn chairs next to the fire.

"What can we get for you?" the girl asked.

"Well, my water bottle is frozen shut. Is there any chance you could warm it by the fire and get it open again?" Josh asked.

"Sure," she said taking the bottle.

Looking around, and seeing only the trailer and one car, it was clear that Josh wouldn't get a ride back to the start from here. No matter how badly injured he was, he'd have to continue to Bearwallow Gap where Jill was already scheduled to meet him. He dreaded telling her but it would be a perfect place for him to get the hell out of this thing.

"How far is it to the next aid station?" Josh asked the man who was walking over to the table.

"This spot is around 35 miles from the start so it's another eight miles to Bearwallow Gap," he responded.

"What's the trail like?"

"Well, I've never actually been on it, but David always says, because of the footing, it's the hardest section on the Hellgate course."

That's right. He said that at the pre-race briefing. I remember it now. Josh thought.

The man continued. "It'll take you at least two hours going hard to get there."

They chatted for another minute or two, then the girl came back over with Josh's bottle. The top was working again and she had already filled it with a sports drink.

"Thanks," Josh said. As the hours piled up, and his desire to race faded, he was feeling more and more appreciative of the volunteers that spent all night huddled in these remote, cold locations just to help a bunch of runners they didn't even know. In a road race, it never seemed like it was a big deal, but at a race like Hellgate, they could literally be life savers.

"I noticed that you were limping a little when you walked up. Are you all right?" the man asked.

"Yeah, I'm fine," Josh answered. "It's just a slight strain on the tendon. It doesn't bother me too much on the flats or uphills."

"Well, then, you might want to take advantage of the next mile or so. It's uphill to the end of this road, then it goes back onto the trail again. I don't know what happens after that."

"Thanks for the info. Hey, if you see a tall dorky looking guy named Scott come through here, tell him that Josh says hello and that he needs to get his ass moving."

"No problem," he laughed. "I'll find him for you and pass the message along. Good luck."

"Thanks again," Josh said as he jogged away from the trailer.

The man had been right about the road. It was slightly uphill, very runnable, and for over a mile Josh took full advantage of it. After that, it switched to single track trail high up near the ridge. Under normal conditions, it would have been extremely difficult to run the trail because of all the rocks. The trail was only a foot across and cut sideways across an incline that sloped left to right at a 40 to 60 degree angle. Today, with the ice encrusted snow, the rocks were covered but if you inadvertently stepped off the trail you could easily tumble or slide a hundred yards or more downhill before stopping.

The view was spectacular and, for the first time, Josh paused to enjoy it before returning to his grind down the single track trail. As the sun rose in the clear sky, he heard birds singing and small animals scurrying through the trees.

A few hours earlier, while traversing a remote dark section on the other side of Headforemost Mountain, Josh had heard a large barrage of noise coming from the woods. Noise seems to amplify in the woods at night, especially when you're alone and all you can see is the small area illuminated by your headlamp, but even taking into account Josh's paranoia, it seemed like a much louder noise than a squirrel should be able to make. Josh thought immediately about the bears that inhabit these woods, just like he would have thought of sharks had he been swimming in the ocean and heard a loud splash nearby. Large predators live on these mountains, that's certain, and the skinny runners are in their habitat, not the other way around. Josh definitely did not want to have an encounter with a bear today or any other day.

In the past, he had seen his share of wildlife on the trails. It ranged from the harmless deer, squirrels, and rabbits to the more frightening variety. He'd had unexpected run-ins with a multitude of snakes, including an adrenaline pumping incident with a rattle-snake while trail running in Texas and a leap into a ravine to avoid a copperhead in North Carolina. For a long time, he was more frightened of venomous snakes than anything else on the trail, but a recent solo run, which had taken him into uncomfortably close proximity to a wolf, had reminded him that there were meat eaters on the trail as well. He was surprised to see it, and it got him thinking about the other predators he never expected to see on a run, like a Florida Panther. They're out there, but so far, Josh had been lucky enough to avoid any confrontations. The wild boar he saw last year and the multiple bobcat sightings had all been brief, and ended with the animal running away from him, but that wolf didn't run, it stared. Josh had no idea what he would do if any of them ever turned and charged toward him, but he supposed that he would do the wrong thing, like scream and run.

In any case, he was very pleased to have made it through the night portion of the run without interrupting a bear or one of the many hunters that were prowling around.

Josh ran easily down the trail, no longer concerned with racing, just trying to make progress toward the next aid station where he still planned to drop out. He mixed in some hiking on the steep sections and tried to run everything else but the poor footing made it hard to do much more than a slow jog anyway. After his brief stop at the trail head, he no longer paid any attention to the splendid views and chose to concentrate on the trail that appeared to stretch to infinity in front of him.

At first, he thought that this section might be flatter, following the ridgeline at his current elevation but, when he hit the first major downhill, he reassessed the situation and prepared himself for a roller coaster ride all the way to Bearwallow Gap.

The downhill was just as steep as the one he ran, boldly, in the dark down to Jennings Creek. Now, his legs were sore and he no longer had the ability to plunge down the trail at the same speed he had run earlier. Instead, he picked his way down, carefully planting his feet to avoid aggravating his knee. The winding trail wrapped around the ridge, following the contours that rain water and melting snow had been cutting into the side of the mountain for thousands of years. Sometimes it was steep and, at other points, it was almost flat. All the while, the trail made a steady decline toward the distant valley. He kept at it and, once he reached the bottom, he looked up to see the ridge over a thousand feet above him. He knew better than to think that he'd been up there for the last time. He jogged for a few minutes and, sooner than he expected, the trail turned skyward again. He took a few deep breaths and began an unrelenting thousand foot climb back to the same ridgeline.

Josh thought about the elevation map and tried to remember the basic profile for this part of the trail but he was, once again, unable to recall it in detail. He was almost sure that there were two more treks to the top followed by descents to the valley floor. The last one would leave him near the road and the second checkpoint. He prepared himself for at least 3,000 feet of climb and a matching amount of descent between his current location and where Jill was waiting with the car. After preparing himself mentally for the challenge, Josh took a drink of water and continued up the steep trail.

He would have stopped at the top, but he never figured out where it was. He was high above the valley when the trail began to undulate with short but steep uphills and downhills that weaved in an out of forested coves. Each one had its own tiny stream and there was an abundance of small waterfalls. He enjoyed this section of the trail and was disappointed when it ended and he was, once again, picking his way down a steep embankment toward the valley.

The trail darted left and right through a series of switchbacks which helped Josh control his speed on the descent. He was breathing hard by the time he reached the bottom and, after a two hour bout with depression since his last fall, he was actually feeling decent and not having much trouble from his knee. So, it was with a hint of enthusiasm that Josh made his way up toward the ridge for what, he hoped, was the last time before the next aid station.

It had literally been hours since Josh had seen anyone, other than volunteers, on the course. So, as he hiked to the ridge, it was a bit of a surprise to see the bright colored clothing a couple of switchbacks above him. Ten minutes later, he overtook a very tired and sick looking Hellgate entrant who was clearly struggling.

Josh felt like he should say something as he approached. "How ya doing?" Josh asked.

The man turned and stepped to the side to allow Josh to pass. "Hanging in there. How about you?"

"Same deal. Just trying to survive at this point." Josh looked at him and wondered if they had met before the race. Maybe it was one of Scott's friends. "You sound familiar, what's your name?"

"Jeff," he responded. Then, as Josh went by, Jeff stepped back on the trail and tried to fall in at the same pace.

"Oh, I remember you. I had fallen a bunch of times, about 30 miles back, and I think you passed me right after I lost my flashlight."

"That was you? Yeah, it seems like a long time ago. I'm glad you were able to get through and keep going."

Josh immediately felt guilty about his plan to drop out. "Yeah, I've had a few bad patches but I guess everyone does in a race like this."

"Maybe it's part of what makes them so memorable. Besides, once you finish, you'll forget the bad parts and only think about the good times."

"Why do you think that happens?" Josh asked.

"That's an easy answer. It's because if you remembered everything, you'd never run another one!" Jeff was laughing. Nine hours on the trail and Josh could see that Jeff was really feeling the effects, and yet, here he was taking time to chat with Josh and even laughing.

"Where are you from?" Josh wondered if he was a local, maybe one of Horton's training group.

"New York. About an hour north of the city."

Josh was surprised. "That's a long way to travel for a race, especially in this weather."

"I wouldn't miss this for anything. I've come down here for all four of Horton's races this year. The Horton Slam," he said proudly.

"That's great." Josh was impressed. He had run a few ultras but to be able to run one every month, like most of these guys did, was quite a feat.

They continued on without talking for a while and then, without any fanfare, Josh slowly pulled away and was on his own again. His legs were getting sore and he could feel the muscles tightening up but there was absolutely nothing he could do to reverse the process. So, he just ignored the steady throbbing from his quads and the occasional twinge in his hamstring and focused on the undulating trail in front of him. Fortunately, he was no longer cold and his knee pain was becoming tolerable. When he looked at his watch, he realized that he'd been on this section of the trail for almost two hours. He had to be getting close to the aid station, but he knew that it was in the valley and he was still high on the ridge. He kept expecting the descent to start and it made him crazy to see the trail continue around corner after corner.

When he finally started downhill, it was a relief. He could feel the aid station getting closer and was already preparing his "I'm dropping out" speech for Jill.

The end of the descent was steep and technical with several switchbacks and a stream crossing. When Josh finally reached the bottom and saw the road, he thought the aid station would be in plain sight, but it wasn't. Knowing that he was close, Josh crossed the road and continued down the trail, which began a very gradual uphill grade through a section of woods with an abundance of fallen trees. It didn't take long to get to a parking lot and the welcome sight of the second major checkpoint. The time limit was twelve and a half hours and Josh was there in just over ten hours. His resolve to drop out was not nearly as firm as it had been two hours earlier. Now, he didn't feel terrible, his knees were marginal, but still good enough to run on and he still had a little left in the legs.

Jill saw him running up and snapped into a blur of motion. She waved him over to the car and started getting his things together.

"Over here Josh!" she yelled.

He jogged up to the car and took a seat in the lawnchair she had set up. "Hey Jillie, have you been waiting long?"

"Yeah! It seems like all night. Oh wait, it has been all night. You guys really need to think about running some 5k's."

"Right now, it wouldn't be hard to convince me," Josh said yawning.

"How's it been?" Jill asked.

"Bad. I'll tell you all about it later. Right now I need to get this duct tape off my feet because it feels like it's coming loose. Can you get my shoes off? I'm going to throw down a can of Boost."

Jill quickly went to work on Josh's shoes but was having a difficult time with the laces. "Josh, the laces are frozen and I can't get the knot out."

Josh looked down at his shoes just as Dr. Horton walked up to the car. He had overheard Jill's comment and had immediately grabbed a fork off of the aid station table. "Let me help," he said as he quickly went to work on the knot. Within a minute he had both laces untied and Jill was back to work on Josh's feet.

She had his shoes off and had peeled the tape back before turning it over to Josh who dried them and slathered on a handful of Bag Balm. A dry pair of socks completed the pit stop and Josh was ready to get back on the trail. He lingered for a few more minutes, chatting with Jill and the race director before rechecking his water bottles and heading back towards the orange streamer that marked the trail.

Watching Jill work so hard to get him in and out of the aid station had convinced Josh, once again, that he could not drop out in front of her. Maybe he could continue just a while longer and then catch a ride back to the start from one of the crossroads. This was the last aid station where she would be waiting. At either of the next two, he could slip out inconspicuously.

Career Ending Workout

"Every runner is just one hamstring injury away from oblivion."

— **Steve Jones**
Marathon World Record holder in 1984

October 1985, University of Florida Track, Gainesville, Florida

Distance running in the 1980's was all about volume *and* quality. The days of Long Slow Distance had passed by and hard intervals were now the rage. The hard/easy system sounded nice for the masses but for the hard core, the elite, it sounded like an excuse to take it easy. For Josh taking an easy day meant only one thing, that a competitor was training hard that day and getting an advantage on him. That was unacceptable.

So, for nine years, Josh had pushed his body to the limit. He ran twice a day, seven days a week, 52 weeks per year. He trained over the holidays and through spring break. If he stayed out late into the evening and had a few too many beers, it didn't mean he had the next morning to sleep in. Instead, regardless of how bad he felt, he was out early for a hard run and usually back to his house before the rest of his friends had woke up. The only time he deviated from the routine was during bouts with illness or injury. But even illness very rarely made a dent in his schedule. He would just run through no matter how bad he felt. Injuries were different, and he had his share, but he even worked through the bad ones fast.

His schedule was simple and effective. He ran leg destroying intervals on the track three times a week and mind numbing long runs every weekend. Nothing was easy. Even the morning runs, which were supposed to be for recovery, were done at less than six minute mile pace. He ran at least a hundred miles a week, every week, even during the racing season. A Saturday race was typically preceded by a desperate attempt to rest and regain some sort of form. After the race, it was right back to hard training, usually the same afternoon. The hundreds of runners he beat, week after week, in road races, never knew that when he stepped to the line he was already exhausted. He knew the type of training his peers were doing and he also knew that he had to work as hard as them if he wanted to remain competitive.

After all of that, the sad truth was, Josh simply didn't have the talent to go to the next level. It's not that he wasn't fast. He was, but there were too many others that were better. He could dominate local events and be highly competitive regionally and to a certain extent nationally. But he would never be able to attain the level of the world class runners. He would never make an Olympic team or a World Championship team. It was out of his reach, but that didn't change the fact that he wanted it very badly. When non-runners judged his ability based on questions like, "are you going to the Olympics?" it hurt. So, he pushed and pushed his body. It was like running a racecar at it's red line for nine years straight. He rode the knife's edge, always in danger of pushing too hard. It was risky and he expected a big crash someday but, somehow he had avoided it for so long that, when it happened, he was caught completely off-guard.

In the fall of 1985, Josh was at the top of his game. He was the fastest he'd ever been and looking forward to his first Florida winter of racing since graduating from college. Reebok had signed him to a modest contract to wear their shoes and apparel. They would even pay travel expenses to a number of races during the upcoming season. He had already run several races including the United States Trials for the World Cross Country Champion-ships. His road races results had been solid and he ran well at the trials but had not made the team. His level of expectation had always been unfairly high and he continued to push his training beyond reason.

Ever since he had made his college team, Tuesday nights had been the hardest night of the week. Josh would be at the track in

Gainesville by four in the afternoon and the interval workout would stretch until six or seven in the evening. Over the years, he had been involved in some Tuesday night classics.

It wasn't just the memorable "Tuesday Night Madness" that made Josh's list of great interval sessions. In 1984, Marathon World Record holder Alberto Salazar came to Gainesville to train in the heat as part of his preparation for the Los Angeles Olympic Games. Josh, and a couple of his teammates, were invited to the track to help pace Alberto on an interval workout. It was extra-ordinary and, at the same time, totally disheartening to see that there were runners in the world that were so far beyond his level. Alberto ran mile after mile like an inhuman machine, each time clocking within a few seconds of 4:25 while only taking a ridiculous 200 meter jog in between for recovery. Josh ran as a pacer on three of the repeats. They weren't consecutive, so he had five minutes to recover and it was still very, very hard. Alberto ran eight of them. It was incredible.

There were others as well. He ran with Rob DeCastella, the man who would break Alberto's world record and with nine-time New York City Marathon winner Grete Waitz. As well as numer-ous others who passed through Gainesville to train in the Early 80's. The common theme was always Tuesday nights. It was special and Josh always felt a chill walking onto the Gainesville track when it was under the lights.

Most of the time, Josh liked to run long intervals and, for the past month, he had been running repeats of anywhere from 1,000 meters to two miles with a couple of friends who were training for a fall marathon. His plan on this particular Tuesday night was to run five repeats of one mile at 4:30 or 4:35 per mile and only take a quick 400 meter recovery jog between each of them. Josh had done this workout before. In fact, ever since watching Alberto run the harder version, it had been one of his favorites. It was difficult enough that it required some help and he had never run it alone. He liked to have other runners jump in and run a couple of laps during the middle to help pace him on the repeats, but on this night, no other runners capable of handling the pace showed up to run.

Resigned to doing it alone, he was about to start his warm-up when he noticed two thin runners enter the stadium on the far end. He recognized them right away. One of the runners was a graduate student at the University and had run for Arizona, while the other was in Gainesville just to train. They were both milers and they had both run well under 4 minutes during the past outdoor track season. He was sure that they'd be running faster than he wanted to go but Josh decided that changing his workout to match theirs would be better than running alone.

Josh approached them as they were switching from training flats to spikes. "Hey Mike, Luis, how's it going?" he asked.

"Hey Josh, who ya running with tonight?" asked Luis.

"I was supposed to run with Ernie but he's not going to make it."

Mike stood up and started doing some stretching. "We're doing quarters. You can jump in with us if you want."

"Maybe I will, if you agree not to kill me," Josh laughed. "How many and how fast?"

"We're just working on turnover so I think about 16 of them should do it. Maybe around 62 or 63 seconds," Luis said as he joined Mike by the fence.

"Kinda fast for me, but I could give it a try. Do I have time for a warm-up or are you ready to go?" Josh asked.

"If you can get ready quick, we'll wait."

Josh was already turning to start a short warm-up on the track. "Thanks, I'll be ready in five minutes."

Josh had several injuries over the past five years but none had required anything more than rest. They were just the usual assortment of stress and strain related aches and pains. It was the sort of thing that you'd expect from thousands of miles pounding on the pavement each year. Tendons and bones can't put up much of a fight against the hard impact that accompanies every step, unless you slowly build up their strength. Josh had done everything he was supposed to do to prepare his body for the rigors of training at the elite level, but not all gifts are handed out equally. Josh had been blessed with many physical attributes that lent themselves to fast running. His heart and lungs were finely tuned machines, but his legs were not the same. The high, rigid arches of his feet caused unusual stress in his lower legs and knees. The result was a steady stream of small fractures and tendon strains. He hadn't been free from pain the past summer as his achilles tendon had become tender to touch and required more and more attention to get through workouts. He had been through it before and was unconcerned when the pain lingered for week after week.

"Are you ready?" Mike asked as he ran past.

Josh had been stretching on the infield. "Yeah, let's do it."

They got together on the back straight and came up with a plan. They'd alternate leading each quarter and try to run under control for the first 10 laps, and then they would run however they felt.

Luis took the first lap. As they leaned into the turn, Josh waited for the shock that always accompanied the first repeat. The body doesn't expect the speed of the first lap. It's too much for the heart and lungs and they struggle to keep up with the requirements being placed on them. It's always the same. By the time you're halfway through the first repeat you really don't think you can do it again at that speed and to think of the entire workout is overwhelming. So, you take them one at a time, counting, but trying not to think about how many are left. They came out of the second turn and ran down the front straight, fast but under control. As they crossed the line, all three runners instinctively looked at their watches for the time.

"64," Luis gasped.

After stopping briefly, Mike was straightening up and walking toward the turn. "Too slow," he said.

Josh didn't want to look like he was having trouble hanging with them but that first repeat really hurt him. "Too slow? Wow, that was uncomfortable," Josh said as they began jogging into the turn. "I've got the lead on the next one"

Josh took them through a smooth 63 and, as his body adapted to the stress, it actually hurt less than the first one. For the milers, who were accustomed to racing at 57 or 58 seconds per lap this was more strength than speed work, but Josh was running at his limit. His race pace in a 5k was about 69 to 70 seconds per lap so this workout was recruiting muscles that were normally only observers during his speed training. To get through it mentally, he broke the quarters down into groups of four. He only thought about running a mile at a time. He followed the other runners around the track and tried to stay close each time they accelerated down the straight away.

The first four went by quickly, but Josh refused to think ahead. He simply planned on running a second mile, four more laps. After each quarter, the runners talked less and less. They were well into lap seven by the time the chatter ceased completely. The reason for the silence was easily explained. If done right, interval training hurts, a lot. Always.

Number nine was a turning point for Josh. So far, he had stayed with Mike and Luis all the way around, but on number nine, he briefly lost contact. Only a spirited run off the final curve brought him back to their shoulders at the finish. He was afraid he could no longer lead when it was his turn. He hated getting dropped on a workout so he pushed himself even harder on number 10 to stay with Mike.

Only six to go, Josh thought. *I lead this one and fourteen. Focus. Hit the first turn hard and make sure you don't miss the split at 200 meters. Get past this one and I'll make it all the way without getting dropped.*

Ten yards from the line, Josh moved to the front and the jog quickly morphed into what must have looked like a full sprint to the joggers in lane five. He leaned into the turn and started hammering. He could hear Mike and Luis right behind him and he was afraid he was running too slowly. What if they moved into lane two on the back straight to pass him? *No way. This is my lap.* Josh pressed the pace and continued to gather speed as the 200 meter mark flashed past. He glanced at his watch and thought he saw a 29. *Whoa! Easy, there's no need to get crazy. Just hit the 62 you're supposed to run.*

No matter what he told himself, it was too late to slow down. He was already on the balls of his feet and flying through the turn. Concerns about running five more of these were washed from his mind when he heard the footsteps behind him. The milers were amused that the distance runner was blasting a sub 60 quarter on his turn, but they could handle it. In fact, they were about to give him a dose of reality. Quite simply, they know that they're faster than Josh and it was abundantly clear that he needed a reminder.

They made their move 20 meters before the end of the curve by silently sliding into lane two and accelerating. It was astonishing to see how quickly the milers changed gears and jumped right to his shoulder. Josh should have conceded right then. They had let him know that, although he was really moving, they were a step higher in the food chain, but he didn't concede. He strained to stay a half step in front and, 50 meters from the finish line, Josh felt something wrong in his left achilles tendon. It started as a burning sensation along with some dull pain but that only lasted about three steps. It was hardly long enough for his brain to register it and process the information. He certainly couldn't stop in those three steps but, for years afterward, he would lie awake at night wishing he had.

When the tendon ruptured on the fourth step the pain was indescribable. That he was running at full speed made it far worse as his momentum continued to carry him forward. The fall seemed to happen in slow motion. His left foot was flopping sickeningly as the ground rose toward him. Without an attachment point, the calf muscle pulled up like a window shade and cramps spasmed through his leg. The impact with the tartan surface felt dreamlike to Josh but, even before he hit, pain rushed through his body. He heard someone screaming and knew it was coming from him.

Josh's nine year flirtation with disaster was over. The catastrophic failure that he had dreaded for so long had happened, and he knew his running career was over. Mike and Luis were already back to where Josh lay thrashing on the ground clutching his ruined leg. His screams were now more from frustration and anger than from pain but he couldn't stop. From the look on their faces, Josh realized that Mike and Luis understood his pain in a way the growing crowd could never comprehend. They knew that, although the tendon had ruptured, the real pain was caused by the loss of his hopes and dreams. He squeezed his eyes tightly shut and fought to keep from hyper-ventilating. In the darkness, statistics were flashing through his head along with a feeling of despair; Four minutes and nine seconds, nine minutes and seven seconds, Fourteen minutes and twenty seven seconds, twenty nine minutes and fifty two seconds. All the numbers, painstakingly accumulated and so important to a track athlete, could be written in ink. He would never erase them. Every "Personal Best" time he had ever run from the mile to the Marathon, would now be lifetime bests. His remaining goals, and the dreams he'd never told anyone about, would remain unfulfilled because he knew, after an injury like this, he would never be able to train his body to this level again.

Josh was just 23 years old.

Purgatory Mountain

"Never really give in as long as you have any earthly chance, and above all don't allow yourself to fancy that you are in this predicament until the gruesome knowledge is absolutely forced upon you. For however bad you may be feeling, it is by no means impossible that the other fellows may be feeling quite as much, if not even more, distressed."

— **Alf Shrubb**

Won over 1,000 races during his career. His 3-Mile World Record, set in 1903, lasted for over 30 years

Dec 10th, 2005, 10:47 am, Jefferson National Forest, VA

The climb back up to the top of the ridge sucked the life out of Josh. It wasn't that he felt a level of fatigue that he couldn't recover from. It was more a question of motivation. He was having a very difficult time finding a reason to climb the ridge. He was cold, tired and sore but the worst thing was his stomach. Ever since he left the last aid station he had felt nauseous. The effort of the climb was magnifying all of his problems.

The trail itself was not helping at this point either. The incline was significant and would have been very hard on him under the best of conditions. Of course, these were not the best of conditions. The trail was covered with snow and ice, which had been broken into chucks by the runners who had already passed though. It was hard to make forward progress since each step up included a slide sideways or back down the hill. There was no way to make decent time and he felt like he had been on this particular climb for hours.

Actually, it had only been about 45 minutes, but his pace had slowed substantially and, soon, he heard the sounds of another runner overtaking him.

"You look like shit," said a familiar voice.

Josh looked back and saw his friend approaching fast. "Hey Scott, I've been expecting you."

"Oh? Sure you have," he said sarcastically, "that was a nice touch at Little Cove Mountain. They guy said you described me as dorky looking. That's just not true. I'm *special* looking."

"No, I was right. You're dorky," Josh said.

Scott was very surprised to see Josh and knew that something had not gone according to plan. "What happened? I never thought I'd see you after the first mile."

"I think it would be easier to tell you what didn't happen," he said as Scott pulled alongside and Josh sped up and tried to match his friends pace.

Scott was honestly interested. "Why don't you try?"

"It doesn't matter. The race is over for me. I'm just looking for a road crossing to find someone to give me a ride back to the start," he said gloomily.

"You're kidding right?"

"No, I'm not kidding. I'm done."

Scott had a hard time believing that Josh was incapable of finishing the race. He knew better than anyone how strong Josh was in the months leading up to Hellgate. "Are you hurt? You're not climbing this hill very fast but I've seen people who've looked a lot worse finish from farther out than this."

Josh sighed. "No, I'm not hurt. I've bashed my knees a few times but I think they're all right."

"Then what is it?" Scott asked.

"Look at what place we're in. I don't think that we're even in the top 10 anymore."

So that was it. Scott had fought this battle with Josh before. "So what?" he asked.

In the past, it had been a hopeless effort to try and convince him that there was any merit in just finishing a race. Josh only thought about times and places. In the mountains, he was out of his element and yet he claimed to love trail running and ultras.

Scott couldn't understand it and, as a result, it had been a topic of discussion on many of their long runs together.

"So, there's no point. I can't catch anyone and it's just going to get worse," Josh responded.

"I can't believe I'm hearing this shit." *One more time.* Scott thought. *I'll try one more time.* "We've been running together for years, literally thousands of miles, and you still don't get what it's all about."

"That's not true! I get it," Josh exclaimed as he quit trudging up the incline and turned to face Scott. "We just happen to disagree on what *it* is."

"Really?" Scott also stopped and he was getting angry. "I'd like to hear what you think *it* is. Why are you out here in the first place? My god, it can't be just to win. Please tell me there's more to it than that."

Josh was in defensive mode now. "Why does there have to be more than winning? Is it so terrible to want to win races or to set records?" He was breathing hard and looking down at the snow.

Scott paused briefly to regain his composure. "Of course not, there's nothing terrible about winning but how does it positively affect anyone else?"

"Jeez, I don't know. Maybe it will inspire others to work hard and reach their potential."

"Maybe," he tried to look Josh in the eye and find a way to reach him, "but you've already done all of that. How many races have you won? Sixty? Seventy? You've set records and held the "top dog" status. The road racers at home just about wet themselves when they see you at the Cup." As he continued, it felt like he was lecturing a child. "I'm sure it feels great but what I'm trying to tell you is that winning isn't the only way to get that feeling you're looking for."

"It's the only way I've ever found," Josh said defiantly.

"Bullshit. It can be felt by anybody. You can get that feeling by setting any goal and accomplishing it."

"Take my word for it; it's a different feeling to cross the line first. Once you've done that, it's all you'll ever want out of racing." He was losing the conviction in his voice and Scott sensed it.

"Is that why you're running ultras instead of road races?" Scott asked indignantly. "You're getting to slow to win there so now you're going to move up and kick our asses?"

"That's a shitty way to put it but I do want to start winning again and maybe this is what it takes."

Scott didn't respond right away. He took out one of his bottles and took a long drink. Meanwhile, Josh's attention appeared to be focused on inspecting his shoes.

Finally, Scott continued. "Do you remember Dr. Horton's briefing after dinner last night?"

"Yeah, Why?"

"I noticed he never called this a race. He referred to it as an adventure."

"I didn't notice," Josh said while looking away from Scott.

"Well, I did, and you should have," Scott forged on. "Let's be realistic Josh. What was your goal for Hellgate? You've been so sick for the past three weeks that I couldn't even believe you decided to run. I know you were in good shape before that but you didn't really expect to come here and win did you?"

Uncertainly, Josh responded. "No, I didn't *expect* to win, but I thought it was a slim possibility."

"So, what you're telling me is there was only a *slim possibility* that you could leave Hellgate with any feeling other than disappointment. Yet, you came anyway. That makes absolutely no sense." He paused briefly and took a deep breath. "I'll ask again. Why are you here?"

He was trapped. "Ok, maybe I had multiple goals," he stammered.

"Well, I think you better go through them for me because it sounds like you're only thinking about one of them."

The older runner was on the offensive. This was the time and the place for his friend, and newbie ultra runner, to come to terms with his personal demons and figure out what he really wanted out of this experience.

Josh was starting to feel like he was on the wrong end of an unexpected inquisition. "Fine, I wanted to win or at least be competitive and finish in the top five."

"There's nothing wrong with that goal but if it wasn't possible, what was your second level goal?" he asked.

"Then, I suppose I wanted to finish in the top 10."

Scott nodded his head. "And what was the next level?"

"There isn't a next level, that's it."

"What about finishing your first 100k race? What about completing a run that very few people in the world are capable of even considering? What about just finishing under the cutoffs? What's wrong with continuing toward those goals?" They'd had this dialogue before and Scott knew what Josh's response would be.

"Well, I've never really considered finishing a goal." Scott was noticeably irritated by the answer but Josh made it even worse. "I think, if you go slowly enough, you can finish any long run. This race is definitely a huge challenge, and I know finishing is extremely difficult, but to call it a goal. I don't know. I think anyone can finish."

"You're wrong. Not under these conditions and not with cutoffs. They can yank you out of these things even if you feel great just because you hit a certain spot a couple of minutes too late. Half the field won't finish today and, believe it or not, finishing is a legitimate goal, even for you." Scott hesitated. "Think back to the several hundred races you've run. Have you ever dropped out without a serious injury forcing the issue?"

Josh thought for a moment. "No, not that I can think of."

"And I know you've never been pulled from a race for being too slow so, if that happened today, it would be a first for you." His eyes were boring into Josh. "I think you want to quit because you're afraid of the embarrassment of being too slow to get under the last cutoff."

"I can assure you, I'm not, as for the rest of this argument, please, what's your point?"

"Jeez Josh, you're killing me with this." Scott had to keep pushing towards a resolution. "Ok, you've run 45 miles, in the snow, and over ice covered roads. Let's see, by my watch, you have been out here for 11 hours which is already a couple of hours longer than your Appalachian Trail debacle a few years ago. Seven hours has been run in the dark, which is at least five hours more than your longest previous night run. I know in a normal race I can't get anywhere near you, so the fact that I caught up to you tells me you've had other difficulties to overcome. Am I right so far?"

"Yeah, you're right."

"It sounds like you're well on your way to accomplishing a lot of goals today. Are you proud of any of them? Does any of it make you feel good?"

Josh conceded the point. "Well, when you say it like that, yes."

"Great! Then forget this *I can't be seen by my adoring public finishing out of the top 10 crap* and get your ass moving again. Keep doing what you've been doing all day, for another 21 miles, and I guarantee, when you finish, you'll be proud of what you've accomplished. Oh, and absolutely no one is going to care what place you're in, in fact, I bet no one will even ask. I've been telling you for years, it only matters to you."

Josh stared down the snow covered trail and tried to imagine the moment. He couldn't.

"You really believe that I'll feel proud of just finishing?" he asked.

In a solemn tone Scott said. "If you don't, I think you should seriously question why you're even here."

"Come on, you know I love running trails."

"I've heard you say that before, but today you going to have to prove it."

Then, Scott did something that caught Josh completely off guard. He looked directly at him for a few seconds, turned, and started to run down the trail.

"Hey! What are you doing?"

Scott slowed briefly and looked back. "I'm finishing this adventure because that was *my* goal."

"What about me? What about this speech? I thought, if you want me to do this so bad, that we might at least run together for a while."

"Hell no!" he yelled. "I can't make the decision for you. This is one of those things that you've got to figure out yourself." He looked at his watch and then back at Josh. "Look, you've got seven hours until the final cutoff. For now, keep moving and use the time to decide what really matters to you. You've got to try and forget about college and all those years of competitive racing and figure out why you're doing this."

Josh was trying to catch up. "Forget about it? Are you kidding, that's all I have! All of my meaningful experiences with running are tied up with racing."

"No they aren't, that's something you need to get past. If you really think about it, you can come up with hundreds of examples. What about the run you told me about from your time in the Scouts? You know, the time you bombed the swim test and ran to the river."

Josh didn't say anything.

"I think that 9-year-old kid *got it* better than you do today. Maybe you need to forget about everything else and just run like that kid again."

Still nothing from Josh.

"I'll see you at the finish," Scott said as he turned away again.

"Yeah, see ya," Josh mumbled.

Thirty seconds later, Scott had disappeared down the trail and Josh was left with nothing but the sounds of the woods and his own thoughts.

It's a good question. *What am I doing here?* Josh was conflicted. He really wanted to be able to enjoy these runs like Scott, but he also wanted to be regarded as one of the best, and that meant that he had to perform consistently at a high level.

He thought back to his first trail runs in Raleigh a few years earlier, where he had met Scott. *Why was I there? I wasn't planning to ever race again. So, why was I there? Why did I latch on to ultra running so quickly?*

Josh was 20 miles from the finish and had plenty of time to think about it.

Trail Running

"Comebacks, like political careers, very rarely end happily."

— **Sebastian Coe**

Twice an Olympic Champion at 1,500 meters, he also set 8 outdoor and 3 indoor World Records

September 11th, 2001, Raleigh, North Carolina

Josh enjoyed being outdoors and the physical activity associated with sports more than anything. Whether it was Fishing, Skiing, Camping or any of a variety of outdoor sports, he loved hanging out in the sun and having a few beers with his friends. During the 15 years that had passed since his achilles injury, and subsequent surgery, Josh had only run intermittently. It wasn't that he didn't try, because he did, over and over. Several times a year, he would train for a month or two. Sometimes, he thought he could feel his legs coming back. It was frustrating that he could only take it to the level where he was just good enough to see a glimmer of hope. *Maybe, if it all goes perfectly, maybe I'll be able to race again, someday,* he would think. He needed that hope because, despite all of his other recreational activities, he missed the feeling of training hard and of winning races. He tried and tried but, inevitably, each time he increased his training intensity, the pain would soon return to his damaged achilles. Josh could never be content to run road races as anything but a competitive athlete and, finally, he accepted that it was out of the question now. So, after a few years, and exactly zero races, he finally gave it up and slipped into a retirement from competition that really began five years earlier while running a long forgotten quarter mile repeat on the track.

His old running buddies faded away as well, uncomfortable being around someone who constantly reminded them that it could all end in an instant. They were still fast and strong while Josh limped noticeably after sitting too long in one position. He had become a pedestrian and was no longer one of them. In the animal kingdom, he would have been killed and eaten.

So, Josh moved on and started a life that didn't include running at all. He had a career in engineering, new interests, and new friends who had no idea he had ever been a competitive athlete. He filled his free time with various activities and began to attack new sports with an overly high level of enthusiasm. He was trying to suppress his loss and find some type of reasonable substitute. That's the simple explanation of why, five years after the injury that ended his racing career, Josh bought a Barefoot Nautique and became a water skier. He didn't even know how much he liked skiing, or if he'd be any good, but some of his friends skied and, as a result, he spent several hours a day, three or four days a week at the lake trying to improve his barefooting skills. That wasn't all. At the same time, beach volleyball took it's place in the rotation, filling in the few empty spots that skiing left open. He played every chance he could during the week and for hours on end over the weekend. And, of course, there was always golf. He had started playing as a kid in Nebraska with his dad, but once he took it up again in Florida, it became an obsession. Almost all of his new friends played and they were beautiful courses all over the state. His plate was full of daily activities that kept his real passion buried deep.

Running was truly part of a forgotten past. All of the trophies and awards were long gone, donated as prizes to the Special Olympics and other charities. The photos and newspaper clippings were tucked away into photo albums that were stashed in closets and boxes. It was so buried, that when he married Jill in 1995, like many of his new friends, she didn't know that he had once run in the National Cross Country Championships or that he had a SEC Championship ring in a small box in his dresser.

Josh never intended to run competitively again but that all changed on September 11th, 2001 when terrorists flew airplanes in the Twin Towers of the World Trade Center. That day, he discovered that his past just needed a trigger to make it resurface stronger than ever.

Josh was in Raleigh, North Carolina on a consulting assignment when he first heard the news. The information he received from another employee was sketchy, and would prove to be inaccurate, but it sent Josh reeling. He went to the office he was using for the week so he could get on the internet and access the news links. After a short time, he left the office and went back to his hotel room to watch live network coverage. Then, like all of America, he watched with growing horror as the towers fell. His emotions were not unique. Most of the country was going through the same thing as Josh. They each had to deal with the anger their own way, but for Josh there was the old standby for releasing anger. When he couldn't stand it any longer, he put on his shoes, went out the side door of the hotel, and started to run.

It had been six years since his last run and, at a solid 190 pounds, he was heavy compared to his racing days when he rarely weighed more than 130 pounds soaking wet.

He ran a mile to the end of the road where he stopped for a few minutes to stretch and catch his breath. He felt overweight and slow, but it was good to be outside. As it had done so many times before, the exercise helped him get his anger under control. After his short break, he jogged slowly back to the hotel. It had made him feel better, so, the next day, he did it again. This time, he went just a little further. Each day, he bumped it up a little more and, within a week, his legs started to feel stronger.

After about 10 days of easy jogging, Josh became bored with the roads around his hotel. He checked the internet for a park or trail system where he could get away from the traffic. He was pleasantly surprised to find a local track club that had an organized group run at Umstead State Park, between Raleigh and Durham, every Saturday morning. He thought it would be nice to run with someone again but, realistically, he didn't expect to be able to keep up with anyone. His primary motivation was to get out there and run without cars buzzing past him. The track club would provide some guidance on which trails to run and, hopefully, someone to follow so he wouldn't get lost.

Josh had never been to Umstead before, so he arrived early and walked to the end of the parking lot to see what the trail looked like. He walked and jogged for almost 20 minutes before returning. What he found was a firm, rock strewn trail that rolled through an endless series of short hills. He wasn't sure how far he could go on the rough terrain but he thought that he should try and run for at least 30 minutes before turning back. When he walked back into the parking lot he saw several runners congregating in one area and figured it was the track club. Josh strolled over and introduced himself to a couple of guys and went through the usual, "where are you from" and "how much do you run", routine. As it turned out, there were actually two groups and you could choose your pace. Naturally, even after a mere 10 days of running in 6 years, Josh's ego wouldn't allow him to run with the "slow" group. So, when they split up, and the "fast" group jogged toward the trailhead, he went along. He began asking their names, and that's how Josh met Jim, Scott, Ralph, Chris, a couple of Steve's and even a Rachel.

As they started down the trail, he fell into line near the back and tried to stay out of everyone's way.

It was clear from the nonstop talking that they were all good friends and that this was a several day per week gathering. The stories were funny and refreshingly raunchy and Josh found himself laughing along with them as the miles went by. Occasionally, one of the gang would drop back to say hello and see how he was doing. He answered a few questions but, for the most part, kept his past to himself. In fact, it wasn't at all easy for him to keep up so he didn't want to talk too much.

He had told them he was only doing 9 or 10 miles and, politely, they had agreed to tell him when he should turn back.

After less than an hour with them, he felt a connection. It wasn't unlike the teams he'd been on in college. They were all very fit and they liked to talk, a lot, while running. It was an extremely comfortable group to fall in with and Josh quickly found himself wondering about their backgrounds.

He didn't have to wait long for information. It came fluttering back to him in the form of a petite blonde named Rachel. Josh soon discovered that Rachel, the self proclaimed "egghead intellectual" of the group, was the designated inquisitor. She probed for data on Josh, as an athlete, while providing similar information on the runners hopping over the rocks and roots in front of him. He tried hard to listen, rather than talk, but had to give in, at least a little, to his persistent interviewer. He was certain that he'd be *Googled*, with all facts checked and verified, before he was back in his hotel. It was amusing, since he hadn't run a race in over 15 years, there would be very little to support or refute his answers. He thought about telling them some of the numbers that all runners would recognize but decided against it. No one would believe the jogger who had joined them for their morning run had ever been competitive, unless it had been in a pancake eating contest. So, for now, he tried to keep a low profile. If he ever got back into shape, he'd share more information and tell a few stories about his college track days.

The pace had been difficult for Josh but they all stayed together through seven miles where a water stop was setup. Everyone continued to talk as they refilled bottles and Josh was unexpectedly drawn into the conversation.

"So, you're heading back in from here Josh?" Jim asked.

"Yeah, that's going to be enough for me," Josh replied. "Maybe I'll be able to go a bit longer next week."

"Super," Jim said, "if you want to join the club, I'll bring a membership form next week."

"Sure, I won't be up here much but I'll join anyway."

From behind, he heard. "What are you training for?"

Josh turned around and saw a tall lanky runner looking at him but couldn't remember his name. "Nothing, I haven't run in a few years so I'm just trying to get my legs back under me."

"Great, well, come back next week and we'll show you some more of the trail," the tall runner said.

"I'm sorry, I can't recall everyone's name yet. Who are you?" Josh asked.

"Oh, I'm Scott Leopard."

"It's nice to meet you Scott. What are you planning to run today?"

Chris and Steve had just walked up and quickly jumped in. "Don't even ask cause you'll just think he's gone mad," Chris said while laughing.

"Ah, you must be training for a marathon," Josh said nodding his head. "I've been through that. You must be doing 20 or 22 miles today, right?"

Scott glanced at his friends and they all shared a moment of laughter at Josh's expense. "No, I'm going 35 today."

"35 miles?" Josh asked incredulously.

"That's right, I'm training for the JFK 50 miler in November so I need to get a five hour run in."

"I've never heard of a 50 mile race. That's crazy."

"It may be, but that would mean everyone standing here is crazy cause we've all run them," Scott said. "There are a thousand people in the JFK race every year."

"Really? I wonder why I've never heard of it?"

Chris chimed in. "Not a lot of people run them compared to marathons or road races and you won't see them written up in *Runner's World* or any road racing magazines."

They had been stopped too long and a couple of the runners had already started to jog off. "Let's go guys," Rachel said as she followed Steve and Chris. A few seconds later, they were all starting to move away from Josh, towards the trail, when Scott turned back.

"You should check it out, trail running is a lot easier on you legs than the roads and the people are less intense. It's just a lot of fun."

"I'll think about it," Josh said.

"Cool. Later," Scott said as he turned and ran to catch back up to the group.

Five hour training runs! What the hell is that all about? Josh thought. It seemed like he had stumbled upon some weird running cult but, at the same time, he couldn't get it out of his mind. He thought about it as he ran back to his car, and even on the drive home.

A couple of days later, he went for another 10 mile run and felt pretty good. After running for two weeks, his achilles wasn't sore and he had lost a few pounds. *Can I race again,* he thought.

He was almost 40 and the more he considered running a road race, the more ridiculous it seemed. He could never, even under perfect circumstances and training, run another Personal Best. So, why train his ass off only to be disappointed week after week. The road and track were out, but these long trail races were intriguing. He didn't need to risk injuring his achilles with speed work, and yet, it was possible that he might still manage to be competitive. He needed to build up to longer runs on the weekend, and there were other training issues to resolve, but the decision was made. Josh would run an ultra-marathon as the first race in, what he now perceived as, his comeback. He studied the calendar and chose a 50 kilometer race in January, three months away, as his first. He told himself this wasn't anything more than an experiment, an offbeat adventure he could look back on later and laugh about, but there was also a voice in his head that taunted him. It kept saying, *"You can win. These guys are slow. You can win."*

He started by increasing the length of his weekend run. At first all he could do was 10 or 12 miles but, after a few weeks, he was up to 20 miles and starting to run faster. The 50 kilometer distance was only five miles longer than a marathon, so he decided to train with the same methods he had used years earlier. The distance of his runs went up but, as he attempted to increase the pace on his long runs, he quickly found out that the 39 year old Josh bore no resemblance to the Josh of 16 years earlier. Now, quite simply, he sucked.

It was tremendously hard to accept the fact that his body was unable to respond to the commands his brain sent but it was understandable. After all, his brain had never witnessed the drop off of his abilities. One day he was fast and strong and, the next, he was injured and a pedestrian. Without the reference of 15 years of gradual physical deteriorization, his mind couldn't comprehend why he was unable to easily cruise at sub six minute mile pace anymore. Most of the time, as he ran on the rocky trails, he felt sluggish and uncoordinated. On the few days that he felt good, and he ran at a pace that he thought was pretty quick, he was always disappointed to find out he had barely been able to average eight minute mile pace. It was frustrating and, as long as it was going to continue, he decided to train alone and keep his weakness a secret. If it ever got to the point that he wasn't embarrassed, he'd show his face back on the weekend group run.

Two months later, he was still running alone. He was improving but had still not gone past 20 miles on his long run. He didn't believe it was necessary, because he was still trying to run faster, not longer. He was back to running tempo runs and had done some two mile repeats at six minute pace but that was all he could do. He wanted to run that pace for the entire 31 mile race, but with less than a month to train, he could only do it for two miles at a time. He wasn't going to make it back into shape fast enough for the race. He needed to either cancel or change his race plan. It was agonizing but, a couple of weeks later, he finally changed his plan. Instead of trying to run six minute pace he would run seven minute pace. It was a compromise, but it was not nearly enough. Although he wasn't even close to being ready for that pace, his brain seemed unable to accept the obvious fact that he was not the same runner he had been.

The race itself was either a success or disaster depending on how Josh viewed it. It was a success because he had finished and, at 31 miles, it was the longest run of his life. It was also a success because he placed in the top three which had been one of his goals. Unfortunately, it was also a disaster. He really believed that he could cruise at seven minute pace all day long. In college, it would have been an easy jog, but those days were long gone. He had only made it six miles before he started receiving danger signals from his tiring legs. Naturally, he ignored them. *It can't be,* he thought. *I've only gone 6 miles. There's no way that I can't run this pace.* So, he continued.

By the time he finished the first 15 mile loop, he was in second place and falling apart. His hamstrings had started to tighten up and he thought that, at any moment, they might cramp. And yet, he was still in denial. As he began the second loop, he tried to increase the pace and catch the leader. Within three miles, he had bridged the gap and was running side by side, in the lead, with a runner named Kurt. Unfortunately, he was now in serious trouble. Both legs were starting to cramp and, after only a mile in the lead, he lost contact with Kurt and quickly started glancing back to see if anyone was closing on him for second.

Within a few miles, he was slowing down considerably but, to his amazement, no one had appeared to pass him. So, he kept running as hard as he could. The effort was there, the pain, which engulfed him, was there, but the leg speed he desired was not. Every mile was slower than the last, until he was grinding along, head down, at nine minute pace. Still, he held on to second place. It was all that kept him going.

The miles passed and finally, as he heard another runner approaching, he saw the last mile marker. He hadn't seen anyone in an hour and this encounter was very short as the runner simply blasted past him. Josh struggled to the finish and held on to third place in four hours and two minutes. Later, when he did the math, he found out that he had averaged just under eight minutes per mile. He didn't understand why he couldn't run fast anymore, but at the same time, he had been competitive. He had led a race for the first time in over a decade and, for that short time, it had felt great. He needed to figure out how to train for these things before trying another one but he had already decided. He was going do it again.

His legs were wrecked for a week. The first couple of days were horrible and he spent all day gobbling anti-inflammatories, icing and laying around the house. Then, having taken some time to let his body recover, he resurfaced in Raleigh for the Saturday trail run. It had been so long that he had to reintroduce himself to everyone but they were easy to talk to and, within a few miles, he was back in the groove, this time, telling stories as well as listening.

"Hey Josh, do you live in Raleigh or Cary?" Jim asked an hour into the run.

"Neither, I'm just up here doing some work. I live in Florida," Josh responded.

"Oh yeah, you said you were a consultant, right?"

"Right," Josh responded.

"You sure seem to be up here a lot," Chris said.

"Yeah, I've got a couple of good clients in the area, so I'm here five to 10 days each month. I don't do it often but I really enjoy running with the group here, back home I have to train alone."

"Really, you know, one of the guys that used to run with us just moved down there," Jim said.

"No kidding, who?" Josh asked.

"His name is Scott Leopard. I don't know if you met him last time."

"Yeah, the name sounds familiar. I think he was here. Hey, wasn't he the guy that was running 35 miles that day?" Josh asked.

"Right! That's Scott."

Chris was just behind them on the trail and spoke up. "If you want to contact him, I have his email address. I'm sure he'd like to find someone to run with."

"Do you know where he's at in Florida?"

"Yeah," Chris said, "he's in a small town somewhere north of Orlando. I think it's called something River."

"Crystal River?"

"That's it!" Chris said.

"No shit. That's only 30 miles from where I live. Yeah, give me his email and I'll get in touch with him," Josh said.

What a stroke of luck. Maybe he could get together with Scott for some runs on the weekend. It would be a nice change after three months of running alone.

From there it snowballed for Josh. He started running with Scott and, over the next couple of years, they traded the secrets of training and racing that they had accumulated over the years. It was good for both of them. Scott understood how to train for ultras and Josh was the only guy around that was strong enough to run with him. For Josh, it reignited the social side of running. He had a friend to go drink beer with and someone who liked to talk about racing. Scott tried to guide Josh through the intricacies of ultra training and racing but that started more arguments than anything else. Josh didn't want to accept Scott ideas on training and when it came to racing they were really not on the same page.

Still, they were becoming good friends and when Josh ran his first 50 mile race, Scott was there as his crew. He would have run the race with Josh but he had a 100 mile race scheduled a week later. As usual, Josh ignored the advice that Scott had given him and he went out too fast. By 30 miles, he was dehydrated and cramping. The last 20 miles were a mess but his time of seven and a half hours wasn't too bad for a first timer.

Scott insisted that Josh would have been an hour faster if he had listened to him. *Whatever,* Josh thought. He didn't want to hear about pacing and holding back. He wanted to go hard and run fast. He wanted to be the "Top Dog" again.

Blackhorse Gap

"I realized recently that when I saw a beautiful golf course my immediate thought was how great it would be to play on it, not run on it."

— Jon Anderson
1973 Boston Marathon winner, speaking in 1991

Dec 10th, 2005, 1:52 pm, Jefferson National Forest, VA

Josh couldn't come up with an answer to the simple question Scott had asked. Why was he here?

He'd been thinking about it for the last 30 minutes as he followed the trail across the ridgeline. The answer that kept working its way to the front of Josh's mind was not one that Scott would like.

Why is everyone else out here? Josh wondered.

He wasn't a former addict out to replace alcohol or narcotics with another form of addiction. He knew there were ultra runners out there that fit that description, but that wasn't Josh. It was easy to see he didn't have some type of handicap or illness which would make completing Hellgate some sort of incredible emotional event. By the same thought process, he considered relatives and friends that might be inspired by his effort but none came to mind. He had not made any promise to himself, God, or anyone else, that he would run Hellgate for them, or in memory of someone. In fact, few people, other than Scott and Jill, who were here, would ever know, or care, that he was in these mountains.

As Josh contemplated his motivation for running Hellgate, he ran up and over a short knoll and was treated to another great view of the valley and neighboring mountains. He paused and really took a look at the landscape. In fact, he turned all the way around several times and took a few deep breaths, really absorbing the entire scene. "Why am I here?" He said aloud. *I'm 43 years old, what am I doing running at all. I quit 15 years ago. Why don't I just go back to playing golf?* Running was so natural to him but he was questioning everything now.

It was inescapable, although he had tried to come up with a better answer, the only motivation he had for running Hellgate was to win or run a fast time. The reason why went back over a decade but he knew the answer. He craved the recognition and attention that he had lost 20 years earlier when his injury forced him into an unwanted, and unacceptable, retirement from racing. He hadn't quit on his own terms, he had been forced out. Ultras were his chance for another round as the guy everyone feared.

He still thought he could get back in shape and dominate. He didn't want to be just another guy in the race. He wanted to be the one everyone talked about before and after. He wanted the glory. It sounded cheesy and insincere for him to say he loved trail running, when the motivation for being at Hellgate was for such a different reason. Scott, on the other hand, was the real deal. Josh realized that Scott was as interested in helping Josh have a good race as he was in his own preparation. Whereas, Josh never concerned himself with Scott's race at all. *Have I ever helped anyone get better? Have I ever taken the time during a race to offer encouragement to someone?* He wondered. *What are they all getting out of this that I'm missing?*

It wasn't an argument that Josh was unfamiliar with. In fact, Scott had questioned Josh's motives on many occasions. Maybe it was the timing. Being alone on the trail, after such a long and difficult night, coupled with his argument with Scott, had put Josh into a reflective mood. It was quiet on the mountain. He could take as much time as he needed to think through the questions from all angles.

Was he physically capable of finishing? Josh thought about it and the answer was a resounding "yes". That meant it was just a mental decision to quit, he didn't really need to. *Is Scott right?* He thought. *Am I afraid of what people will say if I don't finish at the top? Why do I care?*

He had danced around the question for almost an hour but the truth was becoming apparent. Josh was going to have to find another reason to be at Hellgate, because Scott was right, the reason he had when he came here, sucked.

He continued to run and hike along the ridge. As he had been told, the views along this particular stretch of trail were magnificent and he stopped several times to admire them. *This isn't even a race anymore.* He thought. *It hasn't been for the past four hours. I'm just killing time and slowly moving toward the finish. Where is everyone?*

The time he had taken from Bearwallow Gap to the end of the single track felt much longer than the actual time of 90 minutes. At any rate, he was extremely pleased to get back on the fire road because he knew it was only another mile to aid station number eight. Unfortunately, like many before, this mile was all uphill. Josh trudged along, trying to power hike but not really feeling in the mood to push himself.

As he approached the aid station, which was sheltered under a small overpass, he realized that he was about to pass by the Blue Ridge Parkway for the third time. There was a single car parked next to a table and, this time, no one got out when Josh walked up to refill his bottles and get some food. He helped himself to a handful of M&M's and some pretzels. It was cold but he stood around for a couple of minutes, munching on the snacks, before moving on. After his heated discussion with Scott, he had abandoned his plan to drop out. It didn't mean he was excited about continuing and he silently jogged out of the aid station without talking to anyone.

Where am I? Josh wondered. He remembered the pre-race meeting when Dr. Horton discussed this section. He had heard the phrase "going on forever" used. He expected the road to drop about 1,500 feet over the next couple of miles, then it would switch back over to single track until aid station number nine. Josh started to run faster on the downhill and felt the pain building in his quads. It had begun a few hours earlier, but now it was becoming a problem. It wasn't debilitating yet, but Josh knew they would quickly degenerate if he made any mistakes with hydration or caloric intake.

All of the running did nothing to distract Josh from the mental gymnastics that were being conducted in his head. He couldn't get away from Scott's question and, the truth was, he didn't really want to. He needed to come to a resolution. He thought about the first couple of weeks after he began training again. It was before he met the Raleigh group. He hadn't planned on racing anymore. All Josh wanted to do was run because it made him feel good, mentally and physically. After he ran with them and heard about ultra marathons, it all changed, because he started to think he could win races again. That was the root of his problem.

As he ran down to the valley, for what seemed like the hundredth time, Josh made the decision to change his attitude. He felt he could finish Hellgate, but he also decided he would not, under any circumstances, consider dropping out today. He would make finishing his goal. He would become the humble, courteous and friendly poster child for ultra running. He was going to take in his surroundings and appreciate where he was and what he was doing. It was truly an amazing accomplishment to complete Hellgate. He always knew that, but now he was going to allow himself to actually take pride in it.

He tried hard to savor the somewhat painful run down the icy road. He watched for the few areas of gravel that poked through the snow on this side of the ridge. He aimed for them, thereby taking advantage of each bit of good firm footing that he could get. He accepted the pain in his legs, knowing it was the unavoidable result of 53 miles, over two back to back marathons, of pounding over these steep trails. He was no longer deep in the woods. Houses were visible just off of the road and the sunlight streaming through the gaps between trees lit up the road.

The transition from intense racing to "enjoy the experience" is not something that came naturally to Josh but he was trying. He took deep breaths, listened more intently to everything and focused his attention away from the business of trail running. His eyes scanned left and right, trying to burn the spectacular visual images into his memory. As he ran down the road, he fought to become detached from the pain. He forced the thoughts of his night long problems out and nearly ran past the small orange streamer that marked the trail entrance on the side of the road. By the time it had registered, he was 20 yards past and had to stop and jog back. He looked back into the woods and knew that all he had to do was complete this last section of single track and he would be at the final aid station. There was no way that he would drop out there. Not so close to the finish.

For some reason, Josh expected this last piece of rocky trail to be flat. It was a ridiculous assumption. After all, there hadn't been a flat section on the entire course. Why start now? For a couple of hundred yards he ran on a gentle downhill, not even trying to figure out how many sets of footprints were already stamped into the snow covered path. He was at a much lower elevation but the way the trail undulated and twisted, in and out of the crevasses, reminded him of the beautiful path he had been following when Scott passed him on Purgatory Mountain. He had let the scenes slip past without giving them the proper amount of attention. He knew that he should have appreciated the views and, more importantly, the advice that were both right in front of him.

The next stream crossing was only a couple of steps across, but Josh managed to slip off of a rock and plunge his shoes into the ice cold water. His feet had been wet for so long that he didn't even care anymore. He simply trudged up the opposite bank and quietly continued on.

For miles, he repeated the same thing, again and again. He would run up hill for a few minutes, crest a small rise and then drop back down to a small rock strewn creek and cross over. Eventually, he stopped trying to keep his feet dry and started to run straight through the water without any hesitation. It was all about "relentless forward motion". Josh wanted to get to that final aid station. The past hour had done some damage to his legs but he was still moving at a reasonable pace and his knees were going to make it as long as he avoided any more hard falls. The only question now was "Where's the aid station?"

Dr. Horton had been right in his pre-race brief. This section seemed to go on forever. He had counted three significant climbs on the single track and each had a matching descent. Although the temperature was still below freezing, the sun faced this side of the Parkway and had actually began to melt some of the snow, resulting in water runoff all over the trail and a sudden overflow in many of the streams.

After a long morning, and even longer night, a strange thing happened as Josh approached the final aid station. His anticipation escalated. He was becoming excited about finishing. He didn't know how far he'd run but he guessed that he was around 58 to 60 miles into the course. It was by far the longest run he had ever done and, Scott was right, he could sense a hint of the feeling he remembered from those long gone days of winning races. It wasn't quite the same, but it was there, and he hadn't expected it at all. *Can I really get that feeling by just finishing this thing?* he wondered. *Or am I just talking myself into it because of Scott.* He still didn't know the answer, but he was getting more and more curious about how his body would react in a couple of hours.

The water runoff was heavy as he ran through a flooded area at the bottom of a long downhill. In the distance, he thought he could hear voices and his heart raced at the thought that he had reached the end of the single track. When he actually saw the trucks and the tables, he couldn't stop the smile from flashing across his face. He looked at his watch and immediately knew he was going to make it to the finish well under the time limit. After half a day of trying to ignore all thoughts of the distance, or of the finish, for the first time, it seemed real to Josh.

Like Jennings Creek seven hours earlier, the small group of volunteers was extremely vocal and they started cheering as soon as Josh came into view. There was music playing and Josh felt rejuvenated when he ran up to the cluster of tables. *Ok, 60 miles down and only six to go,* he told himself. *This is the final climb. All I have to do is get to the Parkway and its all downhill to the finish.*

"Hey man, you're looking good! Do you need refills for your bottles?" asked an overzealous college student that was working the aid station.

"Sure," Josh said while handing over his water bottles. "One water and one sport drink."

"You got it," the student said as he quickly shifted over to the large coolers that covered the center table.

Josh grabbed handfuls of everything and started stuffing his face with pretzels, candy and sandwiches that were cut into small pieces. Earlier he had no interest, but it all looked good to him now. For the first time, he didn't feel rushed at all. Naturally, he didn't want to linger too long, but the urge to grab food and quickly bolt had left him. He was really starting to enjoy the race simply as an adventure.

Less than a minute later the student returned. "Here's your bottles man."

"Hey, thanks." Josh was staring at the table downing water from the collection of Dixie Cups. "How long have you been out here?"

"Well, since this is the last station, we didn't get here until about 8 a.m. So, I guess I've been out here for about five hours."

Josh nodded his head. "Hey, I really appreciate you guys taking the time to come out here and help."

"Yeah, no problem. I like watching everyone come through late in the race. You're all kinda crazy."

Josh couldn't have agreed more. "I better get moving. Thanks again."

"No problem. Have a good run."

The road immediately began to tilt upward. It was gradual at first but it didn't take long for it to get steep enough that even walking fast caused Josh's heart rate to skyrocket. He kept his arms moving and his back straight, thereby forcing himself to keep good posture and maximize his oxygen uptake. It certainly helped knowing that it was the last climb. Josh worked steadily toward the top but no amount of good form and positive thinking could reduce the pain in his legs or ease the burning in his chest. He tried to keep his eyes focused on a spot 15 yards in front of him but, once every hundred yards, he would glance farther up the hill, looking expectantly for the gate that would flank the Parkway. He hadn't been awake long enough to hallucinate but, on several occasions, he thought he saw cars go past in the distance only to find that he had not reached the road and there were no cars at all. It was just the anticipation of the finish playing tricks on him.

It was the climb he and Scott had been dreading ever since their strategy session at the Tin Cup Tavern a month earlier. It was a harsh and ruthless climb of over 1,700 feet in less than three miles. If it had been the only hill of the day, it would be tough, but dropping it in after 60 torturous miles on this snow covered trail was pure evil.

Josh had no one to talk to, and no one to judge his pace off of, so he just kept grinding away at the distance between himself and the Parkway. Step by step, he closed the gap until he finally saw a gate up ahead. He had been fooled before, but this time it was really there. He looked for traffic, but the storm had closed this section of the Parkway. He started to jog and instantly slipped on a patch of ice. His arms were out for balance again as he stopped and took a few deep breaths. *Take it easy,* he told himself.

Afraid of the ice, Josh walked across the Parkway. Once he was back on the snow and feeling more confident, he started a tentative jog down the road. There was no one in sight in front of him and, as he looked down to the valley, which appeared to be far away, he made a snap decision to run as hard as he could to the bottom. At first, it was just a slight increase in the pace but, as he became more comfortable with the traction, he went harder and harder. Within a mile, he was ignoring the pain in his quads and flying down the hill. *Who cares how bad it hurts now. This is the end and, if necessary, I can take weeks to recover,* he thought.

Ten minutes later, the figure that appeared in the distance looked familiar but it wasn't until Josh was 50 yards behind that he recognized his friend. They were about two miles from the finish and Josh had a lot of momentum. He could easily blast past Scott with one of his classic "take no prisoners" passes. Deep down he wanted to make that move and beat Scott. It would give him bragging rights for the next year and allow him to ignore Scott's advice by throwing the Hellgate results in his face. The decision he'd made a few hours earlier was being strongly tested by 30 years of brainwashing.

Unconsciously, he slowed slightly, not wanting to catch up until he had decided what to do. Scott had challenged Josh to figure out why he was at Hellgate and Josh had thought about little else for the past five hours. He had worked his way through a range of emotions and had finally arrived at an answer that he certainly would not have given a day ago. He had to stick with his answer. Josh sped up just enough to catch Scott and then slowed to match his friends pace.

"Hey," Josh said as he ran alongside.

Scott's head snapped back to see who had run up and you could see the flash of recognition. "Hey Josh. I'm glad to see you're still running. Go on ahead and I'll talk to you at the finish."

"No, we're finishing together," Josh said stoically.

"Are you kidding? You're not going to bury me over this last mile?"

"No."

Scott couldn't believe it. "Why not? What's going on? Are you hurt?"

"I'm not hurt. I've just been thinking about our *talk* on Purgatory Mountain and I agree with everything you said. You're right. I am out here for the wrong reason. Before you bother to ask, I've decided that it's ok to be competitive, and I won't apologize for that, but I want more out of Hellgate than just competition."

Scott wondered where this was going. "All right, go on."

"I have always wanted to win. Not just at this, I'm talking about everything I've ever done. I think, looking back, the reason was obvious. I wanted the attention that comes with winning. I didn't push myself because I loved what I was doing. I just wanted to be better than everyone else."

They had passed a sign that indicated only one mile remained. "What about now?" Scott asked.

"Now? Now, I don't want to be that guy because there's a difference between this sport and everything else I've tried. I really do love this. Ever since I was a kid, I've loved to take off into the woods and just run as far as I could. I love the way it feels to float over the rocks and career down a mountainside at insane, dangerous speeds. I love that I get to see more of a trail in a day than a backpacker sees in a week, or a coach potato sees in a lifetime. This is truly my passion but, a long time ago, I lost track of that and started to treat it like a job. You reminded me of that today. You were absolutely right, when I was a kid, I did run for different reasons. In high school and college, I became convinced that it was all about times. Every workout had to be faster and every run had to be longer than the last time. Each time I raced, I had to defend my position in the hierarchy. The love faded away and my childhood motivation was replaced by a desire for adulation and, intertwined with that, a fear of failure."

They were turning the corner into camp Bethel where the finish was located. Scott had been silent but now he asked Josh again. "So, why are you here?"

Josh could see the race director standing a hundred yards ahead at the finish line. "I don't want to run scared anymore. I don't want to feel like I have to perform like a mouse on a wheel. I want to run free of the expectation and pressure that I've been putting on myself. Out here, when I'm on a trail, I just want to be a kid again and run until I drop."

All Scott said was "Over 66 miles behind us Josh. Do you feel it?"

Josh had noticed it building over the last mile. A slight nausea caused by a rush of adrenaline in his system. His heart was starting to race and he felt overcome by a lightheaded, somewhat detached, feeling. The exact same thing happened each time he won a race. They crossed the line together and were greeted by a jubilant Dr. Horton. Hellgate was over.

"Yeah, I feel it Scott."

Epilogue

"Why am I still running? Well, I know myself: For 15 years, while I have not been a workaholic I have been a runaholic. Some people can't live without booze; it looks like I can't live without running."

— Lasse Viren
4 time Olympic Gold Medalist

The weeks after Hellgate were relaxing for Josh. The holidays came and, for the first time in years, he didn't run at all. He enjoyed visiting with his family, spending time with Jill, and left his shoes in the closet.

When Josh resumed running he vowed to have a new attitude. Scott was understandably skeptical. That didn't mean that he wouldn't be competitive anymore. It just meant that he no longer wanted his racing to define who he was. Instead, he wanted it to be a small part of a bigger picture that showed Josh in a more flattering light. From the time he crossed the finish line at Hellgate, he no longer felt that placing high in the standings or posting a fast time would be his defining moment. If, however, training hard, planning, and running the right way, happened to coincide with a fast time, or a victory, then that was just fine. If not, that was all right as well. He wanted to run for the pure joy of the adventure, to push boundaries and leave his ego out of it.

He decided to put his new perspective on racing to the test during a 50 mile trail race on what he considered his home course in the Withalachochee Wildlife Management Area. The Croom 50 mile Fools Run was an event that, three months ago, Josh wanted to win very badly. Now, he simply wanted to run with Scott and enjoy the experience.

He was preparing for the race, when a call on a Sunday afternoon in February, from his sister, changed his plans entirely.

"Hey, what are doing?" Jennie asked excitedly.

Josh was on his cell phone. "I'm driving home from the Citrus Hiking Trails."

"Were you running out there?" she asked.

"Yeah, I was supposed to do a long run yesterday but I played golf instead and made up the run this morning. What's going on with you?"

"Well, you won't believe it but I'm on my way home from the gym where I just did a five mile run!" she sounded very excited.

Josh was impressed. His sister had never really done any running before and he didn't know if it was a one time thing or if she had been building up to that distance for weeks. "That's great. How'd it feel?"

"Not too bad. I was pretty tired at the end but I'm getting better."

"Keep going and it'll just get easier and easier," Josh suggested.

"I'm going to. In fact, I was wondering if you could give me some advice on a race to run?"

Now that caught Josh off guard. "A race! Are you serious?"

She sounded so enthusiastic that it was infectious. "I sure am. I was thinking about a 5k or something."

"I tell you what. Why don't you keep training this week and then meet me at the Santos Trailhead next Saturday. We'll go for a trail run together and talk about it."

"That sounds great. I'd like to try a trail run."

That got Josh thinking. "You know, I'm signed up for the Croom 50 mile in about five weeks. Maybe you can come down there with me and run a trail race instead of beating yourself up on the roads."

"Are you crazy! I can't run 50 miles."

"No, No, of course not. They have a 50k and a 15 mile race. If you really want to try, I think you could be ready to at least finish the 15 mile. We'd just have to figure out an alternating run and walk plan for you."

236

"That's perfect. I'd love to do that but my longest run has been this five miles I did today. Do you really think I can do it?" Jennie asked.

"I'm sure. Trust me," Josh said happily.

For the next four weekends, they met at the trails and ran together. They experimented with things to drink and with run/walk patterns until they settled on something that seemed to work for Jennie. In fact, they had even done an 11 mile run 10 days before the race.

Then, Josh did something that would have been unthinkable before Hellgate. He called the race director and asked to be moved from the 50 mile to the 15 so that he could run with his sister. He expected Scott to be upset, since they had been planning to run together, but just the opposite happened. Scott was beaming when Josh told him. He was stunned and just walked up to Josh and hugged him. "Finally, after all our arguments, I think you really get what it's all about."

The day of the race, they were fortunate to have good weather early but, by the time they reached the peace sign, which signaled the beginning of the hills, it was getting hot. Jennie was tired, but stuck to her plan and kept going over the toughest part of the course. When they neared the end, Josh ran ahead to let his brother-in-law know she was almost there. They wanted to get a nice photo of her finishing the run. When Jennie came out of the woods a few minutes later and crossed the road to the finish, Josh couldn't have been prouder. He knew how hard it had been for her the last few miles and yet she hadn't given up. She had run like Josh did when he was younger, for fun, and to finish. A few months earlier, on a mountain in Virginia, Josh had said there was no way to duplicate the feeling you had when winning a hard race. At the end of Hellgate, he knew he had been wrong and now it was proven all over again. He felt the familiar knot in his stomach and realized you don't even have to be in the race to feel it.

Only a week later, they all gathered for drinks at the Tin Cup. It was after midnight and the crowd was starting to get loud. They'd been there for hours but Scott had been unusually quiet all night, like he had something important on his mind but didn't want to talk about it.

"What's the deal Scott? You've been mopping around all night," Josh asked.

Scott stared at the beer he'd been nursing for the past half hour and responded quietly. "Nothings wrong, I've just been thinking about asking you something."

"Well, spill it." Josh looked for Jill who was at the next table with some friends.

"Ok, but I want you to keep an open mind," Scott said.

"The answer's no. My wife is off limits," Scott didn't even smile at Josh's joke. "Ok, what the hell is wrong with you?"

Scott still looked unsure of whether or not he should talk. "Back in January, I entered us both into a race without telling you. Our entries were accepted. I wasn't even sure it was something you could do, but now I think you can."

He had Josh's attention. "Oh no. You've waited all night because you want me to have a good buzz when you spring this on me. You want to go back to Hellgate don't you!"

Now Scott laughed. "Of course I want to go back to Hellgate, and we will next December, but that's not it!"

"Then what?" Josh asked.

"Hardrock," Scott said just before taking a long drink of his beer.

"You've got to be kidding. The Hardrock 100 miler?"

Scott became very animated. "Yes, the one and only. 66,000 feet of elevation change, more than double Hellgate. It has an average elevation of over 10,000 feet and, at one point, is over 14,000 feet. Cold, remote, all above tree line, rocky, potentially violent storms, a 60 hour time limit, two full nights on your feet in the dark, sleep deprivation, hallucinations, the whole deal. It's insane!"

Josh was silent for a while and appeared to be deep in thought.

"You sure know how to pitch a race," Josh said. "I guess I could argue, but there's no point. It sounds perfect. I'm in."

Josh looked over at his wife and wondered how he could possibly get her on board with this one. "Well, Jill's never been to the San Juan Mountains. Maybe we could make a vacation out of it."

Printed in the United States
65795LVS00003B/1-99

9 781598 244045